THE
CAREFUL
KILLER

THE CAREFUL KILLER

Murray Carr

To mum and dad. Gone but never forgotten

viewing, he would have been quite disappointed. No blood, bruising or any other signs of injury. The absurdly bizarre thought sprang into Brian's head that perhaps this was a very elaborate practical joke being played on him for his birthday. Any moment his father would sit up and smile. His mother would stop crying and laugh. The man in the white coat would reveal a present. Caroline would come into the room and embarrass him with a kiss. Involuntarily Brian closed his eyes for a split second. When he opened them, the man didn't have a present, there was no Caroline, his mother was still crying, and his father was still dead.

They were led from the morgue, back up in the elevator, and into another small room. Here they were met by a female doctor who invited them to sit down then took a seat opposite. She explained that Caroline had suffered a serious head injury and was in a coma. Brian's mum asked if they could see her, but the doctor said they were still carrying out tests. The hospital would inform them when there was any news.

For the next few days Brian felt as if he was in the eye of a hurricane. Friends, distant relatives and people he didn't know phoned and dropped in continually. His older sister, Elizabeth, who had been on a working holiday during her university break, arrived back home. Brian spent a large part of his day making endless cups of tea for the visitors. He realised that the tea ritual was more important in giving people something to do with their hands and filling in awkward gaps in conversation by taking a sip, than drinking it. The newspapers carried a brief report of the incident and concluded with the usual statement that the Independent Office for Police Conduct would carry out an investigation. His mother spent more time at the hospital with Caroline than she did in the house, and he became weary of telling callers that she wasn't home and trying to remember messages to pass on. Later at night the faint sound of his mother crying would be the last thing he heard before going to sleep. Often, he would dream of the incident and awaken in a cold sweat. Sometimes in his dream his father would reach Caroline and manage to pull her out of the path of the police car. Then he would wake up feeling really good until the reality dawned.

Brian started going to the hospital with his mother, while Elizabeth was left to attend to things at home. The idea was that by talking to Caroline she might be awoken from her coma by the sound of a familiar voice. But while his mother could talk to Caroline for ages, Brian felt very self-conscious, and quickly ran out of things to say. He made up tapes of his sister's favourite music on an ancient recorder, and he played these as a substitute for talking.

After his father's funeral, Brian noticed a change coming over his mother. She had been taking tablets since the accident. At first, she took some at night to get to sleep. Then she started taking others to wake up in the morning. She began to smell of drink, although Brian never actually saw her taking any. He had asked her when he would be able to return to school, but she said that he couldn't go back yet, as she needed him to go with her to the hospital. She began to put letters in the bin without opening them.

Visitors and sympathy calls became less frequent as other peoples' thoughts returned to their own problems. A small report appeared in a daily newspaper stating that no action would be taken against the driver of the police car involved in the accident. A larger feature appeared in a Sunday paper showing Brian's mother sitting at her daughter's bedside. Doctors had declined to comment on the chances of Caroline recovering, and the police declined to comment on the accident, apart from offering sympathy to the family. A spin off from this feature was the arrival of a cheque from the Sunday newspaper made up of donations sent in by sympathetic members of the public.

One day, a few weeks after a very miserable Christmas, an officer from the local authority arrived at the house and politely threatened them regarding what the authority would do if Brian didn't return to school. His mother had had a tantrum, but decided when she had calmed down that he should go back.

Although the familiar sight of the schoolrooms was a relief from the hospital visits, Brian felt like a stranger in many of the classes. His important exams were only a few weeks away and he knew he had little chance of any success. Studying at night was almost impossible, as he had to make up for missing his daytime hospital visits by going in the evenings. Elizabeth had returned to her university work, although she came home every weekend. Their mother talked of Caroline as if she was on holiday or had gone out on an errand. The few people who continued to visit regularly went along with this, and at times Brian felt he was living in a fantasy world rather than the real thing. Inside, every fibre of his being wanted to scream out the reality of the situation, but outwardly he was the dutiful son, making tea and recounting, on demand, past stories of escapades he had had with Caroline.

The local newspaper, the Airdrie and Coatbridge Advertiser, briefly revived the story. The driver of the police vehicle was a constable who was returning to the police station with a witness in the back of the car. He was accompanied by an inspector. Brian had stared at the picture of the smiling constable posing with his wife and son. The boy looked to be a year or two younger than Brian, but he didn't know when the picture was taken. It was a lovely family picture. Father, mother, and one son. The policeman deeply regretted the incident, but insisted that it had been a tragic accident. He had confirmed that he was not using his siren at the time of the incident, but was driving with the blue light flashing. They were rushing to the station with an important witness. The young girl and man had appeared in front of his car in an instant, and there was nothing he could have done to avoid hitting them. *The blue light was flashing!* Brian recoiled from the paper. Frame by frame the picture was explored in his memory. His father pulled his sister off her feet then tried vainly to stop his forward rush. The bonnet of a white car appeared, and his father and sister were thrown up into the air. The car continued across the screen in his mind with the man in the passenger seat holding his arms up to his face and the driver pushed back into his seat as he stood on the brakes. Clouds of thick smoke from the tyres engulfed the back of the car. *But no blue light.* Later, Brian had noticed a blue light reflected off shop windows and had been surprised the police had arrived so quickly. But at the time he didn't realise that the car that had struck his father and sister had been a police vehicle. Had its blue light been flashing, he would surely have noticed it. He must be mistaken. Perhaps he hadn't noticed it in the bright sunlight. Perhaps his attention had been focussed on his family.

Or perhaps the light was only switched on after the accident had happened?

Brian jumped to his feet, dropping the paper on the floor as if it had suddenly become too hot to hold. He tried to get a grip on himself. Whether the light had been flashing or not wouldn't have changed what happened. His sister's desire for the ice cream held her full attention. She wouldn't have noticed the flashing light. But what if she had? Despite the brightness of the sun, she *might* have noticed the reflection from the shop windows. He shook his head as he tried to convince himself that he was wrong. The light MUST have been flashing. There must have been witnesses who testified to that.

Over the next few days, he tried as best he could to stop thinking about the blue light. But he couldn't. Television programmes seemed to be full of scenes involving police cars and flashing lights.

His mother's drinking had become much worse. She was now making no effort to hide the drink and had even been turned away from the hospital on one occasion, as she was considered to be in no fit state to visit. She managed to ensure that never happened again, but she was now taking pills in handfuls. Brian dreaded coming home from school, as he never knew exactly what he would find there. Sometimes his mother would be asleep. Sometimes she would be sitting staring blankly at the television screen. But every evening she would hug him until he felt he would break. The repulsive smell of stale alcohol washed around him as she held him in her grasp.

Eventually, she told him that the doctors had advised her that she should consider allowing the machines attached to Caroline to be switched off. Of course, she would have none of this. Elizabeth's weekend visits became much less frequent. The story was that she was too busy with her university work, but Brian had overheard Elizabeth and their mother arguing on the phone. Now the phone calls had all but stopped, and on the rare occasion when Elizabeth did phone and spoke to their mother, invariably an argument ensued.

Brian's teachers were sympathetic and tried to give him as much help as they could. While they offered advice regarding moving on, Brian simply couldn't. Get up, prepare his breakfast and packed lunch (assuming there was anything fit to eat in the house) and go to school. Come home. Try to find money to buy basic necessities, and then prepare some sort of meal for himself and his mother. Attempt to fit in some studying. Day after day. Now the weekends, once a time for fun, he dreaded more than school days. He tried to tidy the house, do washing and ironing, cook meals, study, care for his mother and so on. The thoughts and ambitions he had always harboured as regards his future became distant memories.

The world Brian had been an active participant in now seemed to be rushing past him like one of those clever television adverts. Everyone else was rushing around getting on with his or her lives and he was stumbling along as if walking through quicksand. The future Brian now thought about was no more distant than a day or even hours ahead. *If mum falls asleep early, I can watch a DVD. If I finish studying the next chapter I can go to sleep.*

He did his best to hide the situation from neighbours, friends, and even the family doctor. His school friends didn't want a morose, brooding pal. They wanted good old Brian back, joking, laughing, and clowning around. So that's what they got. He really, really tried to be back to what he had been. He genuinely hoped this would give him respite from his other life. On occasions it did, briefly, but then the sickness in his stomach would return with a vengeance. The one person he could confide in was Elizabeth, but even with her he played down the situation as best he could. She had offered on many occasions to quit her university course and come home and find work, but Brian would hear none of that talk. In turn, Brian disguised as best he could the deteriorating physical and mental health of their mother.

He even gave religion a try, managing to slip out to attend a few services, then plucking up the courage to seek a one-to-one meeting with a church elder. As with his teachers, the man tried to work things out with him. But the bottom line was that *God works in mysterious ways*, and this did nothing for Brian. He had no idea what God could have had in mind in taking away his father, sister and reducing his mother to a physical and mental wreck. He was told that *suffering was good for the soul*. If true, he reasoned he must have an extremely healthy soul.

The examination diet eventually arrived, and Brian did the best he could. He told himself that the results didn't really matter now anyway. Any thoughts he once had of going to university were gone. He would see what results he achieved, then get a job. That thought cheered him up. *He* would be earning money and would not have to depend on what was left after his mother had fed her increasing drink and drug problem. The doctor had refused to prescribe increased doses of her pills, but she had managed to find a friend of a friend who could get her what she wanted. At a price.

With the exams past, he skipped the last few weeks of school, reasoning, correctly, that his absence would be overlooked. He managed to find casual work which put much needed money into the family purse. He talked to Caroline and told her all his news, but he saw her less and less as his sister. What he saw was an empty shell. The first time that thought crossed his mind he was overwhelmed with feelings of guilt and reached out to touch her hand. The warmth he felt only served to increase his remorse over the thoughts he had had. But these thoughts wouldn't go away. He began to wish she would die. The hospital would let her, but his mother would hear none of it. He was sure Caroline would want to die. She was growing up without living any of her life. *If only she could wake up for a moment and tell them to leave her alone! That's what she would do if she could see herself lying there as he did.*

On one occasion Brian mustered enough courage to catch his mother in a relatively sober moment and tried to reason the situation logically with her. She blew her top. The normally happy, easy-going woman had been replaced with a snarling, stubborn drunk. Her memory of what pills she had taken, and when, became completely confused.

On Saturday, July 13th, just over a year since his father died, Brian took the unusual step of accepting a friend's invitation to a night out at the cinema. Elizabeth had phoned that morning, and she had encouraged Brian to go. Later, he had trouble remembering exactly what film he and his friend had seen. Fortunately, his friend was able to back him up when he was questioned by the police. The questioning was fairly routine and very sympathetic, but the police had to go through the motions. The coroner ruled his mother's death an accidental drug overdose.

Fortunately, Elizabeth had just completed her degree, and she returned home to become the head of the household. She took the decision to authorise the hospital to disconnect Caroline's life support machine. Brian agreed.

A joint funeral of mother and daughter was held on 29th July when they were laid to rest beside James Reid in Old Monkland Cemetery. The house and all furnishings were sold, and Brian and Elizabeth became relatively wealthy young people. It turned out that his dad had various insurance policies which his mother had either not known about or had been in too distressed a state to pursue. Fortunately, his father had had the foresight to make wills for him and his wife. Brian bought a small ex-council house in the north of the town and settled down to restart his life. A former golfing friend of James secured a position for Brian at a small computer software development company situated in an industrial estate in nearby Chapelhall. Elizabeth returned to Hull, where she had attended university.

Brian proved to be a quick learner, and more than pulled his weight in the growing and developing company. He became one of their foremost sales planners, making good use of his natural abilities for logical thought and cool headedness. Just before his twenty fifth birthday, he became the main sales executive for the firm. This gave him relative autonomy to plan his working day as he saw appropriate.

Over the years he had developed his own strategy to beat the nightmares. He would lull himself to sleep with thoughts of exacting revenge on the people responsible for wrecking his family. At first this centred on the policeman, and then gradually expanded to include the pusher who supplied his mother's pills, and the shopkeeper who sold her the drink. They were all to blame in some way for his tragedy. So, he thought of ways to get even. But it was only fantasy, thoughts he turned over in his mind before falling asleep. The pill pusher would be caught by the police, prosecuted and locked up; the shop keeper selling his mother the drink would be caught selling alcohol to youngsters and be prosecuted, witnesses would come forward to testify that the blue light wasn't on and the police car had been driven dangerously leading to the policeman being drummed out of the force. And this fantasising pushed the pain into the background. As the years had passed, the nightmares had receded. Old pictures of his family in happier times could be viewed without feeling the pain. But like a recovering alcoholic, he knew that it would not take much to push him back into the abyss he had slowly climbed out of over the years.

In October, not long after he had been appointed to his new position, an internal memo named a young man who would join the expanding company as a software programmer.

Brian read the memo and froze. His replacement would be a graduate by the name of Roy Turner.

Roy and Brian had never met, but Brian knew the name very well. He remembered it from a newspaper report from years ago when Roy posed for a family snapshot. Could it be the same guy? In an instant, the thoughts that had been gradually receding into the depths of his mind rushed forward, and with them came the pain again.

That old church elder had been right. *The Lord did work in mysterious ways.*

Chapter 2

The man parked his car in the spot he had identified a few days earlier and headed for the park. He felt like skipping with excitement but controlled himself to walk as normally as he could. He walked a bit clumsily, as his shoes were three sizes too big for him.

He walked through the gates that years of rust on the hinges suggested were never closed. Finding the spot he was looking for, he pressed himself deep into the shadow provided by the tall tree and hedges, put on his mask and shower cap and waited. Eventually he heard a soft whistle. The section of the path in front of the hedge was composed of tarmac, unlike many of the other sections in this park, which were red chips. As the whistle drew closer, it was accompanied by quiet footsteps crunching on the chips. He instinctively pushed himself deeper into the hedge and fought the mounting tension and excitement. It was surprisingly hot inside the plastic mask, and it made his breathing sound very noisy. Hopefully it was not as noisy to the approaching man, and with luck the whistling would prevent him from hearing it anyway.

The whistling stopped and was replaced almost immediately by quiet singing.

He had expected the man to be very drunk but judging from the regular footsteps that was not the case. The singing just as suddenly changed back to a whistle, and the footsteps became quieter as the man was now walking on the tarmac. Although the stalker had anticipated his quarry coming into view, the sudden appearance caused him to give a slight start.

He took a quick step forward and threw the nylon rope over the whistling man's head and around his throat. As the rope was tightened, the assailant pulled the man back until his own back rested against a tree. At the same time, he forced his right knee into the middle of the victim's back.

The whistling was replaced by a gargling sound as the man fought frantically to break free. He tried to reach behind, and then he clawed at his neck in a desperate attempt to get some air. Gradually, the struggling stopped, then the twitching stopped, and the man was still. The murderer looked around as he allowed the body to slowly slump to the ground. He found the man's left wrist, removed his watch and replaced it with one he had in his pocket.

The murderer listened intently for a few moments, and then walked briskly to the park gates. On the way, he removed his mask and cap and stuffed them into a pocket of his jacket.

After ten minutes he reached the spot where the car had been left. The oversized boots were removed and replaced with normal shoes. The boots were carefully placed into a plastic bag along with the mask and the cap.

He drove away, carefully staying within the speed limit. When a few miles out of town, he stopped the car in a quiet car park and changed his outer clothes. Everything had been bought from various charity shops especially for this night. The plastic cover that had been on the driver's seat was removed and also put into a plastic bag along with the length of rope and plastic gloves. The bags were dumped in a supermarket rubbish bin.

Reaching home, the murderer carefully hid the watch he had taken. He made himself a cup of tea and tried to relax while the adrenaline worked its way out of his body. This had been his third job and he really felt he was getting the knack of it. But there was so much work still to be done.

It had gone exactly to plan. Leaving the cigarette ends and the few other bits and pieces had been a nice touch. He wished that he had thought of taking the victim's watch from the start, but it was too late to bother about that now. The media were already tentatively linking the previous murders. At the present, the police were not commenting on this. But that was bound to change. Even without his calling card, he felt sure the police would find enough similarities to link them.

He felt proud of his invention. He had always been taught that *if something was worth doing, it was worth doing well*, and he had taken that message to heart. *The Boston Strangler, Son of Sam, The Green River Killer* and, of course, *Jack the Ripper*. All names that, in their day, struck terror into peoples' hearts. What would people call him? He hoped it wouldn't be something like *The York-shire Ripper*, a second-hand name that demeaned the former. But perhaps it was a compliment? Copying is the sincerest form of flattery? No, he wanted something original. *The Clueless Killer?* This was accurate as he did go out of his way to leave no clues, or to be more accurate, to leave misleading clues. But the name sounded derogatory. He quite fancied *The Charity Shop Killer*, but that could only come if his steps to avoid detection were known.

A possible answer was to contact the authorities and name himself, but that was risky. Maybe just one letter? It certainly worked for Jack the Ripper, or James Maybrick or whoever wrote the 'Dear Boss' letter.

It might be an idea just to wait and see what appears in the media. So far, they had only reported his work in the broadest terms. If they come up with a name and he didn't like it, he could contact the media and set them straight.

He had a small shiver of excitement at the prospect. Someone might come up with a name he hadn't thought of but really liked! It was all in the name. But, come to think of it, Ted Bundy, Ian Brady and Dennis Nilsen are names that come to mind when someone thinks of serial killers. Would he want only to be known as a nickname? He shook his head on the pillow. Of course! He would have to be known as a nickname until they knew who he was! He gave a small laugh at his stupidity. But he was getting a bit ahead of himself. After this latest example surely the police would start to link the events. Whether or not they would release this information to the media remained to be seen. The media would be a big help to his purpose. The tabloids always looked to frighten and shock people, and what is more frightening than a serial killer on the loose?

Yes, fame would come if he was patient. And his victims would be glorified in the wake of his fame and would be free of their oppression.

Chapter 3

Brian sat in front of his plasma screen television, completely oblivious to what was showing, frightened to go to sleep because of what was waiting for him there.

Elizabeth had phoned to find out how things were going. After the death of their mother, they had drifted apart. Possibly each would remind the other of the pain they had been through, and they both wanted to start to live some of their lives. So, their contact was now down to infrequent phone calls. Tonight, Brian was glad his sister had phoned. He mentioned, just in passing, that a new guy called Roy Turner was starting in his firm. The line went dead for a few seconds, and then Elizabeth tentatively asked if it was who she thought it was. Brian explained that he wasn't sure. And that was that as far as the discussion about Roy went. Elizabeth did mention that she was planning to come back to Scotland. He couldn't wait to see her again as they had a lot to talk about.

Monday turned out to be an anti-climax. Brian had to go out on a number of local calls, and Roy was closeted behind closed doors, immersed in what was laughingly called the company induction programme.

Tuesday was ending pretty much the same. Brian had returned to the business just before 4p.m. and was filing paperwork when a familiar voice spoke behind him.

'And this is Brian. Brian's the main man as far as sales go.'

Brian turned to face the Head of Personnel, Ian McDonald.

'You'll make Brian's job a lot easier if the stuff you write actually works.'

Ian laughed at his joke as if it were funny. Roy laughed out of politeness; Brian didn't bother as he had heard it before.

'Brian, this is Roy Turner, our new programmer.'

Brian moved his eyes to Roy whilst desperately trying to outwardly display nothing but slight curiosity.

He shook Roy's outstretched hand and was surprised to find the handshake strong and firm. In his mental picture he had expected a handshake somewhat akin to gripping a dead kipper.

Roy smiled, and Brian smiled back. Roy was a few inches smaller than Brian, around 5' 9". His reddish-brown hair was thinning quite noticeable, and what there was of it was untidy and rather unfashionably long. His blue eyes twinkled behind the thick lenses of glasses that seemed too big for his face. While still gripping Brian's hand, Roy used the middle finger of his left hand to push the glasses from where they had slid at the end of his nose up to a more normal position.

'And over here is Lyn, one of our office sales advisors.'

Brian was left staring at Roy's back. But he had seen enough. He wouldn't have recognised the face, but the smile was decisive. Brian was convinced that the smile he had just seen was the same one he had studied countless times in the old newspaper picture. He would have to get to know this new guy and confirm beyond any doubt that he was who he suspected him of being. During his brief meeting with Roy, he had detected the unmistakeable smell of smoke. Brian was at the present time in one of his non-smoking phases. As he turned to head for the door, he decided it was time to start the habit again.

As he made his way home, Brian analysed everything he could remember of their brief meeting. Roy had shown no signs of recognition when they met. This didn't really surprise Brian, as his picture hadn't been in the papers. Even better was the fact that the paper in its story had referred to him as 'James'. In the now somewhat old-fashioned family tradition, Brian had been named James after his father. It quickly became obvious that this would cause all sorts of problems, so Brian became known by his middle name. The chance of Roy learning his identity from people in the company was very low, as to the best of Brian's knowledge no one knew his history. That pretty much left chance as the only factor that might reveal his past. Brian knew enough about chance not to take this lightly, so he had planned a strategy should this eventuality arise. He had considered telling Roy as soon as he met him about who he was but decided that he couldn't judge how Roy would react to this.

Quite contrary to current legislation, the company had allocated a disused storage room as a smoking area for the few employees who worshipped the weed. One or two of the programmers smoked, and due to the sensitive nature of their business, the company preferred their programmers not to smoke outside. Company security procedures meant that if any programmer left his or her post they had to take their removable hard discs with them. Rather than have people standing outside puffing away with the valuable hard disc under their arms trying to shelter it from the pouring rain (the business was in the West of Scotland after all), the company instigated, quite on the hush-hush, the smoking room.

During the following ten days, Brian spent as much time as he dared while at the office finding out what he could about Roy. He had managed to sneak a look at Roy's personnel file, but apart from the application form for his current job, there was little in it. Brian quickly jotted down the basic details. School attended, University, current address, phone number, email address and so on. The address on the form didn't ring any bells with Brian. He was sure that the picture of the policeman and his family had mentioned him living in one of the Airdrie villages. Roy's address was an Airdrie address, but it was quite possible he had moved out to live in his own place. The form stated that Roy was single. He played golf, was interested in football and music, and enjoyed playing chess and solving logic puzzles. He held a current (clean) driving licence and had no criminal convictions. His father was still alive and noted as his next of kin. Brian paused when he read that. He wasn't sure if he had hoped Roy's father would be alive or dead and didn't know whether to feel happy or sad.

Roy had been getting into the habit of spending his breaks in the smoking room and Brian organised his duties to meet up with him. The two young men actually got on very well together. Brian found that they shared the same sense of humour and sympathised with the same groups in society. Brian had carefully avoided any discussion of his own childhood, whilst gathering as much information about Roy's background as he could.

They had a common interest in following the recent spate of murders reported in the press.

Roy mentioned that his father had also been following the reports, and, as an ex-policeman, seemed to have a better insight into what had been happening. The fact that the father was an ex-policeman ticked a major box for Brian.

Out of the blue, Roy had invited Brian to visit his father's house in Glenmavis for a meal. He wanted Brian to meet his dad, and the dinner would take place between Christmas and New Year.

Brian's immediate instinct had been to decline, but eventually he agreed after Roy obviously wasn't going to let the matter drop.

Elizabeth was shocked at the thought of her brother having dinner with the man they suspected had killed their father. But she could tell that her brother was suffering. Somehow, he had reasoned that to confront his demons might lay them to rest, so he had managed to talk her round.

She announced that she would be moving back early in the New Year and he would talk to her about his relationship with Roy. He needed to talk to her about it face to face, not over a telephone. After all, Roy was as innocent in the whole affair as he and his sister were.

The thought of meeting the man who had destroyed his family both disgusted and intrigued him at the same time.

Brian woke on the day of the dinner having slept little the previous night. He was regretting his decision to accept Roy's invitation. During the day he tried to prepare himself mentally for the ordeal. He told himself that he was going to dinner with a friend and his family. That was all. *But what if they knew who he was?* He'd manage to hold it together. He might become upset, but he wouldn't be violent.

He'd have to shake hands. He shuddered when this thought dawned on him. Could he take the hand of the man who had destroyed his family? He had a mental picture of a smiling man holding out a hand. A hand dripping with blood. *STOP IT!* He lit a cigarette and poured himself a generous glass of whisky. Now he was drinking spirits, something he never did, on top of starting to smoke again. The smell of the drink reminded him of his mother. He threw the liquid into the sink and stubbed out the cigarette.

He wouldn't need crutches. He'd handle it. Hadn't he handled everything so far?

It was the Christmas holiday. A time to relax and recharge the batteries before going back to work. But he was more uptight than work ever made him. He shook his head. That wasn't his fault. Once again, he was the victim. The cloud that had drifted into his life years ago was darkening all the time. But it was fate. Roy joining his company, issuing the Christmas invitation. It was all part of a greater plan and he would go along with it. *The Lord works in mysterious ways.* That was what he was meant to do. He owed it to his father and mother. And to Caroline. She'd be twenty-two or twenty-three now. He wondered if she'd have a career, or if she would have settled down with a husband and family. She was always very bright and could have gone on to do anything with her life.

He had been asked to arrive around 7p.m. and, as usual, he was early. In common with many towns, Airdrie has its fair share of satellite villages. Most are the sort of places you only visit if you have a reason to. Not that there is anything wrong with them, just that there is generally nothing there of any great interest. Many of the locals lived there because their parents had lived there, and their parents before them. Although they might be critical of their village, they took offence if an outsider did this. Glenmavis was no exception. The streets had been built in days gone by when there were few privately owned vehicles. Few houses had been built with a garage or even the space to build one. So, the residents had no option but to park in the streets, meaning that these could only be navigated with extreme care. Were you to meet a bus coming in the opposite direction, then you had a major problem. He hadn't imagined there to be much more to Glenmavis than the houses flanking the main road, but now he knew better. As he peered through the windscreen trying to read the names of the streets, he was glad he had noted down Roy's directions. When he left home, Brian had decided not to park too close to the Turner house. He needn't have worried about that, as he couldn't find a parking place in the same street. After exploring a few even smaller streets and cul-de-sacs, he noticed a small car park attached to the bowling club and he drove into it and parked. The clock on the dashboard read 6.55. A light shower of rain began to pepper the windscreen, and he absent-mindedly flicked the wipers to clear his view. He was conscious of his heart thumping in his chest, and he took a few deep, slow breaths in an effort to calm himself down. As he wiped the sweat from his hands with a paper handkerchief he glanced again at the clock. 6.57.

Time to go. He turned the ignition off, got out of the car, locked it, and strode purposefully towards Turner's house. Realising he had left the bottle of red wine on the rear seat, he returned to the car to fetch it.

Brian left as early as politeness would allow and returned to his car. As he made his way home, he turned the events of the evening over in his mind. Outwardly, everything had gone OK, but he had found it difficult. So difficult that he had to go to the toilet on one occasion to fight off the urge to be sick. He felt that he was betraying his family. Normally, Brian was quite a good conversationalist, but tonight had been one of his bad days. The meal had been excellent, but only Roy had drunk any of the wine. Brian had declined since he was driving, and Peter Turner, Roy's dad, had said that he didn't drink.

He glanced at the dashboard clock. Fortunately, he had things to do before he would have to face his nightmares. Time to calm down, clear his head. He turned on his car radio, seeking a distraction from his thoughts.

The station he was tuned to was, predictably, playing Christmas songs.

Have yourself a merry little Christmas,
Make the Yuletide gay,
From now on, our troubles will be miles away.

'Go fuck yourself!' said Brian as he switched the radio off.

Chapter 4

Spread out across his bed on a plastic sheet were his latest purchases from various charity shops. Size 11 boots or shoes were quite difficult to find, but these were essential. It would have been much better if he could have kept the same boots he had worn for the first murder, but that would have been too risky. Everything he wore on his outings had to be discarded. The only thing he kept, and felt a bit uncomfortable about, was the watch from his last victim. But he thought the authorities might expect him to take a trophy. He had done that the first time then threw it away. But he had a much better idea what to do with them now.

He picked up the length of nylon washing line and tested it again for strength. The car was fuelled and ready. He didn't have any need to own a vehicle as he had access to all the cars owned by his company. Using a different one on each of the nights he was working was yet another way to avoid detection.

He changed into the clothes he had collected but put on his own size 8 shoes. The size 11s were put into a plastic bag along with the other items he needed for his work. As he walked to his door, he glanced at the family photograph on the hall table. The mother he had adored, and who had been driven to her death by his abusive father. And the father. Smiling as if butter wouldn't melt in his mouth. He remembered how his father had cried at the mother's funeral, and how he, the devoted son, couldn't shed a tear. Then he remembered how he had cried when, at last, his ogre of a father passed away. His big regret was that his father's passing had been peaceful. He didn't deserve to die peacefully; he should have endured some of the suffering he had dished out to his family. But the death of his father had left such a void in his life, he had no one to hate any more. Then he came up with his master plan. He was sure his father was not unique. He knew that behind closed doors many families were suffering what he and his mother had endured. But he would take his own small steps to rectify this. Men had to learn that going home tanked up with drink to abuse their families would not be tolerated. He had already saved three families from possible suffering, and this was only the beginning. There was a lot more work to be done.

The clutch on the Ford Focus was quite fierce, but he would get used to it before he reached his destination. He had studied the newspaper reports on the killings, but little useful information had been given. This was probably due to the fact that the police had released nothing of significance. And that might be because they knew very little. It annoyed him slightly that his careful and detailed preparations were not appreciated, but in time they would be. He knew that in order for his real genius to be appreciated, he had to be caught. Only then would everyone marvel at how good he was at his work. He would have liked to keep the newspaper articles, but this would be expected by the police, and would have been a give-away. Oh no, barring some really bad luck, they were going to have their work cut out pinning the killings on him! A shudder of excitement ran through him as his mind rushed ahead and visualised the headlines he would get when his identity was eventually released to the eagerly waiting world.

Two hours later, he was driving home after another successful night's work. He had been a bit less prepared than normal, as this time he didn't have a particular victim in mind. However, he knew that many men returning from an evening's drinking at the *Lion's Den* took a short cut through the disused factory. He just had to wait. Annoyingly, the first three possibilities had been with company, so he had to let them pass freely. As usual, he carefully sprinkled cigarette ends around where he was standing. Leaving false clues was important. Perhaps they'll call him the *Fag End Killer*? He quite liked that. It had a rather chummy sound to it.

After again following his disposal ritual, he returned home for the night. He had taken his latest victim's watch but replaced it with the one he took from the previous victim.

On the drive home, he had begun to plan his next event. His business would take him a good hundred miles away over the next week. This was excellent as he could drop into a totally different range of charity shops. He would also need to carry out some reconnaissance for his next victim. To date, he had selected places which would form a nice radius around Glasgow. Hopefully, the authorities would plot the killings on a map with Glasgow as the epi centre and assume he lived there. This, of course, was totally wrong.

The good thing about criminal profiling is that it works two ways. Knowing the methods of the hunters can also help the hunted, if the latter is smart enough. And he was.

Chapter 5

Brian tossed and turned for hours before finally managing to get to sleep. And then the nightmares came back. The same speeding car and flashing light, sometimes on, sometimes off, only this time there was a recognisable face in the car. His fevered mind now added a second reel to the movie. In part two, the car stopped, the side window came down, and a smiling man reached out to shake hands. He woke feeling more tired than when he had gone to bed.

He busied himself getting his house as tidy as he could. This basically involved lots of things being stuffed into cupboards. He prepared the spare bedroom.

Outside, it had started to snow. This was the first of the winter and he hoped it wouldn't get too bad. Fortunately, by the time his sister arrived, the snow had stopped and had only left a light covering on the roads. They exchanged Christmas presents, and after an hour or so of small talk, left to go for a meal.

Their meal hardly followed the Christmas tradition as they dined at the Cafe Spice, an Indian restaurant situated on the town's main street. Elizabeth loved Indian food, and Brian was quite happy to go along with her suggestion, although he generally limited himself to carry out meals. But the naan bread would be warm and moist, not dry and lukewarm as it usually is from a home delivery. They ate the meal and caught up on each other's news, with one very important omission. Nothing was said about Roy.

An hour or two later, and they were both sitting in Brian's small house. Elizabeth had declined the offer of a drink and instead they were both drinking tea.

'And you're not sleeping very well?' said Elizabeth.

'No,' he said eventually, with a sigh of resignation. 'All my nightmares are back, but this time there is a recognisable face looking at me.'

'And you can see the face looking out of the window at you?'

'Yes,' said Brian still pacing up and down.

'Then he didn't destroy our family as he was the passenger in the car, not the driver.'

Brian stood looking at her. He ran the events through in his mind. Then again. Then once again.

'Shit!'

Elizabeth calmly took a sip of her tea.

Brian stomped off towards his bedroom.

A few minutes later he returned with a brown manila folder. He started to carelessly brush everything off the coffee table and onto the floor. Elizabeth quickly rescued her mug of tea from his frantic actions. The folder was opened, and a number of newspaper cuttings spread out on the table.

'I'm sure there's nothing in here that suggests Turner wasn't driving.' Brian spoke as much to himself as to his sister. He picked up the cuttings one at a time and scanned through them. Elizabeth waited until he had picked up the same one three times before getting involved.

'You go and make more tea,' she suggested. 'I'll look at them with a fresh eye. If there's anything worth noting, I'll find it.'

Brian reluctantly headed into the kitchen.

Elizabeth could hear him drumming his fingers on the worktop as he impatiently waited on the kettle boiling.

Eventually he returned with two mugs of tea. She took a sip while still reading a cutting.

'So, I've suddenly stopped taking sugar?' she said, making a face.

Brian snorted, grabbed her cup from her, and returned to the kitchen to sweeten her tea.

Elizabeth waved a cutting in her hand when he returned.

'This one mentions a chief inspector backing up Turner's explanation,' she said.

'I remember that one,' said Brian. 'I assumed that was just a case of the police closing ranks.'

Elizabeth nodded her agreement. 'Unfortunately, neither of us was present at the inquest. Mum was there, but...'

Brian nodded. 'I don't think she would know if it was New Year or New York at that stage,' he said.

Elizabeth put the cutting down and sipped her tea. This time it seemed to be to her satisfaction.

'This makes it a whole new ball game,' she said thoughtfully. 'What if the inspector was driving?'

'Surely someone would have pointed out the discrepancy about the driver?' said Brian.

'Not necessarily,' replied Elizabeth. 'OK, the inspector has a fancier hat, but police uniforms are pretty much the same. Everyone would have been concerned about the injured people. Perhaps no one looked too closely at the occupants of the car.'

'But what about the guy in the back of the car, the one they had as a witness. Surely he'd know which of the policemen was driving?'

'That's a problem,' admitted Elizabeth. 'There's no mention of him in any of the reports I've read.'

'To tell you the truth,' said Brian. 'I hadn't given him much thought.'

'You'll have to consider the possibility that over time your memory of the situation has altered,' Elizabeth said calmly.

Brian got to his feet. 'We need to find out!'

'I can't imagine why this policeman, Turner, would take the blame,' said Elizabeth.

'So, we need to know for sure,' he said calmly. But inside himself he felt nervous and excited. He now had something to act on, although he hadn't a clue exactly what he would do.

Chapter 6

Brian and Elizabeth used the remaining days of the holidays going through old newspapers stored on microfiche in the local library. What they found provided no further enlightenment.

Even a trip to the Mitchell Library in Glasgow added nothing to their research. Apart from the Sunday Special they could find nothing else. They couldn't even find out the name of the witness who was in the car.

'There are three people who could throw light on this,' said Brian as they headed for home in his old black Saab.

Elizabeth gave a short laugh. 'Yeah. But we don't know who one of them is, and I'm not sure if Turner and Chief Inspector Stewart will be happy to tell you the truth. But you could just ask them.'

'Well, why not?' persisted Brian. 'What have we to lose?'

'I was joking,' said Elizabeth.

Suddenly Brian saw the red light and brought the car to a screeching halt.

'Maybe we would be better thinking about this when we get home,' said Elizabeth as she released the pressure of the seat belt following the emergency stop. 'Assuming, of course, that we *get* home.'

'OK,' said Brian, 'sorry about that.'

The rest of the journey was conducted in relative silence.

'We need to approach this from a different angle,' said Elizabeth as she settled into her seat.

It was more of a statement than a suggestion. Brian placed her coffee carefully on a coaster sitting on the small coffee table. He put his own cup of tea (*coffee goes right through me*, he had explained, rather too graphically) on a matching coaster, and then slumped onto the end seat of his two-seater settee. Elizabeth, being his visitor, was given the use of his one armchair.

'Your suggestion, even if it were a serious one, of asking the two people who know the answer is out of the question.'

Brian sipped his tea as he waited on her explaining her new strategy.

'Dig out the photos of the scene again. Let's have a close look at them and see if we recognise any of the onlookers. At the same time, we can check again and see if there's any pictures of the witness they were transporting.'

Once again, the newspaper cuttings were spread out over the table and they examined each of them in turn. Clearly, someone had been at the scene in possession of a camera phone and had taken the opportunity to snap some pics that had then found their way to the newspapers. One picture of the police car showed a figure in the back seat, but the sun was shining so brightly the figure could only be seen in silhouette. The photos didn't show anything of the victims, just the crowd gathered round, but that was what Elizabeth was wanting.

'Do you have a magnifying glass by any chance?' she asked.

Fortunately, for a short period when Brian refused to admit his eyesight was less than perfect, he had bought a cheap glass to read the small print on packets of food. He retrieved it from a kitchen drawer and handed it to her. She studied one photograph carefully.

'I think that's Mrs. White. The woman who lived across the road from us in the house with the metal gates.'

'You mean the old bat who complained every time my ball went into her garden?'

'The very lady. Did you ever speak to her?'

'Only to ask for my ball back. She might even be dead by this time. I remember that she looked pretty old.'

'Everyone looks old when you're fourteen,' explained Elizabeth. 'There's no harm in finding out if she still lives in the same house.'

Elizabeth continued to study the pictures for half an hour or so but couldn't positively identify anyone else. Brian had a go but gave up after ten minutes.

'We should visit Mrs. White,' said Elizabeth jumping to her feet.

'*Now*?' said Brian.

'Why not? Strike while the iron is hot.'

Brian couldn't think of a good reason why they shouldn't go right at this moment, so he took his sister's lead and dragged himself out of his seat.

For some time after he had left the house he shared with his parents, Brian had avoided driving through the area, even if it meant going out of his way by some distance. It was only in the past year that he had found the resolve to go anywhere near it. As they drove the short distance to McKenna Drive, both were silent, immersed in their thoughts.

The street that had been relatively quiet when Brian was a child was now a mass of cars, many choosing to park in this street, as it was a short walk from the Monklands Hospital. Parking in the authorised car park was a nightmare. So people parked in the side roads. The closest Brian could get was fifty yards away. They got out and walked back along the familiar street. Everywhere Brian looked brought back memories. The house where the mongrel dog lived that had been a regular caller to their house; the road he had biked to school; the spot where his grandfather had told him he had found a ten-shilling note as a child.

The small, wooded area where Brian and his pals had played for endless hours was still there, now an oasis of calm amidst a sea of traffic, but the tall hedges that had lined it had been removed. Then they came up level with their old house.

'I wonder who's living there now?' he said, as much to himself as to Elizabeth.

Elizabeth gave a shrug, and they crossed the road to the house still bearing the metal gates Brian remembered from his younger days. Elizabeth looked for the latch, but Brian instinctively found it and opened the smaller of the two gates. They walked up the path to the front door and Elizabeth rang the bell. They had almost assumed no one was at home when the door was unlocked, and opened very slowly, still held by the security chain.

'Yes?' said an elderly white-haired woman.

'Mrs White?' said Elizabeth with a smile.

'Yes?' said the woman.

'I'm Elizabeth Reid and this is my brother Brian. I wonder if you might be able to spare a few moments to talk to us.'

'Well, I don't know. It's getting quite late...'

'We wanted to ask you something about the accident,' said Elizabeth. 'Something very important.'

'Oh, the accident. A terrible thing. And then later....' The old woman looked at them, then smiled.

'Your mother was a very fine woman. Please come in.'

They followed her inside. Brian had expected to find the house furnishings dating back twenty or thirty years and was surprised to find it bright and modern.

As if she sensed his surprise, Mrs White explained.

'I've just finished decorating the whole place. Well, my son did the work. I've lost track of the number of times he's tried to persuade me to move in with him and give this place up, but he has a wife and a young family. The last thing he needs is his old mother cluttering up the place. '

'I didn't know you had a son,' said Brian, accepting her invitation to sit down.

'Well, he was a fair bit older than you if I remember correctly. And in any case, you only spoke to me to ask for your ball back.' Then the woman laughed.

'I did find it so difficult to act very sternly every time that ball came into my garden, but I had to think of the damage to my plants. Once or twice I apologised to your mum when you were at school. She told me not to apologise, but to keep harping on at you about it. I think she hoped you would get involved with your school team and stop simply kicking the ball about the streets.'

The thought of his mother and this old battle-axe conniving against him left Brian speechless.

'And I bet you thought I was just put on this earth to ruin your fun?'

She laughed, and Brian laughed, thus avoiding confirming that that was *exactly* what he had thought.

'I wonder what you remember about the accident,' began Elizabeth, keen to get the pleasantries over and down to the reason for their visit. 'I noticed you in one of the pictures taken at the scene.'

'Really? I didn't know that.' said Mrs. White. 'As I recall, I was just about to leave the newsagents when I heard the screaming. I rushed out of the shop and noticed people running to the corner opposite the ice cream parlour. I hurried over to see what had happened and people told me there had been an accident. I was quite content to stay a reasonable distance back, as there was nothing I could have done. It was only later that I learned who had been involved in the accident. I was shocked, totally shocked.'

She sat back in her chair shaking her head as she recalled the event.

'If I remember correctly, I heard that it was your birthday.' She looked at Brian.

Brian nodded. In spite of all the grieving he had done over the years, for some reason hearing a different account from someone else who was there hit home very hard.

Mrs. White stared at him, and then her face took on a look he had never seen before and would not have imagined possible from the ogre he remembered.

She reached over and patted his hand gently.

'A terrible, terrible tragedy. I am so, so sorry.'

Brian could only nod his appreciation.

'We were wondering if you could add anything about the accident to what had been reported in the newspaper,' said Elizabeth.

'I don't really know what they said in the press,' said Mrs. White. 'I never read newspapers, and certainly wouldn't have taken any pleasure in reading about the tragedy. But ask me anything you like, and I'll help if I can.'

'We were wondering about the police officers in the car. The official report said that an officer by the name of Turner was driving the car. We wondered if that was correct?'

Mrs. White shook her head. 'I'm afraid I don't know that man, but I did hear he had been driving the car. In fact, I didn't recognise either of the policemen.'

Elizabeth sighed. 'It was a bit of a long shot, Mrs White. We were hoping you might be able to give us some information, even something small and seemingly insignificant that had been missed. I hope you don't mind us coming here to ask?'

'Of course not. It was nice to see you both again after all this time. It's just a pity your visit wasn't under more cheerful circumstances.' She paused for a moment. 'There was something I heard that might help you.'

'Yes?' said Elizabeth.

'Well, I was quite friendly with Mrs. Hamilton. Do you remember her? She and her family lived just at the top of Centenary Avenue. Well, I saw her quite often, as we both were members of the same bowling club. Her husband was a policeman. I remember her telling me that he had talked about the accident and said that the officers had been attending a function earlier that evening. Anyway, he had commented that there had been a fair bit of drink flying about, and that the chief inspector had a reputation for liking a drink. He said it was lucky that Turner had been driving, as the inspector was a bit merry when he had seen him last.'

'Do you know if he told any of this to the inquiry?' asked Brian, finding his voice.

Mrs. White shook her head. 'I know for a fact that he didn't. Jean Hamilton said that her husband wasn't involved in the inquiry, as he had had nothing to do with the incident.'

'And did anyone contact you for your recollections of the incident?' asked Elizabeth.

'Me? No! There was nothing I could have told them anyway. The accident had happened while I was in the shop. Even when I was rushing over to the scene, I couldn't see... I couldn't see your father and sister on the ground. I just saw the men getting out of the police car. One officer was using the radio, I think. And putting the blue light on.'

'Putting the blue light on!' said Brian, much more loudly than necessary.

'Yes. Well, I assume he did this, as there was no light one-minute, and the next it was on. Then he got out of the car and ran over to the scene.'

She held up a finger and waved it slightly. 'To be perfectly accurate, he started to make for the crowd, then turned back, took his hat off, threw it into the car, then made for the crowd. I don't really know why he did that. It was quite a fancy hat.'

Chapter 7

'It was quite a few years ago,' said Brian. 'Anyway, I always thought she was a few raisins short of a fruit cake.'

'But *if* she's correct!' Elizabeth stood up and started to pace around Brian's living room.

'Do you really think the police wouldn't have carried out a thorough inquiry?'

'I don't know. Do you?'

Brian shook his head.

'But what's got into you?' said Elizabeth, stopping her pacing to face him. 'Why is it that as soon as we get evidence which might prove our suspicions correct, that all of a sudden you start to have doubts?'

'OK,' said Brian. 'Do you think the police are going to investigate the accident again in the light of what an old woman tells them about it ten years later?'

Elizabeth stopped and stared at him. 'What *has* got into you?'

'I'll tell you what's got into me! What if I had done something really extreme to Turner assuming that he was the driver. Then we find out he wasn't driving. How would I feel then?'

'OK. He might not have been driving, but he covered up what happened. He may have been lying for years to protect a superior officer. And someone who might have been drunk while driving!'

Brian decided not to pursue the subject until she calmed down a bit.

But Elizabeth was displaying something of his old venom. Perhaps she was right about Turner? Perhaps he was still as responsible as if he had been behind the wheel?

As if reading his mind, Elizabeth sat down and continued, but calmer and more controlled than before.

'I can understand why you have doubts,' she said. 'But they were in it together. Even if the inspector *had* been driving, Turner would have been complicit in helping him get away with it.'

Brian knew she was correct. They might have covered up the identity of the driver, a driver who may have been drunk. There was little doubt that if this was true, and if this information had come out at the time, the careers of the officers would have been over. Even worse, they could have ended up serving time.

'The bottom line is, do you believe what Mrs White told us?' asked Elizabeth.

'I believe that she believes it,' he said. 'But believing is not the same as knowing.'

'Doesn't that just bring us back to where we started?' said Elizabeth.

'Yes,' agreed her brother. He jumped to his feet and took up the pacing ritual. 'I'm going to ask Roy's father straight out. Then I'm going to find this chief inspector and ask him!'

Elizabeth shook her head. 'I thought we had been over all that. What good will it do?'

'They're the only people who can reveal the truth, except for the witness and we haven't a clue who he was.'

'OK, say you ask them, and they deny it?' said Elizabeth.

'Then we're just back where we started and have to come up with something else.'

'And what if they admit it? What will we do then?'

Brian looked at her blankly.

'What will we do then? Will you act all indignant and tell them they were bad boys and not to do it again? Or will you be happy you know the truth, and settle down to a normal life?'

'I don't really know,' admitted Brian.

'Of course, you don't! Because the whole point of...of... everything, has been that you didn't *know*! That's what's been driving you! The need to know! And when you *do* know, you won't have a clue what to do then.'

'Once I know, then I'll figure out what to do,' said Brian stubbornly.

'No,' said Elizabeth, 'once *we* know, *we'll* figure out what to do! I believe it happened just as Mrs. White told us.'

Chapter 8

He softly closed the book, laid it gently down on the coffee table and then slumped back into his armchair. After a few moments thought, he got up and walked the few steps to a display cabinet. In the second drawer from the bottom, he found what he had been looking for. He tucked the desk diary under his arm, closed the drawer, retrieved two pens from his jacket pocket and then sat back down in his chair,

Although there continued to be heated debate over the authenticity of *The Diary of Jack the Ripper*, he had decided to read it anyway. He had read the book once and had just finished reading it for a second time. The arguments over the book's origin had been many and varied; the ink used; the writing style; the location references, and so on. But none of this mattered to him. What had impressed him was the text. If *he* had been Jack and had written a diary, he would have written it exactly the way it was. And this was an area the so-called experts were not in a position to comment on, unless any of them happened to be a serial killer. The moments of anger, rage even; the commitment to the task.

It had inspired him. So, he would write his own diary. No one would then be in any doubt regarding what he did and why he had done it. The authorities, the press and anyone else could say what they liked, but the definitive account would be there to set the record straight.

He leaned forward and opened his diary. He lifted a pen and prepared to start. Perhaps he would be better to do a draft before starting on the diary? No. Part of the Jack diary's appeal was the spontaneity. The scoring out, the ranting, the half-finished sentences, the attempts at poetry all gave the document an authentic feel. If this was good enough for Jack...

However, he would take one small liberty with his creation, hence the two pens. Hopefully no one would realise he had written some of the work in retrospect.

Now I can start to make a difference. My one regret is that this comes much too late to save the one person who really loved me.

I should have done more against the brute, but to my everlasting shame I failed.

But my failure is behind me now and there it will stay.

After writing another few lines, he changed pens and began to write about his first murder.

An hour or so later he decided to call it a night. He wasn't quite up to date, but he would take care of that tomorrow. The book was carefully placed inside a thick plastic bag, and then put under a floorboard that had been removed previously to allow engineers to install a replacement central heating system.

Chapter 9

'Did you enjoy your holidays?' asked Roy.
'Yes, not bad at all,' lied Brian. 'What about you?'

'Didn't do anything special,' said Roy. 'Took my dad out to visit some people, and that was about it.'

'Do you see your dad often?'

'I drop in on Wednesday, and spend some time with him over the weekend. He doesn't do much on account of his health. He retired from the police due to his heart problems. He's had one or two minor heart attacks over the years since. The quacks reckon the problem is a leaking valve, and they plan to operate. They talk about complications that they're trying to correct with tablets before the op.'

Brian made a mental note of the Wednesday visit.

'I knew a guy who had the valve operation. It made quite a difference to him, a new man in fact.'

'That's what we're hoping,' said Roy. 'Some days he's as right as rain, others he has absolutely no energy. He spends most of his time in the house reading. He's still very interested in police work. He'd have liked to have been a detective, but that didn't work out for him. Talking of police work, did you see that the media are now classing the murders around Glasgow as the work of a serial killer?'

'Yeah, I noticed that, but I wasn't sure if that was what they reckoned, or if they had got that from the police.'

'As far as my dad knows, the police are not publicly saying it *is* a serial killer. But I think they know a lot more than they're telling the press. I asked my dad for details, but he wouldn't say much. I know the SCAS are involved.'

Brian gave him a puzzled look. 'The Serious Crime Analysis Section,' said Roy. 'They're used to identify serial killers at an early stage. They have a database, ViCLAS, which stands for Violent Crime Linkage Analysis System which can help with identifying if the offender has previously been known. It can also help with a breakdown of the behaviour exhibited by the offender.'

Brian nodded his understating. He looked at his watch.

'Oh well, back to the grind,' he said, starting to tidy up the remains of his lunch.

'Out and about today?' asked Roy.

'Yeah, and I'll be down in the north of England tomorrow, so I'm afraid you'll be eating lunch on your own.'

'No problem,' said Roy. 'I'll have to bring in extra grub tomorrow. We're working on that new financial package and have fallen a bit behind. I've told my dad not to expect me.'

Brian nodded. Once again the Gods seemed to be smiling on him.

What Brian had told Roy wasn't a lie. He did have business in Newcastle that prevented him from being back at the office for lunch, but he was home around six. He made a call to the office on the pretext of wanting a word with Ian. As expected, Ian had left for the day. In the course of his call, he happened to mention to Isobel, one of the switchboard operators, that a customer had asked about the new financial package the company had been forecasting. She confirmed that the programming section was working late, but she didn't know if that was what they were working on.

He changed, and then drove to Turner's house. He parked where he had on the night of the meal and walked the short distance to the ex-policeman's door.

'Hello Brian,' said Turner senior, obviously surprised to see him. 'If you're looking for Roy he's not here. He has to work late tonight.'

'Yes, I know,' said Brian. 'It's actually you I need to speak to.'

Brian followed the older man into his lounge, declined the offer of a cup of coffee and sat down.

'I think I know why you're here,' said Turner.

Brian was a bit taken aback but said nothing.

'Reid is quite a common name, I suppose, but I had a feeling when you came for dinner that there was something not quite right. Am I correct?'

Brian nodded. He had rehearsed what he would say, but Turner's opening remarks had forced him to throw the script away.

The policeman's eyes took on a faraway look. 'It was a terrible day,' he said eventually, 'and not only for you, although your family suffered in a way I can only try and imagine. But it affected me, too. I want you to know that. It probably affected my wife more than me in some ways, but that's..., well, that's another story. But it did affect me. Policemen *defend* the public they don't...well, you know what I did.'

He paused. There was obviously more he thought of saying, as he opened his mouth to speak a few times, and then thought better of it.

Brian decided to wait until it was clear Turner had finished.

The ex-policeman shook his head sadly. 'I really don't know what you want me to say,' he said eventually.

'I want to hear you say that you weren't the driver,' said Brian calmly. He watched as his words sank in. The man seemed to consider what Brian had said.

'Would that make you feel better?' asked Turner.

'I don't think anything you can say would make me feel better,' said Brian, 'except that I really want to know the truth.'

'The truth?' said Turner. 'The truth is that your father was killed, and your sister left seriously injured by a police car. We have all suffered since that day.'

'Suffered!' Brian got to his feet. 'Tell me exactly how you have suffered! As far as I know, the incident was investigated, and then brushed under the carpet. You would have had a few weeks of discomfort, and then it was forgotten!'

Brian walked to the window and looked out at nothing in particular. He felt a mixture of anger and sadness. There was a danger the sadness would overcome his anger and cause him to break down, and he didn't want Turner to see that.

'Forgotten?' said Turner quietly. 'Do you really think I just forgot about what had happened and carried on as normal? Do you really think I'm such a cold-hearted bastard? The times I woke in a cold sweat after a nightmare…'

'You had nightmares!' Brian turned to face the man, his anger now in control. 'But when you woke up your wife and son were still there. When I woke up, my family had been destroyed! So, let's compare nightmares! I'd swop mine for yours any day of the week!'

'I'm sure you would,' said Turner quietly.

Turner looked at Brian with sadness in his eyes. Brian returned the stare, but with anger burning in his eyes. Slowly, the anger abated. Turner was now looking at his slippers. He looked older than he had when he met Brian at the door. He slowly lifted a shaking hand and wiped away what might have been a tear. He looked grey, old and ill. Suddenly, Brian felt pity for the man. No! Pity wasn't in his plan! Why should he pity this man? If anyone deserved pity, it was Brian.

Brian sat down again. 'I need to know about the accident,' said Brian. 'I need to know if the chief inspector was driving. And I need to know if he was drunk.'

'What gives you that idea?'

'A former neighbour, Betty White, was there. She has very vivid memories of that day. She knows who did what and even that your boss had quite a bit to drink earlier in the evening. So, do you accept that what she told me is true?'

'If I agreed with her,' said Turner slowly, 'would it make you feel better? You need to know who to blame? I'm to blame. I was in the car. The car that hit two innocent people crossing the road. Should they have been crossing the road? No. Should the car have hit them? No. Were they, and did it? Yes. And that's it.'

Brian was struggling to focus. Images of the accident, his mother, funerals, visitors, sympathy cards, pills, hospital, Caroline, more cards, more pills. His mind was going into overload. Suddenly he felt that he had to get out of the house. Without another word, he got up and left. He got back into his car and tried to put the key into the ignition. His hand wouldn't stop shaking. He tried steadying it with his other hand, but it too was shaking. He gave up and started to cry.

Back in the house, Turner stared for a while at the seat Brian had occupied. Then he picked up the phone and dialled a number.

After a few rings, a male voice answered.

'It's Turner, we have a problem.'

Brian eventually calmed down and regained control enough to drive home. He was pleased to find that Elizabeth was out. He poured himself a glass of whisky, took a slug, and recoiled at the disgusting taste. He threw the rest down the sink and lit a cigarette. That hadn't gone as planned. He wished he had taken Elizabeth with him. She might have been able to use her intuition to see behind what was being said. Basically, he was none the wiser, just as Elizabeth had predicted. And he had forgotten to ask who the other man in the car had been. Perhaps he would have more luck with Chief Inspector Stewart. He debated whether or not he should wait for Elizabeth. After making a fool of himself with Turner, he decided he should go alone. In any case, he had no idea where she was, and he wanted to get this over with as soon as he could. If he had better luck with the chief inspector, he could relay this to Elizabeth and skimp over the disastrous meeting with Turner.

Brian had the chief inspector's address in Motherwell, but this was in an area he wasn't familiar with. However, with the aid of his SatNav he found his way there quicker than he had anticipated.

He paused outside the house and had a look at the area. He had no idea what kind of money a chief inspector made, but the house was impressive. At one time the house may have been two semi-detached properties which had then been joined. Brian opened the large iron gate and walked up the gravel path to the imposing set of double doors. The chimes of the doorbell echoed inside and before Brian could ring a second time, a very tall man opened the door.

'Mr. Stewart?' said Brian politely.

'Yes,' said the man in a very deep voice.

'I wonder if I might have a word with you.'

'Are you selling something?' said the former chief inspector.

'No, nothing like that. It has to do with an accident you were involved in a number of years ago.'

'Really?' said Stewart, 'well you'd better come in and tell me what I can do for you.'

Brian followed the man into a long hallway. They passed one door on the right and another on the left, and then entered the second door on the left which was ajar.

'This is my study,' explained Stewart. 'Have a seat and give me a minute to tell my wife that I'm busy, and then I'll be right with you.'

Brian sat down in a comfortable armchair and heard muffled voices from further down the corridor. He looked around the room. Although decorated in a fairly modern style, the high ceiling betrayed the age of the house. Bookshelves lined two of the walls, and they were packed with mostly hardback volumes. The large bay window behind the desk had multiple panels of glass to blend with the old building, although the window frame was obviously quite modern. A computer and telephone sat on the old mahogany desk. A few moments later, Stewart reappeared and sat down on his leather swivel chair behind the desk.

'Now Mr...?'

'Reid,' said Brian.

'Well Mr Reid, what can I do for you? It's getting quite late, so I hope this isn't going to take too long.'

'I'll only take a few moments of your time,' said Brian. He took a deep breath. 'I just need you to confirm that in the accident you were involved in a decade ago in which my father was killed and my sister gravely injured that you were driving the car that hit them. And that you were driving the car while under the influence of drink. I would also like you to tell me the name of the witness you had in the back of the car on the day in question.'

Stewart leaned back in his large chair and eyed Brian carefully. Brian battled hard to maintain his outward appearance of calm.

'I believe you're referring to the tragic accident in Airdrie. The accident in which a police car was rushing back to the station with a witness, and which was then involved in striking two pedestrians who had ran out into the road with no warning whatsoever. An accident which was then investigated very thoroughly with no charges made against the officers involved. Is that the reason for your visit to me at this hour of the evening?'

Brian was determined not to be undermined by the former chief inspector's glib and confident manner.

'That's exactly the reason I'm here, but I have information that wasn't available to the inquiry at the time. This information would, I believe, force another inquiry. One that would get to the truth of the matter.' Brian felt very uncomfortable discussing the event in such matter-of-fact terms, but he sensed that calm discussion might be more effective than hysterical outbursts.

'So, you have new information?' said the Inspector. 'I suppose you have uncovered CCTV footage, or previously unseen video or photographic records of the incident?'

'Not exactly,' said Brian, 'but I do have a witness who saw certain things which throw revealing new light on the fairy-tale that the inquiry upheld.'

The Inspector raised his eyebrows. 'New witnesses? Ah.'

'No, one new witness.'

'Oh sorry, only one. I see. Someone quite reliable I suppose. A professional person who would be in a position to undermine the evidence taken by the committee?'

Brian nodded.

'And this lady, she's...?'

'I didn't say it was a woman,' said Brian, relieved he had the sense to avoid what he took to be a trap.

'A former neighbour of my family. Someone who knew my parents very well, and who was unlikely to forget what they saw even after all this time.'

'I see. A friend of the family, and able to give a totally unbiased view of things. And what did this person see that has caused your appearance on my doorstep?'

'You turning on the blue light after the accident, and you throwing your fancy cap into the car to avoid anyone at the scene being in a position to easily distinguish you from Turner. You were also seen emerging from the driver's seat, and not the passenger seat as the inquiry believed. My visit is simply to give you a chance to admit your deception. Is that reason enough?'

'And you expect me to break down and admit that this story you're telling me is the truth?'

'I didn't really know what to expect when I called on you,' admitted Brian. 'I suppose I thought that someone who had been a senior officer might have some shred of honour and decency, and even after all this time be prepared to admit that he *had* been driving and *was* drunk at the time. However, if that's too much for you, we'll just have to await developments.'

'Are you threatening me, Mr Reid?'

'Yes. I suppose I am in a way.'

'I'm used to being threatened, Mr. Reid, and by much more serious and dangerous people than you. So, do what you have to do, but please, before you bother me or Mr Turner again, make sure you have something a bit more substantial than a half-baked story given to you by a neighbour.'

Brian sat in his car. He was shaking again, but not as badly as when he left Turner's house. If he was honest with himself, he didn't really expect to have any more luck with the chief inspector. But he had remained in control, and the visit hadn't been a total waste. He may have learned one thing - Stewart appeared to know that he had spoken to Turner. If he hadn't, how did he know to refer to Mrs. White as a lady before Brian had said the witness was a female? Was he just fishing?

Chapter 10

The killer held open the library door to allow a middle-aged woman to enter. She smiled at him politely, and he returned the gesture. He was feeling very good. It now seemed that his work was being appreciated. Although he had a computer at home, he preferred scanning the newspapers online at the local library. He knew how to delete his viewing history on his own computer but wasn't sure if some smart arse in the police might still be able to retrieve it.

Feeling a surge of enthusiasm, he started the one and a half mile walk home to continue his preparations for his latest outing. Snow was forecast for the Glasgow area over the next day or so, and that might force him to call off his plans. He had considered making additional allowances for snow, but all things considered, he had decided it would be too risky. Tricky driving conditions, tracking footprints, clues being covered, etc. No. He didn't want to blow things just when he was becoming successful. Still, he might be able to squeeze in one more outing in case the weather put him out of business.

As he started his walk home, he considered what he had read in the library. The police were now advising the public that the killings might be the work of the same man. They were also suggesting that mature men were the targets, with all the victims being attacked as they made their way home. They didn't mention that all had been drinking and were going home to abuse their wives and families, but he didn't expect them to release that information. They needed the public to feel sympathy for the liberated families, even to the extent of encouraging them to give quotes to the papers saying how sad they were at their loss. The killer snorted and increased his pace. It was all a big front to paint a picture of him as the bad guy. Only in time would the truth come out. Until then he would continue his work undeterred by anything the papers might say. One disappointment was that none had come up with a decent name for him. They were content to use emotive language and describe him as *depraved, demented, an animal and a psycho.* This made him laugh! They didn't know him, so what did they base their description on? But it was only as he expected. The more the papers screamed a sensational headline, the greater their sales. And the public lapped it up.

The police had been vague regarding the type of person they were looking for. They tried to make this sound as if they were not in a position to release information. That made him laugh! They hadn't a clue! Well, they did have clues, but only the ones he wanted them to have. There had been a suggestion that the man was likely to be big and powerful. He smiled and congratulated himself on his choice of footwear. He laughed out loud when the image of the police escorting clowns into police stations flashed into his mind.

The police were advising men out and about in the evenings in the Glasgow area to travel in groups, or at least in pairs. But he knew this advice would be largely ignored. When the prostitutes were being murdered in Yorkshire, similar advice was issued and ignored.

The fools! Do they really think that advising men to stay home will work? No chance! Their desire to drink and then abuse their wives would prove a much greater draw than advice given via a newspaper.

Chapter 11

Brian dreaded going into work the next day. The bravado had deserted him for the time being, and he didn't fancy a confrontation with Roy. As fortune would have it, he arrived to find a minor emergency had arisen with one of their biggest clients based in Aberdeen.

It was the weekend before he was back home, and there were no messages from Roy.

'So, you had to go and confront them, even though I said it would be a waste of time?'

Elizabeth stood with her hands on her hips.

Brian had been waiting to speak to her for three days. It turned out she had gone back down South to attend to some matters.

'Yes,' said Brian defiantly, 'I needed to see how they would react.'

'And did their reactions come up to your expectations?'

'It was quite strange. Turner probably did what I expected. He seemed genuinely upset about the whole business but wouldn't confirm or deny what I was telling him.'

'Of course he didn't! Have you considered the effect on Turner and Stewart if the truth comes out? Even after all this time they could still end up in jail. Loss of pensions and God knows what else! There's no way they'll admit what happened!'

'Stewart was quite different,' continued Brian, ignoring what Elizabeth had said. 'He was very calm and didn't show any signs of remorse about the accident. He talked about it in a very clinical, detached way. But there was something else. I got the distinct impression that he was expecting me. Although he pretended to, he didn't have to try very hard to recall the accident.'

'Well, it *was* a fatal accident; I'd imagine only a very emotionless individual would be able to forget about that.'

Brian shook his head. 'No. It was more than that. I felt he knew what I was going to say before I said it. He talked about CCTV and pictures. But even as he was talking about this, nothing in his manner suggested he expected for a moment that I had that sort of evidence. He seemed to know about Mrs White, and he could only have got that information from Turner.'

Elizabeth sat down. 'So?' she said. 'It's no great surprise that Turner called him, if that's what happened.'

'Possibly,' admitted Brian.

'Anyway, what do we do now?' asked Elizabeth.

'I think we go to the police,' said Brian. 'Even if they don't do anything right now, at least we'll have registered our complaint. If we turn up anything else in the future, it will back it up.'

'We should check with Mrs. White to see if she's happy talking to the police,' said Elizabeth. 'Plus, we've given her some time to think about it; we need to check if she's still confident about what she saw.'

'That's fair enough,' agreed Brian. 'There's also the fact that Stewart is a very tall man, much taller than Turner. That could help to confirm the identification she'll make.'

An hour later, and they were at Betty White's door.

'Perhaps she's out shopping?' suggested Brian when there was no answer.

'Perhaps,' agreed Elizabeth. 'Do we wait or come back later?'

'Let's sit in the car for a few minutes and see if she returns,' suggested Brian. 'Or we could ask some of the neighbours?'

As if on cue, an elderly man emerged from a house two doors up.

'Are you looking for Betty White?' he called loudly.

Brian and Elizabeth walked down the three steps from Mrs. White's door and moved closer to the old partition fence.

'Yes,' shouted Elizabeth.

The man moved to lean on his fence.

'I'm afraid she's gone,' he said in a quieter voice.

'Do you know when she'll be back?' asked Brian.

'Oh no,' said the man. 'She won't be back. She's dead.'

Brian and Elizabeth looked at each other.

'But we only spoke to her the other day,' said Brian to the man. 'When did she die?'

The man shuffled and tried to lean even closer over the fence. He opened his mouth to speak, and then gestured for them to come closer.

'Last night,' he said. 'It happened last night. It must have been just after the gasman left. She could have lain for days if another neighbour hadn't called on her. This other neighbour had been expected, and she was surprised to find no one at home. She tried the door, and it was open, so she tried to go in, but the door wouldn't open enough. Then she found out why. Betty was lying behind it. She had fallen down the stairs. I suppose she had broken her neck.'

'So where...' Brian started to ask a question.

'The police arranged for an undertaker to take her away. The police were here for quite some time. I suppose they have to investigate any sudden death, even if it is an old woman and the cause seems pretty obvious. Did you know her well?'

For some reason, Brian felt guilty. 'We've known her for years,' he said, 'but I wouldn't say that we knew her well.'

The man nodded. 'I haven't lived here very long,' he said, 'but I knew her quite well. A terrible thing to happen. She was very nice, and still very active in spite of her age.'

Brian and Elizabeth thanked him and turned to leave.

'Do you want me to let you know when the funeral is?' said the man.

'Yes, of course.' Brian reached in his pocket, dug out one of his business cards and handed it to the man.

'If you could give us a ring on any of the numbers on the card, we'd appreciate it.'

'You know,' said the man, 'it's fortunate she left her door open.'

'Yes,' said Elizabeth as she turned to walk away.

'But it's strange,' said the man. 'She never left her door open.'

Brian and Elizabeth paused.

'But you said she was expecting her neighbour,' said Elizabeth.

'Yes, she was. But she never left her door open. I asked her about this once. You know, in a joking manner. I asked her if she thought someone might come and steal her or something. She laughed and told me that you can never be too careful.' He paused and seemed to be thinking.

'And even if the door wasn't actually locked, she'd always have the security chain on. It puzzles me a bit. It's probably nothing, but you know how your mind turns things over after a shock?'

Brian agreed. 'But you said the gas man had just been.'

The man nodded. 'True, very true.'

'Maybe he had left, and she was coming down the stairs to lock her door when she tripped?'

The man continued to nod. 'But her gas meter isn't upstairs,' said the man. 'It's in the same place as mine, under the sink in the kitchen.'

'Are you sure?' said Brian.

'Oh. I'm sure,' said the man. 'I know where my gas meter is!'

'No,' said Brian. 'I mean, are you sure her meter is in the same place?'

'Positive,' said the man. 'She told me. When I moved in a few years ago she dropped in to see me. I think she was just being nosey, but I don't like to speak ill of the dead. Anyway, she insisted on telling me where everything was, the fuse box, the meters and that sort of stuff. She knew exactly where these were as she said my house had the same layout as hers.'

'Did the police ask you anything about this?' asked Elizabeth.

'No,' said the man, shaking his head. 'They just asked when I had seen her last. They only talked to me for a minute or two. They seemed to be quite busy as their radio things kept interrupting us. Do you think I should tell them?'

'Did you tell them about the gas man?' asked Brian.

'Oh yes. I thought that would be helpful in working out when she had her fall. I don't think I'll go out of my way and call on them. They might think I'm being a nuisance.'

Elizabeth and Brian drove home in silence.

'So, what do we do now?' said Brian, placing a cup of tea in front of Elizabeth. He lit a cigarette, much to Elizabeth's disapproval.

'I don't know what we can do,' said Elizabeth, returning to her seat after opening a window to let the smoke out. 'We're back where we started. We could go to the police and tell them what she told us, but without her to back us up it would be a waste of time.'

Brian nodded. 'There's something about Stewart that bothers me,' he said thoughtfully.

'There's a lot that bothers me, too,' said Elizabeth.

'I don't mean the accident. He lives in a huge house. When I arrived, I couldn't believe I was at the correct place. You really want to see it, it's a mansion. He's obviously well off. I wonder where he got the money?'

'I'm sure a chief inspector's pension is very good. And his family may have had money, or his wife's family. I don't think we can read anything into the size of house he lives in. There's lots of ways he could have got the money.'

'Possibly,' agreed Brian, 'but I think I'll sniff around a bit.'

'If you like,' said Elizabeth, obviously doubtful of where this would take them.

'I'll try again and come up with someone else like Betty White. The accident happened on a Saturday morning, there must have been lots of people about. Didn't Betty say she had been in a shop?'

Brian confirmed that the old lady had said that.

'Well,' said Elizabeth, 'it won't do any harm in asking in the local shops.'

Brian agreed it was worth a try, and they settled down to watch something on the television. If asked later what it was they watched, Brian wouldn't have had a clue. His mind continued to turn things over and over, and he suspected his sister was doing the same.

Sunday dawned, and Brian didn't have any enthusiasm for the day. The neighbour of Mrs. White they had been speaking to, a Derek Nelson, had phoned to say the funeral would be on Thursday.

'I suppose we really should go,' said Brian as they ate breakfast. 'This'll be the first funeral I've been to since mum's.'

'I'll go,' said Elizabeth. 'I'll tell anyone who asks that you had to be away on business, but I'm sure no one will ask.'

'No, I feel I should be there,' argued Brian.

'You'll cramp my style,' said Elizabeth. 'This might be a good chance to see some of our old neighbours. I might pick up a few bits and pieces if I get them chatting. You would probably put them off. All they'll remember of you is you trying to get your bloody ball back!'

She did have a point, so Brian decided not to argue with her.

'You'll get some flowers? We don't even know who to send a card to.'

'I'll take a card with me,' said Elizabeth.

Brian took a swig of tea. 'The way you talk about it sounds so cold.'

'It's a funeral,' said Elizabeth. 'They tend to be that way.'

'No, I meant...'

'I know what you meant. Listen, the old lady tried to help us, I doubt if she'd be upset at me trying to get to the bottom of things now that she's not here.'

'I suppose so,' said Brian unenthusiastically.

Elizabeth got up and walked round to put a hand on his shoulder.

'You're my brother, and I love you to bits, but you were always soft. I imagined all these thoughts of revenge would have changed you, but they haven't. You're still the same soft guy you've always been.'

She headed off to her room.

'And I wouldn't change you for the world,' she said under her breath as she left.

On Monday morning, Brian had no reason not to be at his work. He decided to take the bull by the horns and turn up for lunch as normal. At least if he and Roy were going to have a blazing row it would be relatively private. The lunch break came and went with no sign of Roy, so Brian went to investigate.

'Oh, he's not in today,' said Lyn, the font of all knowledge. 'Didn't you hear? His dad's had a heart attack. Roy's at the hospital.'

'Is it serious?' said Brian.

'Well, it is a heart attack.'

Brian thanked her and left.

It crossed his mind that he should go to the hospital, but then he decided against it. If the discussion he had with Turner was in any way the cause of the attack, the last thing likely to help matters would be him turning up at the hospital.

He checked his diary, and found that he had nothing scheduled for the rest of the day.

On an impulse, he borrowed one of the office phones and, after withholding the number, phoned former Chief Inspector Stewart.

'Mr. Stewart, please,' he said in his most polite voice when his call was answered.

'I'm sorry, Mr. Stewart is at work, can I ask who's calling?'

'No, it's OK; I'm just an old colleague. I'll try him at his work. Thanks.' Then Brian hung up.

He assumed the person who had answered was Stewart's wife. He cursed himself for not having the foresight to ask for Stewart's work number, but that might have forced him to make up a name for himself and a reason for his call.

Changing his mind about working in the office, he left and went to the local library. Stewart's house was still bothering him, and he had an idea how to check on this.

Unfortunately, the local history librarian informed him that they were no longer allowed to display electoral rolls. Something to do with data protection. Brian cursed quietly and went home.

Elizabeth arrived just after four and was surprised to find him in the house.

'Turner's had a heart attack,' said Brian.

Elizabeth paused. 'Is it bad?' she said.

'I've no idea,' said Brian.

'Have you spoken to Roy?'

'No. I went looking for him. That's when I discovered his dad had taken ill. Roy's at the hospital.'

'You didn't go there, did you?' asked Elizabeth.

'I thought about it but decided it best not to.'

'That's sensible. Do you know if Roy knows you went to see his dad?'

'I've no idea,' confessed Brian.

'I know what you're thinking,' said Elizabeth, 'you're blaming yourself for the heart attack. Well, you can get that out of your mind. If anything caused the attack, it would be his conscience. Serves him right, if you ask me.'

Brian didn't want to get into an argument, so he didn't reply.

'I've found out something interesting about our Chief Inspector Stewart,' said Brian. He picked up a sheet of paper he had been writing on.

'Stewart bought his current house six years ago, while he was still with the police. Stewart's mother and father both worked for the Department of Agriculture and lived in a council house all their days. They're both dead. His wife was formerly Maureen Donnelly, the only daughter of a fireman and a cleaner who also lived all their days in a council house.'

'So perhaps he got the house at a bargain price?' suggested Elizabeth.

Brian referred again to his notes. 'The house was on the market at offers over £450,000. The Stewarts did own their own home before buying the current property. I haven't been able to track down what they sold their old place for, but an equivalent property in the same street sold for £120,000 about a year ago.'

Elizabeth had been listening while she packed the last of the food in the refrigerator.

'So, they would need to get a mortgage for the difference, £330,000. A big loan at their age.'

'Assuming that they had cleared off their old mortgage,' added Brian. 'Stewart and his wife seem to have a lot of cash. Apart from the house, there were two cars in the driveway when I visited. One was a BMW and the other was some type of 4 x 4.'

'Do you think Stewart could be getting money from Turner? Something to do with the accident?'

'I'd have thought it more likely to be the other way round,' said Brian.

'Yeah,' agreed Elizabeth. 'It all does seem a bit suspicious.'

'Stewart seems to have another job,' said Brian. He then told her briefly about his phone call.

'Perhaps he's in a much better job than the police,' suggested Elizabeth.

'Better than a chief inspector?' said Brian, 'it could be worth finding out, just to satisfy my curiosity.'

'You'll not get that on the Internet, will you?'

'Unlikely, and I wouldn't know where to start. No. I think the answer is for me to get involved in a bit of police work. Of the detective style.'

'OK. I'll be Dr. Watson.'

Chapter 12

As Brian had little on for the next few days, he phoned his work first thing in the morning and asked to take a couple of days leave. This wasn't a problem, as his employers usually had to persuade him to take time off. He spent the day trying to find out more information about Stewart. He also decided to look into Turner's past but didn't turn up anything of use.

His old Saab had been acting up a bit, so Brian arranged for this to be looked at by his usual mechanic who had a small garage on the road out of the town. The following day he borrowed Elizabeth's car and drove round to Stewart's house. He parked a few houses away, then got out and walked casually past Stewart's home. There were no cars parked in sight, but they could have been housed in the large double garage, a modern brick building which looked quite out of place against the much older house. He went back to the car and pondered what to do. Another phone call would be very suspicious, so he decided to wait for a while and see if anything happened. He studied the buildings more closely. Every one that didn't have a large hedge shielding it from view possessed a large driveway. Some could have served as a small hotel or boarding house. He remembered noticing how high the ceiling was in Stewart's house, a sign that the house was built in a bygone era. As far as he could tell, the house was completely double-glazed. Brian remembered back to when he had his place fitted with double-glazing and the cost involved. He estimated that the Stewart house would have at least eighteen windows, possibly more, and shuddered to think what double-glazing that lot would have set them back.

'What are you looking at Robbie,' said Maureen Stewart.

Stewart pointed out of the attic window at the car parked some way down the street. 'It's the young man who called on me the other night.'

Mrs. Stewart peered out of the window.

'How do you know? Can you see him inside the car?'

'He walked past the house and then returned to his car.'

'What do you think he wants?'

Stewart shrugged. 'I've no idea,' he said.

'Should we call the police?' asked his wife.

'And tell them what? That a man is sitting in his car? It's not parked illegally, there's nothing they can do. There's no need to worry, he may just be waiting to pick someone up.'

'That would be too much of a coincidence! Why don't you tell me what he wanted?'

Stewart shook his head. 'It was nothing, he wanted me to help him with an old case, but I told him there was nothing I could do. I'm not in the Force anymore and it was a long time ago. Don't worry, dear.'

Maureen Stewart frowned, but said nothing and returned to the kitchen.

Stewart went downstairs where he could get a better look at the car. He needed to get a note of the registration number before making his phone call.

Brian eventually gave up and headed for home, frustrated at the waste of time. Tomorrow was Mrs. White's funeral, and with luck Elizabeth might turn up something useful.

Elizabeth had spent the time while he was out tidying up. At least that was what she called it. Brian tended to view it as a couple of hours spent hiding things. Elizabeth had smacked him on the arm when he asked for a guided tour. Fortunately, she had been unable to hide his television, so they watched it for a few hours. Elizabeth didn't want to watch sport, and Brian didn't want to watch soaps, so they started to watch a crime film. Elizabeth became fed up with Brian constantly pointing out flaws in the plot, so she decided to have an early night. For once, they both agreed. The funeral was first thing in the morning, and Brian wanted to try his luck outside Stewart's house again, a bit earlier this time. Fortunately, his car was now repaired, and he would be able to collect this any time after 8am.

Brian woke and sat up. He looked at his bedside clock. Just after 3. He shrugged and settled down to sleep.

'Brian!'

He jumped up and swung himself out of the bed. The lounge light was on, so he headed there rather than Elizabeth's room.

He squinted, trying to get his eyes used to the light. Elizabeth was standing in her nightdress in the middle of the living room.

'What's all the fuss?' asked Brian.

Elizabeth pointed to the window.

Three of the segments of the vertical blind were hanging loose. He walked to the window, and then stopped.

Lying just behind the couch was a large brick. Attached to the brick was a piece of string and attached to the string was a piece of paper.

Brian bent to pick it up as Elizabeth moved to join him.

'Watch your feet,' said Brian. She stopped. He picked up the brick carefully and retreated until he was clear of the glass.

75

'The smash woke me up,' explained Elizabeth.

'Me, too,' said Brian, as he opened the sheet of paper. 'Or at least it must have.' He read the note, and then handed it to his sister.

She read it out loud. 'Leave it. Or else.'

She handed it back to her brother. 'Turner?' she said.

'He's still in hospital as far as I know,' said Brian.

'Roy?'

Brian shrugged. 'I don't even know if he's aware that I've been to see his dad.'

'So, who does that leave? Stewart?'

'That's about it, assuming this is linked to the questions we've been asking.'

'Well, you'll need to call the police.'

'And tell them what?' said Brian. 'They'll ask lots of questions. Do we really want to tell them the whole story?'

'It wouldn't be my first choice,' admitted Elizabeth, 'but you'll need to report it to claim on your house insurance. You'll need a crime incident number.'

'Let's split the difference,' said Brian, 'we'll report it, but say nothing about the note. We'll just say we've had a brick thrown through our window.'

Elizabeth nodded.

They were a bit surprised that the police arrived within a few minutes of being phoned. They said that they were having a quiet night. After twenty minutes of asking fairly standard questions they left, saying they would cruise around the neighbourhood a few times, looking for anyone acting suspiciously. They had just left when the glazier arrived, responding to the emergency number Elizabeth had called. She had thought it more likely they would come out in the middle of the night if they heard it was a woman in distress.

Brian tidied up the glass, and they went to bed to try and get some sleep in what was left of the night. Brian's plan of watching Stewart's house was snookered, as he would have to deal with the insurance company. There was no reason for Elizabeth to wait with him, so she would go to the funeral as planned. Brian was very happy not to be going to the funeral. It was being held in the Old Monkland Cemetery, the same place where his family were buried.

As he tried to fall asleep, Brian thought about the message they had received. There was little doubt in his mind it referred to them snooping about. But who could have sent it? He could only think of three possibilities, the ones he had discussed briefly with Elizabeth – Peter Turner, Roy Turner and Robert Stewart.

Things were tied up surprisingly quickly with the insurance company and the glazier, and by the time Elizabeth returned there were no signs of the incident, apart from one window that was much cleaner than the others.

'Do you remember Terry Scott?' she asked.

'The name rings a bell,' said Brian.

'He's a few years older than me and lived across from the hospital. He wasn't around his home much, as he was at university. But he got a part time job during the holidays in Provan's the Butchers. A strange job, cutting up cows, since he was studying Animal Science and Welfare. Anyway, he was working on the day of the accident serving at the counter as they were short staffed. He didn't go out at the time of the accident as he didn't want to leave the shop, but a customer came in after some of the fuss had died down, and this woman told him basically what had happened.'

'So?' said Brian.

'Well, she said that a police car had struck two pedestrians and that the officers had got out to try and help. She recognised the passenger as Turner. She knew his wife quite well.'

'So why didn't she tell the inquiry that?' asked Brian.

'Maybe she wasn't asked. Terry has no idea where she is now.'

'So why didn't Terry tell the inquiry what she had told him?'

'Because he was back at university.'

'He'd have read about it in the papers.'

'Not down in Suffolk. That's where he was at university. He didn't even know until much later that there had *been* an inquiry. You've got to realise that when someone isn't directly involved in an incident like that, they forget about it pretty quickly.'

'I don't know if his evidence would be any good anyway,' said Brian. 'Isn't that what they call hearsay?'

'I haven't a clue,' said Elizabeth. 'But I could only chat to him for a few moments, there might be more that he can tell us. Just in case, I took a note of his address and phone number. He'd be quite happy to talk to us if we want. He's married and living up here again.'

'It certainly wouldn't do any harm,' said Brian. 'Let's give him a ring and drop in on him this weekend if convenient. Tomorrow I'm going to track down Roy.'

'And his dad?'

'No. I'd rather find out the position with Roy first.'

Elizabeth agreed. 'Do you think there's any way we could find out who the guy in the back of the car was?'

'I suppose the police would have a record of it,' said Brian. 'But I don't know if they would tell us. Since it was so long ago, they would probably need a very good reason even to try and find out.'

'We could hunt through reports of court cases and see if these would give us a clue.'

Brian shook his head. 'That's a real long shot. Stewart claims the passenger was only a witness.'

The paper on Friday morning had a headline screaming 'Serial Killer at Large.'

Brian read the report while having his breakfast. The police were now looking for a man who was believed to have killed at least four men in the Glasgow area.

This latest 'atrocity' was the work of a 'deranged psychopath' who 'prowled the streets' around Glasgow looking for his 'prey'. He then strangled his victims, 'discarding their bodies' to be discovered by 'innocent people who happened upon them'. All the victims to date had been 'loving family men' with no criminal records of any kind. The crimes were motiveless and were obviously the work of a 'sadistic maniac'. Nameless people were interviewed, and all told how shocked, stunned and terrified they were. Everyone in the area stated that they were afraid to go out at night and wondered how long it would be before the police could 'cage' this killer.

The police were quoted as saying that they were not in a position to release any specific details of the crimes but were convinced that they were hunting for a serial killer. The murders contained a sufficient number of similarities for them to draw this conclusion. They appealed for the public to report any strange men seen lurking around the town (Brian laughed at that bit. Glasgow. Strange men lurking around? Never!).

The public were strongly advised not to approach any such individual, but to contact the police, in confidence if desired. The article was beefed up with details of previous murders in the Glasgow area, including, of course, Bible John.

At last! So, the police have now recognised my work! The brakes will be off the papers now. They will try as best they can to feed the public's hunger for news on the killings. I need to time my events to maximise the publicity. The 'loving family man' statements made me laugh. Still, I suppose it is asking too much for the press to probe beneath the surface of these men's lives. No matter. But I need to be careful. It's possible the police will have officers on the streets under-cover. Research is the key to continued success.

Chapter 13

Brian phoned the hospital and learned that Peter Turner had been released. He felt relieved at the news. In all the revenge scenarios he had rehearsed over the years, Turner having a heart attack and dying had not been one of them. In fact, nothing that had happened recently fitted in at all well with what he had imagined. In spite of Elizabeth's view that Turner was just as guilty as Stewart, he was having problems with that. He was swinging towards Stewart as the main focus of his hatred, not only because of what he suspected, but also because of the demeanour of the man.

The phone rang just as he was preparing to leave for work. It was Roy.

'I need to speak to you,' said Roy coldly.

'Where are you?' said Brian.

'I'm at home. Can you come round?'

'I'll be there in fifteen minutes,' said Brian.

Roy hung up.

Brian took a deep breath then made towards his door. Realising that he still had the phone receiver in his hand, he returned to replace it. Eventually he made it to his Saab and left.

Reaching his destination, he could see Roy looking out of his window. Brian parked and walked up to the door as casually as he could. The door opened before he could knock, and Roy stood aside to let him enter.

'How's your dad?' said Brian.

He turned to face Roy and didn't see the punch coming. Surprise as much as the force of the blow caused him to stumble back against a small hall table and then onto the floor. He instinctively put his hands over his face to protect himself against further blows, but Roy just stood looking down at him.

'Feel better?' said Brian, rubbing his jaw.

'A bit,' replied Roy, breathing heavily.

'If I get up, are you going to knock me down again?' said Brian.

'I'm not sure,' said Roy.

'Well, I reckon I'll just sit here until you make up your mind. How's your dad?'

'Do you really give a shit?' said Roy.

Brian looked up at Roy but said nothing.

'My dad told me who you are, and about your visit,' said Roy. 'He said that you needed to talk about the accident. We've never talked about the accident because it caused him so much pain, then you arrive and reopen old wounds. Did you really have to do that?'

Brian didn't attempt to get up.

'How's he keeping?' he asked.

'It was another minor attack, much like he's had before. They kept him in as much for observation as anything else. Brought on by stress, they said. Stress caused by your visit, I've no doubt.'

'I'm really sorry about that,' said Brian, and he meant it.

'Look,' Roy sat down on the floor opposite Brian. 'They're still hoping to do the operation in the next few months, but every time he has one of these attacks it weakens him. We're trying to build him up, mentally as much as physically. I don't want you to talk to him again until he gets through his op. But...' Roy looked a bit uncomfortable. 'I know my dad, and I know there's things about the accident he's not telling me.'

'I *bet* he doesn't!' said Elizabeth. 'And you said you were sorry! Jesus Christ! What have you to be sorry about!' She put on a soppy voice. 'Oh, Mr Turner, I'm really sorry to bother you, but can you explain to me why you lied about the incident in which you were responsible for murdering my father and sister. Please, if it's not too much trouble!'

'It wasn't like that,' said Brian.

'Christ, you're so soft! You let people walk all over you!'

She turned one way, then the other. 'I'm going to see this Roy guy and get a few things straight!'

'No, you're not!' said Brian, jumping to his feet. 'You'll sit down and listen to me!'

'No, I won't!'

'*Yes, you will!*' Brian's face was red with rage as he screamed at her.

She stared at him for a moment, and then sat down.

'This isn't about revenge for the sake of it,' said Brian, trying to sound a bit calmer. 'Is that what you want? Revenge?'

'*And what if it is?*' shouted Elizabeth, getting to her feet again.

'*Sit down!*' shouted Brian. She hesitated a moment, then sat down.

'Do you really think it's revenge I want?'

'You told me you did,' said Elizabeth.

'I was wrong,' said Brian. 'That's what I always told myself, but I was wrong.'

'So, what *do* you want?' asked Elizabeth in a calmer voice.

'I want them to take responsibility for what they did. For them to stand up and say *I did it. This is how it happened.* That's what I want.'

'And you'd be satisfied with that?' said Elizabeth.

'Yes,' said Brian in a soft voice.

'Well, that's not what I want. That's not good enough for me, and it shouldn't be good enough for you either.' Elizabeth got to her feet and walked away.

Brian tried to put their argument out of his mind and busied himself making a few calls to line up his schedule for the coming week. He called Ian.

'Listen Brian,' said Ian, after the preliminary small talk was over, 'the new financial package is at the trial stage. This is going to take at least a week. I know you've been pushing the package with your clients and they're probably getting a bit impatient at the delay. It might be an idea if you stayed clear of them for a while. When this has been debugged, you can start to push it.'

Brian agreed.

'Great!' said Ian. 'I know you've taken a few days holiday recently, but you're due lots more. Why don't you take some more time and get yourself psyched up for the big push? We could really do with you being on the top of your game.'

'OK,' said Brian. 'I'll keep the appointments I've made next week and leave it at that.'

Brian put the phone down but couldn't decide how he felt. All things considered, he'd probably be better cutting back on work for a while, but work gave him a focus in his life.

'Listen Brian,' said Elizabeth, interrupting his thoughts. 'I think we need to take a few steps back for a while. Things are getting confused. We both need to think things over.'

'What are you saying?' said Brian.

'Just that,' said Elizabeth. 'I'll go and see Terry tomorrow and then I'll need to go back down South. I need to sort some things out. There's just too much going on at the moment and I can't concentrate on one thing for others getting in the way.'

'I know how you feel. Can I help?' asked Brian.

She shook her head and smiled. 'Thanks, but no. I need to sort this for myself.'

'So how long will you be gone?'

'I've no idea. I just need time to evaluate my life. Do I go back to Uni or find a job? I've not reached a decision about that, and the money I've stashed away won't last forever.'

'If it's money you need...'

'No, no. I'm OK. I just need to sort things out, that's all.'

'I hope you're not going because of our argument,' said Brian.

She shook her head. 'Of course not! When have we ever agreed on anything? Don't worry about that. I think you could do with a break, too. We've lived with the situation for years; another month or two won't make much difference.'

'A month or two? Is that how long you'll be away?'

'I've no idea,' said Elizabeth. 'Perhaps not, perhaps longer.'

She was beginning to sound irritated, so Brian decided to drop it.

'Well, keep in touch,' he said rather lamely.

She smiled. 'Don't worry. I'm not away yet. Why don't we go out for a meal tonight?'

'Yes,' said Brian. 'That'd be nice.'

The next day Elizabeth packed up most of her things and left. She was going to see Terry on her way down south.

Brian sat in the house on his own. He began to experience a feeling he hadn't felt for years - loneliness. He got up and wandered into Elizabeth's room. Only the lingering smell of her perfume betrayed the fact that she had been there. He turned to leave, and then he noticed a small picture sitting on the bedside table. He picked it up and looked at it. It was an old photograph of the whole family together and had been taken many years ago. He didn't remember having seen it before, and had no idea who took the picture, but it must have been taken not long before the accident. He sat down on the bed and began to sob.

Chapter 14

'So how are you,' asked Elizabeth.

'Fine,' lied Brian. 'I thought I might hear from you on Sunday night.'

'I'm sorry,' said Elizabeth. 'I should have phoned to say I got down OK, but I've been rushing about since I got here, and the time seems to have just flown by.'

'Did you see Terry?'

'Yes, but he really couldn't add anything to what he had already told me. He said he would ask around some of the old neighbours if he saw them, but I think he said that just to get rid of me. His wife was drawing me daggers all the time I was there, and his daughters were being a bit of a handful.'

'Oh well,' said Brian, 'I suppose it was worth a try.'

'And what about you?' said Elizabeth. 'Are you looking after yourself OK?'

'And why wouldn't I be?' asked Brian. 'I managed fine before you came to stay.'

'So, the place is a shambles then!' said Elizabeth.

'Don't you believe it,' said Brian, visualising the dishes piled up in the sink. 'Everything's fine.'

'I'm glad to hear it,' said Elizabeth.

'Listen,' said Brian, 'do I have to call you on your mobile or do you have a landline?'

'Just the mobile, I'm afraid. Are you worried about the charges?'

She laughed, and then continued before he could reply.

'Listen, I'll need to go. I'll call you soon, OK? I love you to bits.'

Another week passed, and Brian was again having lunch with Roy. They talked as if nothing had happened, but there was an undercurrent of tension. Brian had asked after Peter Turner's health, and Roy confirmed that he was much better and was back home, but that's as far as the conversation went regarding the older man.

Roy now had a girlfriend, Marion, and it sounded to Brian that he was seeing quite a lot of her.

'I'll need to meet her,' said Brian, without feeling any real enthusiasm.

'Yeah. We could arrange to go out some night,' said Roy, with an equal amount of apathy.

The next week he noticed a newspaper report of a house fire in which two people had been badly injured. The fire was described as 'suspicious'. He scanned through the report and was about to turn the page when something caught his eye. The injured couple was a Mr. and Mrs. *Terence* Scott.

He grabbed the phone and dialled.

'Elizabeth, where does Terry Scott live?'

'In Calderbank, why?'

'What street?'

'Just off Main Street, Cedar Crescent. Why?'

'Because they've been injured in a house fire.'

'Are you sure?'

Brian picked up the paper. 'A fire almost took the lives of Mr. and Mrs. Terence Scott and their two daughters last night. A neighbour noticed flames flickering at the windows of the house in Cedar Crescent, Calderbank, in the small hours of the morning. Tom Callaghan was returning from his job at a local bakery when he noticed the flames. *I quickly phoned the emergency services, said Mr. Callaghan, and then rushed to the house to see if there was anything I could do. I broke in through the back door then ran in shouting to Terry and Pamela to get out quick. The place was filled with smoke and I couldn't see my hand in front of my face, so I had to rush back out. Fortunately, the fire brigade arrived very quickly and they managed to get everyone out.* The fire was quickly brought under control, and Mr. Callaghan was praised for his courage. Mr and Mrs Scott and their two daughters, Alison and Ann aged six and three respectively were the only people in the house at the time of the incident. The parents are suffering from the effects of smoke inhalation, although the children have suffered some serious burns. The spokesman continued, *there is no doubt that Mr. Callaghan's quick thinking in alerting us when he did saved four lives.* A Police spokesman stated that *the fire was being treated as suspicious. They did not rule out a gas leak being responsible, but stressed that there did not appear to have been an explosion.*

'One hell of a coincidence, don't you think? And who had been at Betty White's house just before she died? Yeah, a gas man.'

'What are you saying?' said Elizabeth.

'I'm saying that there's something really weird going on here! And you'll remember the brick through the window?'

'Now, wait a minute,' said Elizabeth. 'I think you're jumping to conclusions.'

'You're bloody right I'm jumping! As soon as I finish talking to you, I'll be straight onto the police. Then we'll see who's jumping! What was it Ian Fleming wrote in Goldfinger? *Once is happenstance, twice is coincidence and thrice is enemy action?'*

'You're not going to tell me that Peter Turner is running about setting fires and murdering old ladies? In any case he was in hospital when Mrs. White died. And I know Roy wouldn't have anything to do with the fire. That leaves Stewart. Do you think he's the type to go about throwing bricks through windows and setting fires? Why would he be doing that?'

'To frighten us off. To stop us getting to the truth of the accident, that's why!'

'So why doesn't he try something with us? We're the ones who've been stirring it. Why target people we've spoken to? And how would he know we've spoken to these people in the first place?'

'Turner probably told him we spoke to Mrs. White,' said Brian. 'As for Terry Scott, I've no idea. I don't know all the answers. But you have to admit it's all adds up to one hell of a coincidence?'

'Now Brian, you need to calm down. I hope to be back up soon. Don't do anything until we can talk about it. Think how silly you'll sound if you go to the police with your suspicions and the fire turns out to be an accident. If they can prove foul play caused the fire, then that's a different matter. Let's wait and see what their investigation turns up before you do anything.'

Brian had to admit that she made a good point. He agreed to wait until they could discuss the matter.

He got up the following morning, feeling as if he hadn't slept at all.

On an impulse he phoned Roy's home, but there was no answer. He glanced at the clock - 7.45. Roy was getting an early start. Quickly downing the dregs of his coffee he dialled work.

'Hi, it's Brian. Is Roy Turner in yet?'

'Sorry, Brian,' said Isobel, 'Roy won't be in today. He's had to go to the hospital.'

'Is his dad ill again?' said Brian.

'I don't know. He just said he had to go to the hospital. It was an emergency.'

Brian pondered for a moment over what to do. He decided he would go to the hospital, so he quickly finished dressing and left.

'There's no note of anyone called Turner being admitted,' said the receptionist.

'Are you sure?' said Brian.

Her look said *of course I am*, but she saw his obvious concern.

'There's a chance that the admission hasn't been entered on the records yet. You could go round to the accident and emergency and ask there.'

Brian thanked her and exited the building. He remembered that the accident and emergency reception was round the side of the building, so he quickly hurried in that direction.

As he approached the entrance, he noticed Roy's car.

Across from the reception desk was a set of doors barring admission to the main area of the department. Brian fought against the memories which were flooding back and waited impatiently at the reception desk while a young woman rattled on a keyboard.

'Yes?' she said with a rather bored look on her face.

'I'm here with Mr Turner,' said Brian.

She didn't answer but referred to her screen.

Brian glanced around then saw Roy on the other side of the doors.

'That's him!' said Brian. 'That's Roy Turner, I'm with him. I really need to speak to him urgently.'

The young woman could tell from his face that he was serious. She didn't answer but leaned below the desk and nodded towards the doors.

Brian rushed to the doors and pushed them open.

Roy didn't see him coming as he was peering intently through a glass window. He only became aware of Brian just as Brian reached him.

'It's Marion,' he said. 'She's had an accident.'

Brian looked through the glass.

'Elizabeth!' he said.

'No,' said Roy, 'it's Marion.'

'Marion's her middle name,' said Brian. 'That's Elizabeth... my sister!'

Chapter 15

Roy and Brian sat in the hospital cafeteria with cups of vendor-dispensed liquid in front of them. Brian was fighting his urgent need for a cigarette and imagined Roy would be doing the same.

'So,' said Brian, 'can you tell me what's going on?'

'I think I should be asking you that question,' said Roy. 'Don't you find it a bit strange that my girlfriend turns out to be your sister?'

'Strange isn't the word for it,' said Brian. 'As far as I knew she was down south sorting out a few things.'

'What happened? The accident I mean?'

Roy took a sip of his drink and made a face. 'All I know is that her car crashed. She set off from my house and I had just gone inside, and I heard the smash. She seems to have gone through the junction at the bottom of the hill and a lorry struck her car. I ran out to the gate when I heard the racket and...' Roy began to shake visibly.

'Take it easy,' said Brian. 'Whatever happened, the main thing is that she'll be OK,' said Brian. 'Have the doctors told you anything?'

Roy shook his head. 'Only that they're running tests. I still don't get what she was doing with me?'

'There's only one person who can answer that question,' said Brian, 'and I think we both want to hear the answer.'

'Listen Brian. I'm not stupid. There's more to this whole business than my father, you, or Marion is telling me. What's going on?'

'Before I answer that,' said Brian, 'do you know a Mrs. Betty White?'

Roy shook his head.

'What about Terry and Pamela Scott?'

Brian watched Roy carefully as he again shook his head after thinking for a moment.

'Should I know them?' said Roy.

'Possibly not, but I'd like to find out if your father knows them.'

'My father? What's he got to do with all this?'

'He may have a lot to do with it, or, then again, perhaps nothing. I don't know. But I'd like to ask him.'

'So, ask me,' said a voice behind them. Brian spun round to face Peter Turner. The former policeman looked quite healthy. He was well wrapped up against the cold, but there was a fair bit of colour in his cheeks.

'Is there anything in that machine worth drinking?' he asked.

'Not that we've found,' said Roy. 'Dad, you shouldn't be here!'

'Oh, don't fuss,' said Turner senior. 'Let me get something hot, then I'll join you.'

'How is she?' asked Peter Turner as he sat down.

'They're still doing tests,' said Roy. 'We really don't know anything. But Brian here dropped a bombshell. Marion is his sister.'

The old man raised an eyebrow. 'Clever,' he said, 'very clever.'

'What do you mean *clever*?' said Roy. 'Look! I'm getting more confused by the minute. What *is* going on here?'

Peter Turner smiled at his son but didn't answer him. He looked at Brian. 'I think I'm ready to answer your questions now Brian.'

'Before we get into that, do you know Terry Scott?'

Turner stared at him. 'Never heard of him,' he said. 'Should I?'

'Have you been reading the papers?' asked Brian.

'Not really,' said Turner, 'I'm not much for reading newspapers.'

'Did you read about the fire in Calderbank?' asked Brian.

Turner shook his head. 'No, I must have missed that. What was it all about?'

Brian ignored his question for the moment. 'What about Betty White?' he asked.

'Isn't that the woman you mentioned when you came to see me?'

'Yes, that's right. Do you know that she's dead?' Brian watched Turner carefully.

'I had no idea. When did she die?'

'The day after I had spoken to her. She's supposed to have fallen down the stairs in her house. The Terry Scott I mentioned, Elizabeth, or Marion as you know her, had visited him and his family. Then a few days later they are badly injured in a house fire. I've had a brick through my window. Now this accident involving my sister. How are you on coincidences?'

If Turner was aware of the reasons behind these happenings and not saying so, then Brian reckoned he must be the best actor never to have set foot on a stage.

His stare never wavered while Brian was telling him the story, and he continued to look him in the eye.

'Brian,' he said, 'whatever you may think of me, believe me when I tell you that I had nothing to do with these incidents.'

'I do believe you,' said Brian. 'But I don't know where this leaves me.'

'Look! Will someone tell me what the fuck's...'

Turner held up a hand to quieten his son as a doctor approached their table.

'Mr Turner?' he said. Roy and his father both answered *yes* at the same time.

'I'm Roy Turner, this is my father, and this is Marion's brother.'

The doctor nodded to each of them and sat down.

'Well,' he began, 'we've finished our tests. She doesn't have any broken bones or internal bleeding. We can find no organ damage. Her main injuries are head injuries, but there appears to be no blood clot on the brain, eye damage or anything of that nature.'

'That all sounds good,' said Roy.

'It is,' agreed the doctor, 'yes, it is. But she's still unconscious.'

'But when she comes round...'

'Mr. Turner,' the doctor interrupted Roy. 'I'm afraid she's in a coma. We don't know when, or indeed if, she'll come round. I'm sorry. There's nothing else I can tell you at the moment.'

'But if she has no obvious injuries?' said Roy.

'There's still so much we don't understand about how the brain functions,' explained the doctor. 'Many comas are due to brain damage, but others seem to be a body defence mechanism. As I said, there is still so much we don't know.'

'So how do you plan to proceed?' asked Turner senior.

'We have ruled out the more extreme causes of the coma, such as a traumatic brain injury, subarachnoid haemorrhage, things like that. We're currently assessing the level of consciousness, but all indicators are that this coma is deep.'

'But she could snap out of it at any time?' asked Roy.

The doctor frowned. 'Contrary to what you see in films, Mr Turner, coma patients rarely *snap out of it*. In rare cases this can happen, but recovery is normally much slower. The patient may regain consciousness but will then fall asleep very quickly. Gradually the waking period will increase. The patient is also likely to wake in a very profound state of confusion.'

'Have you any idea when you will know more?' asked Brian.

'It's very difficult to say. A coma rarely lasts more than 5 weeks. If she hasn't responded by then... Well, her chances of a full recovery diminish as time passes.'

'But we hear of people coming out of comas after years of unconsciousness,' said Roy.

'In the very rare occasion,' explained the doctor, 'that's why you read about these examples. At any point in time, there are probably thousands of people in comas around the world. You don't read about remarkable recoveries every day, do you? I'm not trying to paint a bleak picture, gentlemen, I'm just telling you the way it is.'

'We appreciate that,' said Peter Turner. 'Is there anything we can do?'

'We're going to transfer her to a specialised neurological unit,' said the doctor. 'There are no physical signs causing the coma, so there is no reason why she shouldn't make a full recovery. Some people advise as much attention from friends and family as possible. Other specialists doubt whether this does much good.'

'And what do you think doctor?' said Roy.

'I can't see how it could do any harm.'

The doctor stood up. 'In the meantime, I suggest you go home and get some rest. The hospital will let you know when the transfer has taken place. The Queen Elizabeth operates quite flexible hours regarding visiting coma patients.'

They provided him with contact phone numbers, thanked him, and he left.

Later that morning, they met at Turner senior's house.

'I had a call from the police earlier,' said Brian. 'They're treating Elizabeth's accident as suspicious. They said they would tell me more when they've completed their investigation of the car.'

Roy shook his head. 'I really haven't a clue what is going on here.'

'Roy,' began his father, 'I'm afraid you're going to hear some things that I hoped you would never hear. Your mother went to her grave with no inkling of what I'm going to tell you. But things have changed.'

He looked at Brian. He gathered his thoughts, took a deep breath and started talking.

'You're correct, Brian. I wasn't driving the car on that night. Chief Inspector Stewart was driving. And he had been drinking.'

'And the light, the blue light?' said Brian.

'Stewart switched it on after the collision. People were running from everywhere, it was bedlam.' The old man shook his head.

'I've asked myself a thousand times since that day. Had I been driving, could I have stopped in time?'

'And?' asked Brian.

The old man shook his head again. 'Things happened too quickly. We were going too fast. Would I have been driving as fast? I really don't know. Our attention was on getting back to the station and then out again to another call.'

He took a sip of the coffee he had made.

'I've never been a drinker,' he continued, 'I don't like the taste. Oh, I can force down the occasional non-alcoholic lager if in company, but I've never been drunk. I don't understand the effects. Stewart had been drinking, yes, but was he fit to drive? I've handled many a drunk in my years on the force, but these guys were falling all over the place. Stewart seemed OK.'

He took another drink.

'He had asked me to give him a lift home after the function. The station had called to ask if anyone was available to pick up a witness. I offered to go, and Stewart said he would go with me and then get me to drop him off at his house. At the last minute he said he would drive. I asked him if he thought that was wise. He said he hadn't been in a patrol car for years and he wanted the thrill of driving one again. I didn't understand where the thrill was, but then I was out in them every day. Anyway, I gave him the keys and we set off. He was driving normally, not speeding. We collected the witness, and then calls started to come through. We could have ignored these, as we were both off duty. But Stewart wanted to *get his hands dirty* he said. I reckon that giving out all the awards to beat policemen made him long for his old days out on the streets. So, I picked up the radio and told the dispatcher that we would respond after we dropped off our witness. After that, we were locked in. I admit that I was curious to see how he would handle the incident. When we reached the town, I told him that we should have the light and siren on, but he couldn't remember where the switches were. I had just finished telling him when the accident happened. After we hit the people, all I could think of was trying to help them. I didn't realise Stewart had put the light on. I noticed he wasn't wearing his cap but assumed he had lost it rushing out of the car. After the ambulance arrived, he took me aside and explained that I must say that I had been driving.'

Turner paused and looked at his son.

'You were still at school and your mother wasn't fit to work. Stewart painted a bleak picture of what would happen to me if the truth came out. He laid it on thick how he would say that he had told me to slow down, told me to put the light and siren on. Who would believe me over him? He said that there would be an inquiry, but he would see to it that this was a mere formality, assuming I followed his lead. How would it help the people who had been injured, he told me? I know...' Turner acknowledged Brian wanting to say something, but continued.

'So I went along with it. I may seem to be laying all the blame on him, but that wasn't the case. I knew the outcome for me and my family would be serious if I didn't back Stewart up. I would have gone to prison; of that I have no doubt. There would be no pension. All material things, I know, but at that stage of my life they were important to me. And because of that, I put my own interests before that of justice. Stewart was grateful. After a few years he managed to smooth the way for me to step up to sergeant, meaning more money and a bigger pension. I was taken off the streets and given a nice secure desk job. Constant day working and regular hours. Stewart saw to all of that. What he was really doing was keeping an eye on me. It wasn't for my benefit; it was for his security. He didn't become a chief inspector by accident. He's a clever man, much cleverer than me, and a scheming one.'

Turner finished his tea and leaned back in his chair.

'So, there you have it. That's the whole story. Roy...'

'You disgust me!' said Roy jumping to his feet. He rushed to the kitchen, pausing only to sweep a collection of displayed pictures off the sideboard.

Brian got up and retrieved the pictures. They were mainly family pictures. None were broken, and Brian placed them carefully back on the sideboard.

'They say confession is good for the soul, Brian. Perhaps if I had done it years ago, or even when you asked me recently. I don't feel any kind of relief, and I don't think I deserve to. At least Roy has had a chance in life, a better one than he would have had if I had ignored Stewart's advice. If you want to talk to the police, I won't try to dissuade you. I'll tell them everything. It's up to you.'

'But what about the witness you had in the back of the car? How did Stewart manage to persuade him to go along with it?'

'His name was Steve Collins. At the time he was involved with a counterfeiting mob, importing fake designer stuff, all that kind of thing. Rather than sell these at markets, Collins persuaded small shop owners to handle the goods. He reckoned that people were more likely to buy from a shop and less likely to suspect what they were buying wasn't the real thing. We hoped we could get him to squeal on his bosses. But everything changed as soon as the accident happened. Stewart had managed to get a quick word with Collins, and they had reached an understanding. I was too uptight about the whole thing to ask any questions.'

'And what would Collins get out of it?' asked Brian.

Turner looked quite uncomfortable. 'Collins would be kept in the loop regarding any raids that were planned. This would make him invaluable to his bosses.'

'So that's where Stewart got his money from,' said Brian.

'Yes. It's likely he was getting money from Collins.'

'And what happened to Steve Collins?'

'I haven't seen him since,' said Turner.

Brian got up and went into the kitchen. Roy was standing at the backdoor, looking out at nothing in particular.

'Roy,' said Brian.

Roy glanced round. 'No wonder you hate him! I hate him!'

'That won't help anything.'

'It helps me!' said Roy. 'Christ! And I lectured you on upsetting my father!'

'Roy, come back in, please. There are some things I want to say.'

Reluctantly, Roy followed Brian back into the lounge. He sat down with his back to his father as Brian started to speak.

'I always hoped this day would come when I would find out the truth, and I tried to imagine how I would feel. Triumph, I suppose. Elation. All these sorts of things. But for some reason I don't. Right now, all I can think about is Elizabeth. There have been enough victims in this sorry story. I don't want my sister to be one more.'

'I'm sorry to change the subject, but I had a call from the hospital earlier. They need me in for some tests,' said Peter.

'A call?' said Roy, 'I thought they usually sent out letters for appointments?'

'They've had a cancellation at short notice. They asked me if I can go in on Monday. It'll only be for one overnight. I said that'd be OK.'

'Are you fit enough for these tests?' asked Roy.

The old man shrugged. 'They want to try out some other drugs and need to check my blood pressure regularly. I guess I'll just be lying in bed all the time.'

'What ward are you going in to?' asked Roy.

'I'm not sure. In any case, there's no need for you to visit. I can get there and back by myself. You two will be better off visiting Marion.'

'And leave your car parked there overnight?' said Roy. 'That's taking a chance! No, I'll drop you off tomorrow morning then pick you up the next day.'

'If you think that's best,' said his dad.

'Right, so that's settled.'

Brian was pleased to see the two Turner's talking again, even if they were only discussing travelling arrangements.

'I'll head home,' said Brian. 'I'll have a rummage about and see if Elizabeth has left anything at my house she might need in hospital. If not, I'll nip out and buy some things.'

They agreed that if no one had heard from the hospital by 6pm that Brian would phone and try and get some information.

At just before 5, Brian's phone rang. Elizabeth was now in the Queen Elizabeth and was showing some signs of improvement. He checked when the visiting times were, and then phoned Roy. The relief was apparent in Roy's voice. Brian said he would set off immediately to pick up Roy and then the two of them could head into Glasgow to the hospital. They knew that the journey which would normally take around thirty minutes was likely to be well over an hour at this time of day, given that the M8 was regularly nose to tail for a good few miles in both directions, particularly at the junctions leading to the city centre, but they had no option, and they hoped the hospital would make an exception for their visit under the circumstances.

Their estimation of an hour to reach the hospital was out by a good twenty minutes, but the visiting time for the particular ward Elizabeth was in didn't finish until 8.30, so they had plenty of time.

On the journey into Glasgow, Roy and Brian had discussed the possible effect on Elizabeth of both of them visiting at the same time. They discussed whether the knowledge that her deception had been discovered might adversely affect her recovery. When they arrived at the ward, they still hadn't decided what was best. However, when they asked a nurse for the location of her bed, she showed them into a side room to talk to a doctor.

'I believe you were advised that she is showing signs of recovery,' said Doctor Dunn.

'Yes,' said Brian, 'but we don't know how significant this is.'

'Oh, it's very significant,' said the doctor. 'This first step is crucial, and in cases like this it's very important that the patient shows signs of recovery as early as possible. However, I should explain to you that, while we have detected signs of recovery, you may not.'

'I don't understand,' said Roy.

'The chances are that you will only see her unconscious during your visit. In fact, over the next day or two the chances of you visiting and finding her conscious are very slim. On the occasion where you do happen to find her conscious, she will be unlikely to display any signs of recognition of who is present.'

'She won't know we're there?' said Brian.

'I believe she'll know you're there,' said the doctor, 'but she won't be able to show this.'

'The important thing is that she knows we're with her,' said Brian. 'We don't expect her to be sitting up and chatting for some time, but as long as she gets there in the end. That's what we want.'

'Excellent,' said Doctor Dunn, 'I felt it was important to make you aware of the situation. I didn't want you to expect a marked improvement in her condition only to be disappointed when you see her. At this stage in her recovery she needs encouragement. Everything you say or do should be positive.'

'Do you expect her to make a full recovery Doctor?' asked Brian. It was the sixty-four thousand dollar question.

'If you promise not to sue me if I'm wrong,' said the doctor, 'then, if pushed, I would say yes. But...'

He held up a hand as Brian and Roy started to grin at each other. 'All I'm saying is that's what I *expect*. I may be wrong. It's early days, but the signs are good.'

They thanked the doctor for his time and were shown to Elizabeth's bed. She was lying on her back with various tubes and wires feeding from her to a variety of machines. Brian and Roy both said hello to her, but there was no response.

Brian sat down and held her hand. He fought off the feelings of déjà vu and started to talk to her as if she was awake. First of all, he explained that he was with Roy and he made a joke about him finding out that Roy knew her as Marion. He didn't want to go into too much detail about what they had been up to but tried to constantly reassure her that things were working out well.

Then it was Roy's turn. They had agreed that they both shouldn't talk to her at the same time.

Brian moved away from the bed to allow Roy to take his place. Roy was becoming quite emotional which in turn was affecting Brian. He left the bedside to leave the two of them alone. As he turned to walk away, he noticed her mobile phone sitting on a small table. He discreetly lifted this and put it in his pocket. Walking back to the nurse's station, he checked to see if there had been any missed calls and was relieved to find there were none. He checked with the nurse to see if it was OK for him to take the phone. She noted it on a form and asked him to sign at the bottom.

'I found that quite difficult,' admitted Roy when they were back in the car heading home. 'I don't know how you managed to think of so much to say.'

'Practice,' said Brian. 'Although it was a long time ago.'

'I'll need to rehearse a bit,' said Roy.

'If you like,' said Brian, 'but I think what you say is less important than how you say it.'

Chapter 16

'Did you get your dad to the hospital OK?' asked Brian.
'Yeah. No problem. I just dropped him at the entrance as he asked.'

'So, how's things? I mean between the two of you?'

'We've both agreed to let things lie just now, at least until Elizabeth's better.'

'That makes sense,' said Brian.

'But after that? Well, we'll need to do a lot of talking. And a lot will depend on what you do.'

'That will depend a lot on Elizabeth,' said Brian honestly. 'I've spent some time getting to know the pair of you, hearing your dad tell me what happened, seeing his and your reactions. So, my feelings on this have changed quite a bit from what they were. But Elizabeth, well, she's not been a part of any of this. She's way behind me on the forgiving road. And I'm not giving anything away when I say that in many ways, she feels even more strongly than I did. I just don't know what she'll think.'

Later they again found themselves sitting at her bedside, holding her hand and talking to her quietly. The nurses had washed and changed her, and she looked clean and fresh. She was now wearing a nightdress Brian had found in a drawer in her room. She looked more natural with her hair washed and combed and wearing something of hers rather than the hospital issue gown. But still she slept. The duty nurse had informed them that they continued to notice very slight improvements.

Brian was out of the office on business the following day. It was the evening before he saw Roy.

'Did you pick up your dad?' asked Brian.

'Yeah, a bit of a rush, but I made it.'

'How is he?'

'He looks fine. He didn't say very much on the way home. I thought he looked quite tired, but I suppose he wouldn't have got much sleep if they had to continually wake him up to take his blood pressure. Did you know there had been another murder last night?'

'You mean another serial killer murder?'

'Yeah. It was on the radio. The police weren't issuing details until relatives had been informed, but the papers were saying the same guy did it. And it was in Motherwell.'

'How many's that now?' said Brian.

'I think that's five.'

That night, they left the hospital feeling much more optimistic than on previous visits. While talking to Elizabeth, Roy said he felt as if her hand had moved while he was holding it. He laid it gently back on the bed and they both watched intently. Just when they both were agreeing that Roy must have imagined it, she moved again. It was all they could do to avoid jumping up and running around like idiots. Brian took a turn talking to her, and he too felt her hand twitch.

'Yes, that's quite normal,' said the nurse when asked. 'Earlier on she had her eyes open. She didn't attempt to say anything, but she was clearly aware of things happening around her. It was only for a few minutes, but I was moving her to avoid her getting bed sores.'

'Did she look frightened?' asked Brian.

'No. Not at all. I spoke to her, but she made no effort to talk back, then she closed her eyes and went to sleep again. But it is an improvement. There's no reason why it won't continue.'

Brian dropped Roy off at his house and headed home. He had only been in the house for a few minutes when his phone rang.

'Have you seen the news?' said Roy.

'I've just come in the door, what news are you talking about?'

'The latest murder, have you seen anything about it?'

'I've told you I've just arrived home.'

'The police have released the identity of the victim. It was Stewart.'

'Stewart? What, the chief inspector?'

'The very man.'

'Are you sure? It'll be a common name; there could be loads of Stewarts.'

'I'm pretty sure it's him. A retired police officer who lived in Motherwell. How many people fitting that description will there be?'

'Let me switch the TV on then get back to you.'

Brian sat down without waiting to take his jacket off and switched his TV onto one of the 24-hour news channels. He waited a few minutes impatiently while they broadcast the weather forecast, and then came the headlines with the latest murder as the top story. As he listened to the brief summary, Brian realised that Roy was one hundred per cent correct. It was their guy. Details were still sketchy, and the news didn't carry a picture of the victim, but everything else tied in. Former Police Chief Inspector Robert Stewart who had worked for Strathclyde Police, now retired and living with his wife in Motherwell. His age was given as sixty, and

he was described as 'tall and distinguished looking'. They had cob-
bled together a brief background of his career and had managed to
find a former colleague who described him as 'a well-respected and
liked officer'. A woman walking her dog early in the morning had
found his body in a park close to his home. The report concluded
by stating that their reporter suspected that this crime was the
latest carried out by the serial killer who had been terrifying the
West of Scotland. A police spokesman confirmed the identity of
the victim. He would not confirm the cause of death but did say
they were treating it as murder. He appealed for any witnesses who
saw anyone acting suspiciously in or near the park on the previous
night to contact their local police station.

Brian waited until the report finished then phoned Roy.

'Yeah, it's him all right,' he said. 'Poetic justice, if you ask me,
but one hell of a coincidence. How's your dad taking the news?'

'He's pretty calm about it,' said Roy. 'He seems more concerned
about how you feel.'

'Right at this moment I'm not sure how I feel,' admitted Brian.
'I'm a bit pissed off that I never managed to get him to admit to
what really happened.'

'Where do you go from here?' asked Roy.

'I haven't had a chance to weigh things up,' said Brian, 'If
Stewart was behind Elizabeth's accident and all the other stuff,
we've little chance of confirming that now.'

Brian sat quietly for a while after putting the phone down.
Elizabeth had always told him he was soft. Was that why he had
lost the urge for revenge? Or did he just not have the bottle to see
it through? He imagined the story being released to the media and
the resulting police investigation. What would his parents and Caroline think? If they were watching somewhere, they would have

seen him turn into a vengeful and angry young man. But he was pulling himself back from the brink just in time. He would have to try and do the same with Elizabeth.

Suddenly he felt very tired. He undressed and climbed into bed. Soon he was fast asleep. And for once the nightmares didn't come.

Chapter 17

The papers the following day carried a full account of the latest murder, including a picture of the victim. There was no doubt it was Stewart. The headlines screamed about the serial killer, about how the police were powerless to stop him, about vigilante groups scouring the neighbourhoods, even how much this was affecting the pub takings. One positive spin off was that taxi firms were reporting that they were run off their feet. The tabloids were devoting six or eight pages to the story. Most carried a map of the area showing where the crimes had been committed. They surmised that the killer might well live in Glasgow. The police had followed up a number of leads, but so far had nothing conclusive. There was another appeal for members of the public to come forward with any information, no matter how irrelevant they might think it to be. To jog peoples' memories, they reprinted pictures of all the victims, together with maps of the routes they had followed before meeting their deaths.

A senior policeman had commented on television the night before that this killing of a former police officer was a particularly evil crime. His comment had sparked public outrage. Members of the previous victims' families had been offended by the comments that seemed to suggest a former policeman's life was worth more than any other person. The police were quick to deny that this was what had been meant. They lamely pointed out that to attack a police officer, even a former one, showed a blatant disregard for authority.

Brian had bought a paper, intending to keep it for Elizabeth. He wondered if mentioning this event to her might help to snap her out of the coma but decided against it. Neither he nor Roy had mentioned anything about their investigations, instead keeping their conversations on a much more positive and cheerful level. Had Stewart been responsible for Betty White's death, the fire at the Scott's house, Elizabeth's 'accident'? These events still troubled Brian, but what could he do? He didn't know for certain if they were related.

Not far away, another individual was reading the same edition of the paper. Or he *had* been reading it; now he was ripping it to shreds in a fit of rage. The number of killings attributed to the Glasgow serial killer had now reached five, and this *really* pissed him off.

He had only committed four.

Chapter 18

'Roy? Hi, it's Brian. She's awake!'

'Let me call you right back on my mobile,' said Roy before hanging up. He left his desk and walked out into the corridor where his call would be a bit more private.

'How awake?' he asked, 'I mean, is she fully conscious, drowsy or what?'

'I don't know. I just had a call saying there had been a significant improvement.'

'Do they expect this improvement to continue?'

'They hope so.'

Roy found that he was starting to tremble as he held the phone. He realised he was holding it too tight and tried to release his grip.

'The doctor told me that we'll have to be ready for her asking all sorts of questions. If she remains conscious and doesn't fall asleep for too long, they've no doubt she'll start to try and work out what's happened to her. They told me that we should still refer to the crash as an accident. They don't want her to get too upset or worried at this early stage. Christ! If they only knew that questions about her accident would be relatively easy, it's all the other stuff she might ask about that has me uptight.'

'I'll try and get away from work a bit earlier,' said Roy. 'If I manage it I'll give you a ring and we can head in a bit earlier. Then we can try and work out what we should say to the questions she asks.'

Brian agreed, and then hung up.

For the first time that winter, snow had begun to fall quite heavily. While some areas of England had had some quite severe snow falls, most of Scotland had survived with only the occasional flurry. The forecast had been for snow, and although it was expected to continue for most of the week, temperatures were to remain above freezing, so there was every chance the snow would largely disappear between showers.

The gritters were out in force as Brian and Roy left for the hospital. They made surprisingly good progress on the M8, and it appeared that many people had set off early on their journeys to avoid the snow, mindful of the severe winter of some years past when the country was brought to a standstill. They managed to get parked a good forty-five minutes before the visiting was due to start. To kill the time, they walked the short distance to the restaurant and ordered two meals.

They both settled for steak pie, although Brian had commented that he wasn't so keen on the pastry they cooked separately and then sat on top of the pie.

'It explodes when you cut it,' he explained. 'More of it ends up around your plate than on it.' As if to illustrate his point, he attacked the pastry much more aggressively than necessary and a lot of it ended up on the table.

'I don't think we should tell her about Stewart unless we can't avoid it,' said Brian, while trying to clear up the flakes of pastry off the table.

'Christ, it'll seem strange calling her Elizabeth,' said Roy. 'Or do you think I should call her Marion as I did the last time I saw her?'

Brian gave a soft whistle. 'I'll pass on that one I'm afraid.'

'I think I'll call her Elizabeth,' said Roy, 'she'll have enough bother without people calling her different names.'

Brian agreed.

They discussed topics they felt would be safe to bring up. Roy was in the fortunate position, or unfortunate depending on how you viewed it, as to be working with some young women who were soap addicts. He had little option but to listen to their conversations. As a result, he knew who had been killed, died, injured, married, divorced, got pregnant, had an affair with, and every other significant event. The only problem was he didn't know which event happened in which soap. They decided he would just mention the events and the names he could recall, and Elizabeth would work it out from that.

She was sitting up in bed when they arrived at her room, but her eyes were closed. Brian suggested that Roy should go in alone at first. As Roy walked quietly into her room, Brian turned and headed off down the corridor is search of a drinks machine. He reckoned that her relationship with Roy had to be sorted out before he came into the picture. He found the machine he was hunting for, paid for a cup of soup, and tried to work out what the floating things were, then just gave up and started to drink it. Someone had left an evening paper on the small table, and he sat down to browse through it. The latest murder continued to feature as the headline, but the report offered little he hadn't read earlier. The only significant statement was that the police were treating this killing as the latest to be carried out by the *Glasgow Killer*. He wondered if anyone else would find the title a bit strange as none of the murders had actually been carried out in Glasgow. He finished his soup, which was surprisingly good, and stopped short of eating the sludge that inevitable gathers at the bottom of vended drinks. Roy had been in with Elizabeth for twenty minutes, and Brian reckoned it was time he made an appearance. There was every chance she would have fallen asleep by now and if this were the case, Brian would just sit quietly hoping she would come round again.

'Were you the one who picked this nightdress?'

Elizabeth asked Brian the question as soon as he walked in her door.

'Yes,' he said, somewhat stunned, 'what's wrong with it?'

'It's two sizes too small and makes my boobs look huge, and the colour is awful! If I'd known what I was wearing, I'd have woken up ages ago and got changed!' Then she smiled.

At that moment, her smile was the most beautiful thing Brian had ever seen. She put her arms out, and Brian went over to give her a hug.

'Welcome back,' he whispered in her ear, and then he kissed her gently on the cheek.

He felt tears beginning to come into his eyes, so he held into her a little longer until he had control of himself.

'I've got a lot of explaining to do,' said Elizabeth when Brian had sat down. 'I didn't want to deceive you, but I thought I'd get some useful information if I tried the unorthodox approach. This was only meant to be for a day or two, but then I started to enjoy Roy's company.'

She looked at Brian. 'I now know why you were finding things so difficult; it's one thing to theorise and plot, but quite another when you get to know the people involved. I'm really sorry I deceived you.'

'Don't worry about that,' said Brian, 'you're a big girl; you can do what you want.' The remainder of the visiting time continued in the same vein, although Elizabeth began to look very tired, and her responses slowed down quite considerably.

'The problem they'll have now is trying to keep her in,' said Brian, as he and Roy headed back home.

'Rather them than me,' said Roy, and Brian agreed.

They were both feeling quite elated and were totally unaware of the clouds gathering on the horizon.

Chapter 19

'What do you want?'

'It's nice to see you too.'

Detective Constable Greg Anderson peered at Angela through the gap allowed by the security chain.

'I need to talk to you, Sarge' he said.

'You could have phoned,' said Angela.

'I did,' said Greg, 'but you didn't answer.'

'I'm on gardening leave, remember? There's no reason for me to answer a call from the station.'

'Well, there is actually,' said Greg. 'But,' he added, just as Angela started to close the door in his face, 'let's forget about that just now. I need to talk to you.'

The door closed, the chain was released, and then the door was opened to allow him to enter.

The young Detective Sergeant left Greg to close the door behind him.

'I like what you've done with the place,' he said.

'I haven't done anything with it, and, in any case, you've never been here before so how would you know?'

'Haven't I? Perhaps you're right.'

Angela gave a small grunt. 'Some fuckin' detective! So what do you want?''

'The Boss wants to see you.'

Angela slumped into a chair and looked curiously at the detective. She didn't invite him to sit down. Greg Anderson was twenty-three years old, but looked younger. He was slim everywhere and had a major handicap in that he had been born in Edinburgh. Normally, that wouldn't be much of a problem, but he was now working in the Glasgow area. West of Scotland folk say it's easy to tell the tourists from the locals in Edinburgh, tourists are the ones who smile occasionally. Greg smiled now and again, but he had learned that skill since moving west.

'Which boss would this be who wants the pleasure of my company? Is it the Boss Boss or our temporary boss?'

'It's Russell,' answered Greg.

Angela shrugged. 'I was quite enjoying my gardening leave. What's happened to cause him to seek the pleasure of my company?'

Greg ignored the obvious sarcasm.

'I really don't know Sarge,' he said.

His private school upbringing baulked at him using the abbreviation *Sarge*, but he felt this would help him fit in with his new environment. An environment his wealthy parents totally disproved of, as they had no idea why he wanted to be a police officer. Being a detective made things slightly better, but only slightly. A doctor or a lawyer would have suited them down to the ground, but they had failed to persuade him to go that way. They believed he chose his profession just to spite them, and they were partly correct in that assumption. Only partly, because Greg had always wanted to be in law enforcement. His parents' objections just made it that bit easier for him to go that way.

Angela, on the other hand, was a totally different kettle of fish. She had been born and bred in an area of the West of Scotland that had the reputation of being tough. Becoming a lawyer or doctor appealed to Angela when she was younger, but she had one major obstacle to overcome - she hated school. As a teenager, her hatred overcame her ambition, and she left to get a job as soon as she could. Looking back, she regretted this, but the past was the past and she had moved on. She was now in a job she loved, and this fact, combined with her natural abilities, meant that she had become very good at it. But she had never gotten over her dislike of authority, and often had difficulty in keeping this feeling under control, as demonstrated by the situation she was currently in.

'Bullshit!' she said. 'He wouldn't change his mind so quickly without at least hinting at a reason. What's been happening in the two days and six hours I've been removed from duty?'

'I think he's reconsidered your theory.'

'Christ, that's a first! Admitting he was wrong!'

'I think the *admitting he was wrong* bit is pushing things a bit far, but I think he believes you might be on to something.'

'So, couldn't he have thought of that before biting my head off?'

'I don't think he bit your head off because of your theory,' said Greg. 'I think it was because you called DI Lambert a prick.'

'I didn't call him a prick!'

'You said he was acting like a prick. I heard you. In fact, I think the whole of the station heard you. Even the guys in the car park.'

'That's not the same as actually *calling* him a prick. I mean, he *is* a prick. An overbearing, arrogant, *bully* of a prick. So, in saying that he was acting like a prick I was actually being quite reserved.'

'Well, whatever.'

Greg didn't really want to get into a discussion of whether DI Lambert was a prick or not. He was simply asked to collect

Detective Sergeant Angela Porter and bring her to the station. It sounded like quite an easy task, but things weren't going exactly to plan. He thought of simply telling her that she had been ordered to go back with him, but past experience had taught him that Angela did not take too kindly to orders, especially second hand ones. He had learned a lot in the short time in his present posting. Most of what he now knew he had learned from Angela. However, he doubted if his tutors at the Police College would approve of his expanded education.

Angela was only in her late twenties and had risen rapidly due to her impressive success rate as a detective. However, her methods invariable landed her in hot water with her superiors. She was very much a *the end justifies the means* type of person.

Their Chief Inspector, on the other hand, played things exactly by the book. Detective Chief Inspector Jim Russell had been transferred to their station a few months ago, but from the first day sparks had flown between him and Angela. Russell actually had a very good record as a detective, hence his continued promotion. However, irrespective of how good a detective he was, his rise through the ranks meant he had to deal with people, and in this aspect, he was sadly lacking. Other officers made allowances and recognised his authority. Angela didn't. She called a spade a spade no matter who she was speaking to. Hard working, yes; dedicated to her job, yes; determined to catch bad guys, yes; arse licker, definitely not. Russell expected people to give him respect due to his rank. Angela believed that respect was earned, and in her book, Russell hadn't earned hers yet, so she gave him very little.

The object of her anger, DI Lambert, fell way behind Russell on Angela's respect meter. The two of them had never hit it off and neither made any secret of their intense dislike of the other.

John Lambert was a fair bit older than Angela and resented her for three main reasons. Firstly, he felt she had been promoted much too quickly. Secondly, he took exception to her lack of respect for authority. Finally, although he would never admit to this, he felt that women had no place in the CID. To find himself working closely with a woman, and a young woman at that, was just too much for him to take. Her outburst had been provoked but was at the very least, unprofessional. Rivalry or dislike between officers, and indeed any group of people working closely together, was inevitable. In most cases this could be kept under the surface, but Angela had had enough and reacted in exactly the way Lambert had hoped she would.

'So...will you come back with me?' asked Greg.

'You could say I wasn't at home,' said Angela, being awkward just for fun. She sat back in the chair and brushed her jet-black hair out of her face. She tilted her head to one side and stared at Greg through her greeny-blue eyes. He recognised the pose. It said *convince me*, and he felt a bit uncomfortable.

'You could tell him that the neighbours told you I had gone on holiday,' said Angela.'

'That would make matters worse,' said Greg. 'You know that on gardening leave you have to be available for work if called upon.'

'True,' said Angela. 'But my neighbours could be mistaken. I might just have gone shopping. There's nothing in the handbook to say I must sit in my chair waiting on a call. I still have to eat you know.'

'I doubt if you've read the handbook, Sarge,' said Greg, beginning to feel quite exasperated. 'I don't think you would recognise the handbook if you saw one.'

Angela smiled and jumped to her feet so suddenly that Greg was startled for a moment.

'You know Greg, I like you.' Angela put her shoes on as she spoke. 'Out of all the people at the station I've worked with, I must say that you're my favourite.'

She grabbed her keys and headed for the door.

'And exactly how many people have you worked with?' asked Greg.

Angela paused at the door and thought for a moment.

'One,' she said as she opened the door and left. 'Lock the door behind you please.'

Greg did as he was asked, and hurried out behind her. She was standing at the driver's side of the car.

As he approached, she put her hand out.

'Give me the keys,' she said, 'I'm driving. You get in and tell me exactly why you think our DCI has had a change of heart.'

Greg did his best to enlighten her during the trip to the station, but he failed quite miserably. He was having great difficulty in concentrating as he was expecting them to crash at any moment. Angela didn't exceed the speed limits by much, but she did accelerate and decelerate very quickly. She also took corners at what Greg considered a very dangerous speed. Judging by her demeanour, this was her natural driving style. Normally, when they were working together, Greg would drive. He assumed this was because he was the junior officer. Angela sensed his discomfort.

'Don't worry,' said Angela with a rather mischievous grin, 'we're coming in for a landing soon.'

Greg glanced over at her as she concentrated on not hitting anything. She was very attractive, although Greg would never have dreamt of telling her that. He rarely saw her out of uniform, and had never seen her wearing a skirt or dress. Angela tended to wear functional clothes when working. This comprised of a pair of trousers, a shirt and sensible shoes. Someone at the station had commented once about her shoes. The officer had described them as unladylike. 'You can't chase arseholes in high heels,' had been Angela's response. 'But of course, you'll know that,' she had added, much to the amusement of onlookers and the annoyance of the officer who had dared criticise her. Her skin was lightly tanned, and she had sparkling white teeth. Greg knew next to nothing about her family or her friends, and he reckoned that's the way she liked it.

Angela brought the car screeching to a halt, more abandoned than parked, and they got out.

Greg followed behind her into the station, fully expecting to be taking her home after her meeting with their boss. He had thought of asking Angela to stay calm but reckoned that she might be tempted to do exactly the opposite.

He sat down at his desk and watched as Angela entered the chief inspector's office, without knocking as usual.

'Sit down please, Angela,' said Russell pleasantly.

Angela did as she was asked.

The DCI thought for a moment. 'Although we haven't known each other for long, we've never found it easy to work together,' he began. 'I've always been concerned regarding your lack of respect for authority,' he continued quickly before Angela had the opportunity to confirm or deny what he had said.

'But you have a very fine record. Your intuition in many cases has been admirable. I think I may have overreacted to your comments. But to have such a public blow out with a fellow officer was inexcusable.' He carried on without waiting for her response. 'I've taken action to protect the authority of my position, but in doing so I may have hampered the investigation. Whatever else we may disagree on, I'm sure we both accept that nothing should get in the way of solving these cases.'

He paused and Angela nodded. At least she could agree with the last bit.

'I'm prepared to accept that what happened was a result of frustration and leave it at that. I haven't instigated any formal proceedings, as I wanted to think things over. I would like you to come back immediately and work on this from your own angle. How do you feel about that?'

'Well, sir,' began Angela. (She felt the *sir* was a nice touch, even if she didn't mean the respect it implied.) 'There's no doubt about the level of frustration I've felt; in fact, I believe we all feel frustrated. I would certainly welcome the chance to get back to work and examine the evidence to see if it backs up my theory.'

'I will expect you to apologise to DI Lambert. Not over the phone or in writing, but personally. Is that going to be a problem for you?'

'No Sir.'

'Excellent!' said the DCI. He got to his feet. 'I'll send a memo to all officers immediately informing them that you are back with us. There will be a briefing at 16.00 and I expect to see you there. One thing, Angela, it might be worth reminded you that we have a lot of officers working on these cases. A lot of officers who, collectively, have amassed a considerable amount of experience. You are one small cog in a big wheel. For the time being, I'd like you to report directly to me. One last piece of advice, we work as a team and I really need you to be a team player.'

Angela smiled and left. *Team player? No problem*, she thought, *as long as they play by my rules.*

The chief inspector sat down and brought up on his computer screen the memo he had already written. He was very pleased at the outcome of the meeting. In many ways he admired Angela, but he couldn't allow indiscipline amongst his officers. He had to be seen to stamp on this if and when it arose. Angela was a loose cannon in his team, but even in the short time he had known her, she had displayed a high level of intuition. And he knew that this could be an invaluable asset for a detective, especially when a case appeared to be going nowhere. He would continue to allow Detective Anderson to work with her. They seemed to work well together, or at least he wasn't aware of the two of them ever fighting. Yet. Detective Inspector Lambert, Angela's immediate superior, had been interviewed and stated that he would accept an apology from his junior officer. However, he had made it quite clear that he felt he would be unable to continue with her in his team. No matter how sincere her apology may be, his authority had been undermined publicly. Russell had accepted this and rather than assign her to another DI the DCI had taken the unusual decision to ask her to report to him. He prepared to send the memo and deleted the alternative one he had written just in case things hadn't turned out so well.

Angela headed for where Greg was sitting, nervously sharpening a pencil which was already honed to a fine point.

'Ok, Greg my boy, we're almost ready to roll! You're taking me back home to get changed, and then it's back to work.'

She set off for the door and Greg rushed after her.

'Do you need to get changed?' he said. 'You look fine the way you are.'

'Oh Greg, you say the nicest things. But unless you want me to go out with a pen stuck in my bra and my notebook in my knickers, I need to get something with pockets in it.'

'Couldn't you have thought of that before we left?' asked Greg.

'OK,' admitted Angela, 'perhaps I should have, but I didn't know that I was going to be staying. In any case, we'll be heading to Motherwell, and that takes us past my house, so it's no big deal.'

'Won't we be stepping on someone's toes going to Motherwell? Shouldn't we at least let the local boys know we're coming?'

'Greg, we're part of a team investigating these serial killings. That gives us license to go wherever we like and ask for co-operation. Remember, we're all part of the same team.'

Greg doubted if he had ever heard Angela use the words *co-operation* and *team* before, but he decided not to mention this.

'Are you driving?' he asked.

'Why?' said Angela. 'If I am, do you need a toilet break?'

'Well, you are a bit, eh, reckless Sarge.'

Angela stopped in her tracks and spun to face him.

'I'll let you know that I've passed the advanced police driving test.'

'If you say so, but I'm a bit surprised you've passed *any* driving test.'

'Greg. If I want wit and humour, I'll talk to myself.'

'Why are we going to Motherwell?' asked Greg.

'To do what we're paid to do, Greg, to detect. To try and throw some light on this latest killing, the one our more experienced colleagues believe was done by the *Careful Killer*. Does that answer your question?'

'Not really,' said Greg. 'For a start, I've never heard of the *Careful Killer*, and I don't see how going back over the crime scene will add anything to what we already know.'

'Then let me enlighten you. The *Careful Killer* is, of course, the serial killer we're all trying to catch. You've never heard of the name because I only made it up yesterday. The reason we're going to Motherwell is to talk to some people who might throw some light on why this latest murder suggests the *Careful Killer* is becoming a bit careless.'

'Is he?'

'Of course he is. Although the Boss doesn't seem to think so. Lambert is quite sure I'm wrong, but his view is as worthless as an ashtray on a motorbike. So we're going to do some detecting.'

She hurried down the steps from the station leaving the baffled detective in her wake. Greg had been working with her for a few months, but he still couldn't figure her out. She seemed to do everything on impulse, but this worked out to her advantage so often he wondered if it only *appeared* to be an impulse. He knew that his inexperience showed, not just in analysing crimes, but also in dealing with witnesses and suspects. Greg had not long left the uniformed branch and found the more informal conduct of the CID difficult to get used to. Most other Detective Constables called their sergeants by their first names. In fact, they usually did the same with their inspectors, but Greg hadn't got used to this. He had never worked with a superior officer who mocked and teased him so much, and he was sure it would be classed as some form of harassment. However, what she said never *really* offended him, and he suspected her reason for tormenting him was to toughen him up.

Angela seemed to have a sixth sense when dealing with people. She knew when to push something and when to back off. Greg didn't think this was a skill he would be able to learn easily or quickly. Sometimes he doubted if he could learn it at all, but to Angela it appeared to come naturally.

She would be very offhand with suspects, almost like the way the old TV detective Colombo acted. Lulling people into a false sense of security, making them think she was a bit dizzy and unfocussed, but Greg now knew better. He almost felt sorry for suspects in Angela's clutches. They were like flies caught in her web. When she lost her temper and shouted, it was almost always an act. However, there were times when she was calm and collected and Greg was sure she was seething inside.

Greg knew that many of their colleagues were waiting on Angela falling flat on her face. Waiting for her to follow one of her hunches, and for this to turn out to be totally wrong. But this hadn't happened yet, and Greg hoped it never would. DI Lambert had been one of the main men who looked on putting her down as a crusade. Angela had described Lambert as a bully, and Greg had to agree with her assessment. And like most bullies, as soon as someone stood up to him, he wilted. In the specific case which landed Angela in hot water, Lambert had run bleating to his superiors. Even the other officers who enjoyed sparring with Angela had taken exception to that.

Anderson also came in for a fair bit of teasing. He was sure the new boy usually did, but because he was working with Angela, this was more focussed. A day or so after he had been assigned to work with her, he had arrived at the station to find a bag of paper nappies and a baby's rattle on his desk. He put them in the bin. A few days later he arrived to find a packet of condoms on his desk with a note saying *for your first big stakeout…with Angela*. Some of the guys had pretended to be busy, but were obviously watching him. He had thrown the note in the bin, but put the condoms in his pocket. That was the last time he was left any form of present.

Greg took the wheel this time and drove to Angela's house. He waited in the car while she got changed, then they headed for Motherwell.

'When do you plan to apologise to Lambert?' said Greg.

'When I run into him, I suppose.'

'So, you're not going out of your way to see him?'

Angela didn't answer, but just gave Greg a look he was beginning to know quite well.

'But you'll have to do it sometime,' persisted Greg, 'so why not get it over with sooner rather than later?'

'If it makes you happy, I'll try and catch up with Lambert after we've been to Motherwell. There. Happy now?'

'Are we going to the crime scene?' asked Greg, changing the subject.

'No. I don't think we'll find out much from that.'

'So where are we going exactly?'

'We're going to visit the deceased's wife to ask her a few questions.'

'Why?' asked Greg.

Angela gave a sigh. 'Greg, let me ask you some questions. Let's say we are investigating a murder. What do we do?'

Greg suspected this was a trick question, so he thought carefully before answering.

'We would examine the crime scene for clues...'

'Correct,' said Angela.

'Looking in particular for a possible murder weapon..'

'Correct.'

'We would try and find out if there were any witnesses who may have seen something significant...'

'Correct.'

'As most murders are committed by someone who knows the victim, we would then interview all friends and relatives...'

'Correct again.'

'Then we would check their alibis and see if they hold up...'

'Right.'

'We would consider a possible motive for the murder...'

'Full marks so far.'

'Depending on the autopsy results we might interview some people again...'

'Right, stop there. That's very good, straight out of the text-book. Or at least I think it is. If it's not in the textbook, then it should be. So, what's different about this murder?'

'Well, it's part of a series. It looks like another one done by your *Careful Killer*.'

'It *looks* as if it is,' said Angela, 'but what if it isn't?'

'I don't see what you're getting at Sarge,' admitted Greg.

'Have you seen the preliminary reports on the crime?'

'Yes.'

'Did you see the notes of the interview with Mrs Stewart and other people?'

'No. I didn't see them.'

'Did you look for them?'

'I'm afraid not, I didn't see the point.'

'Spot on, Greg! You didn't look for them because you didn't see the *point*. And if you had looked for them, you wouldn't have found them, because the officers investigating the case didn't see the point of carrying them out. They assumed right from the off that Stewart was another victim of the serial killer. And if he were a victim of the serial killer, they would not be looking for a motive for his murder closer to home. So no one wasted time questioning these people.'

'And you don't think it was?'

'I accept the possibility that it might not be. And if he didn't do it, it's a whole new ball game. There are dozens of detectives going through what clues we have from the previous murders over and over again. We're going to start with a clean slate and *investigate* this latest murder.'

'OK, now I understand.'

'Excellent! Now, let me ask you another question. Why do you always drive so slowly?'

Chapter 20

'We're sorry to bother you Mrs, Stewart. I imagine you've already answered a lot of questions.'

'Not really,' she replied, showing them to seats in a spacious lounge, 'no one has asked me very much at all.'

Angela shot a quick glance at Greg as they sat down. They declined the offer of tea or coffee and waited until Mrs Stewart had made herself comfortable.

'I see you're planning a trip,' said Angela indicating the suitcases visible in the hallway.

'I can't make up my mind,' said Mrs Stewart. 'My son has asked me to go and stay with him for a few days. But I don't know if I should.' She looked round the room. 'I feel I should stay and sort through Robbie's things. I know that the longer this is put off, the more difficult it becomes. I need to busy myself doing things. At my son's house, I would just be sitting around.'

'Why doesn't your son come here for a while?' asked Greg. 'He would be able to help you if you decide to sort things out.'

The woman smiled. 'I know this will sound bad,' she said, 'but he's too busy with his work to afford to be away for even a few days. He'll be up for the funeral. To be honest, he and my husband didn't really get along. Richard, that's my son, moved away the first chance he got. We haven't seen much of him and his wife recently. They live in Brighton, so they're hardly within easy reach. I just don't know what to do.' She stared at the suitcases.

'I know this will be difficult for you, Mrs Stewart, but are you able to answer a few questions?'

'Yes,' said the woman looking at Angela, 'anything to help. They're saying it is this serial killer again?'

'Well, that's a possibility,' said Angela, taking out her notebook, 'but at this stage we like to keep an open mind.'

The woman nodded.

'Did your husband have any enemies you were aware of?'

'None I know of. But he had been a policeman. And I suppose in your line of work you will always make enemies.' She shook her head. 'My husband never really talked about his work very much.'

'On the night when he was attacked, do you know where your husband was going?'

'I've no idea,' said the woman. 'He just told me that he wouldn't be long.'

'What time did he leave?'

'Just before ten I think.'

'Could he have been going to the pub?'

'Oh no, my husband never went to the pub. It's no secret that he liked the occasional drink, but he would take that here.'

Angela wrote in her notebook.

'Was it normal for him to leave at that hour?'

'Now and again he would get a phone call and have to go out.'

'Did he receive a call on that night?'

'Yes he did.'

'And do you know who called?'

'No, I'm afraid not.'

'But he was retired, was he not?'

'From the Police Force, yes, but he was doing some part time work for a friend.'

'Do you know what type of part time work?'

'No, I'm afraid not.'

'Do you know who his friend was?'

'Again, no, I'm afraid not.'

Angela paused to write in her book again.

'I don't think I'm being of much help to you,' said Mrs Stewart. 'I don't seem to know anything useful.'

'To be honest, Mrs Stewart, we don't know what might be useful at this stage. We're just trying to build up a picture of that night. Even minor things may become significant as the inquiry continues. Now, did your husband seem troubled when he left?'

'I'd say he was thoughtful, but not troubled.'

'Now I don't want you to take offence, Mrs Stewart, but I have to ask. Did you and your husband have any money worries?'

'Oh, no. We are fairly well off.'

'And did you have any marital problems? Excuse me again for asking.'

The woman smiled. 'No, we had no problems of that kind, and there's no need to excuse yourself. Contrary to what my husband seemed to believe, I do live in the real world. I have seen crime programmes on the television. Next you'll be asking me if there as any possibility my husband was having an affair?' She carried on without waiting for Angela to confirm her statement. 'The answer is no, I'm pretty sure he wasn't. No tell-tale lipstick on his collars or long strands of hair on his jacket. No smell of perfume on his clothes. He didn't change his appearance to make himself look younger. No, there was nothing to make me suspect there was another woman, or man for that matter.'

Greg looked startled and Angela smiled.

'Thank you for your openness,' said Angela, 'it makes our job so much easier when people are willing to be frank with us.'

Mrs Stewart made a small gracious bow in acknowledgement.

'Now, in the days leading up to your husband's death, were you aware of anything unusual happening?'

'Not that I can think of. It had been a pretty uneventful week. He went out a few times to meet with friends, but that was normal. We received some phone calls, but again nothing out of the ordinary.'

'Did you receive any visitors?'

'A young man called and was here for ten or fifteen minutes.'

'Did you know who he was?'

'No, I'm afraid not.'

'Did your husband know him?'

'I don't think so.'

'Do you know what his visit was about?'

'Robbie said that the young man wanted help with an old case, but that there was nothing my husband could do.'

'Did that sort of thing happen often?'

'No, never before that I'm aware of. I didn't think much of it at the time, except that a day or so later the man came back.'

'To see your husband again?'

'He didn't come to the house; he just sat in his car outside.'

'Can you describe the man?'

'I'm afraid not; my husband let him in on the day he called, and I remained in another room. My husband said he had walked past the house, but I only saw him when he was sitting in his car.'

'Can you describe the car?' asked Greg with urgency in his voice.

'All I can tell you is that it was a blue one. It looked fairly big. It had four doors, I'm sure of that. It wasn't a sports car and it wasn't an estate car.'

'Was it light or dark blue?'

'It was quite a light shade of blue, and it had a Scotland badge on the number plate.'

'You noticed that?' said Greg.

The woman smiled. 'Strangely enough, yes, I did.'

'I don't suppose you remember the registration number?'

'No, sorry. I wouldn't have been able to make out the badge except that Robbie came downstairs for a closer look at the car and I followed him. Then I became bored and went back to reading my book.'

'Can you show us where you first saw this car?' asked Angela.

Mrs Stewart took them to an upstairs room and pointed out where the car had been parked.

'It was facing up the road, the rear end was just ahead of that walnut tree in the next garden,' she said, 'so from here you couldn't tell there was anyone in it.'

'And where did you go for a closer look?' asked Angela.

The woman led them back downstairs into Stewart's study. She pointed out the window.

'From here I could see the Scotland badge,' explained the woman. 'And I could tell that there was one person in the car.'

'There's one more thing while it's in my mind, Mrs Stewart, would it be possible for us to have a fairly recent photograph of your husband?'

'If you don't mind waiting I'll see what I can find.'

When the woman left, Greg wandered about the room while Angela remained at the window.

'Pretty highbrow stuff,' said Greg, reading the title of a book on the bookshelf.

'By *highbrow* do you mean *shite*?' asked Angela in a low voice.

Greg ignored her comment.

'Shouldn't you be looking around?' said Greg, 'you know, doing some detecting.'

'Sshh, I'm busy,' she replied.

Greg wandered over to where she was bending over the small table in front of the window. She was scribbling with a pencil over the top sheet of a small notebook. She finished scribbling, ripped off the top sheet and stuffed it in her pocket.

'Any sign of a diary?' she asked, still in a low voice.

'Not that I've noticed,' said Greg, 'but it might be in one of the desk drawers.'

'I'll have a look,' said Angela, 'you let me know if Mrs Stewart's coming back.'

She quickly moved to the desk and opened the top drawer, then the second one.

Greg was nervously glancing between Angela and the hallway as she closed that drawer and opened the third and last one.

'Here it is,' she said. She brought a large A4 book out of the drawer and laid it on the desk.

'Sarge! She's coming back!' whispered Greg urgently.

'Stall her,' said Angela.

Greg walked out into the hallway to meet the woman.

'I'm sorry to trouble you Mrs Stewart, but is it possible I could use your toilet?'

Mrs Stewart started to give Greg directions and he seemed to be having difficulty in following them. Eventually he left her and headed up the stairs.

'Here's a picture,' said Mrs Stewart to Angela. 'It was taken at his retirement dinner and he hadn't changed much since then.'

Angela took the photograph and carefully placed it in her notebook.

They waited on Greg returning, then thanked her and left.

'I don't think I've been of much help,' said Mrs Stewart as they walked towards the gate.

'You've been a big help,' said Angela. 'We'll keep you informed of developments. And I don't see what harm it would do for you to go and stay with your son for a few days.'

'OK. Let's go and I'll buy you lunch,' said Angela.

Angela took the piece of paper out of her pocket while Greg went to the burger van with the tenner she had given him.

'Not quite what I had in mind when you mentioned lunch,' said Greg as he got back into the car and handed her a cheeseburger and coke.

'Well, we're on duty. It would have taken too long to get served at the Hilton.' She glanced over at Greg. 'Is that you eating a burger? That's a change from the rabbit food you usually eat.'

'You know I'm a vegetarian.'

'You say that as if you're a superior being,' said Angela. 'But I had your deviant tastes in mind when I brought you here. They do have veggie burgers, don't they?'

Greg held up a rather limp looking roll with something brown in the middle of it.

'Looks delicious,' said Angela as she took a bite of her burger. 'I'll maybe get one of those the next time.'

She nodded at the small grassy area in front of where they had parked the car. 'If you don't like it, you could always go over there for a graze. I'll wait. So, what have we learned?' asked Angela, brushing crumbs from her jacket.

To an observer, it would appear as if Angela was constantly quizzing him, as a teacher would do with a pupil. By asking questions and listening to Greg's responses, Angela was able to organise her thoughts. Sometimes she would ask him to question her, usually when she felt she had missed something. Greg was now quite used to this procedure and had long since dismissed the thought of it having any demeaning intent.

'Assuming we treat this murder as unrelated to the others,' began Greg, 'I'd say there is no obvious motive for it. There appears to be no financial or sexual suggestion of a motive. However, she doesn't seem to know much about what her husband was up to regarding his part time work. She couldn't tell us much about the phone calls he had been receiving. Then there's the visit of the young man which might be worth looking in to.'

'I'd say that sums things up quite nicely,' said Angela, taking a drink of her coke. 'So how would you suggest we proceed?'

'I'd get the phone records, look for recurring numbers and find out who they were from and to. I'd be particularly interested in the call Stewart received just before he went out on the night he was killed. I'd also be interested in tracking down the man who visited him recently, and whose car was seen parked along from the house. It could also be worthwhile finding out exactly what type of part time work Stewart was involved in, and who he was working with. I would also like to know where Stewart was going, or had been, just before he was killed.'

'You know Greg,' said Angela, 'sometimes I think you might make a detective.'

She reached in her pocket and pulled out the bit of paper she had taken from the Stewart house.

'What do you think of this?'

Angela handed the paper to Greg. Inside the pencil scribbling, Greg could make out part of what appeared to be the registration number of a car.

'Did you get this idea from a Sherlock Holmes story?' asked Greg.

'Don't knock it, Greg my boy. Crime detection owes a lot to Sir Arthur Conan Doyle. What can you deduce from the piece of paper?'

Greg frowned. 'It's a car registration number. Stewart wrote it down, and then ripped the sheet with the number written on it from the pad, presumably to try and find out who owned the car.'

'And?'

'And that's it, as far as I can tell.'

'Not quite. You assumed the driver of the car is the same person as the owner, not necessarily true. Also, if Stewart was as disinterested in his visitor as he told his wife, why take a note of the registration number?'

'I meant to ask you about the diary; anything of interest in it?' said Greg.

'I'm not sure,' said Angela. 'He noted quite a few appointments, but usually he just wrote the time. On the odd occasion he had written things like *2.30 Dentist.* But that also tells us something. It tells us that he was meeting with people he knew quite well, otherwise he would have written more than just the time.'

'He might not have wanted his wife to see who he was meeting,' suggested Greg.

'A good point. Perhaps we'll know more when we examine the diary in more detail.'

'Are we going back for it?'

'Yes, but not today. Have we ruled out Mrs. Stewart as a suspect?'

'I doubt if she had anything to do with her husband's death, but I'd have to say no, we haven't ruled her out yet.'

'Spot on, but it might well be advisable that she doesn't know we're interested in the diary.'

'So that's why you didn't ask her for it?'

'That's one reason. A more far-fetched reason is that if we had asked her for it, and she had denied one existed, we would have lost it. By the time we returned with a search warrant, even assuming we could get one, she could have disposed of it.'

'So how are we going to get it without asking?'

'Well, she's likely to be going away for a few days...'

'You're going to break in!'

'I'm not planning to break anything, Greg. That would be malicious damage and against the law. I'm shocked you even thought that!'

'But you are going to *get* in?'

'*We* are going to get in. I want to look at the diary, and I'd also like to take a look at his computer.'

Greg shook his head. 'And there was me thinking that you were showing a sensitive touch by advising her to visit her son. I should have known you had an ulterior motive.'

'You do me an injustice, Greg. My advice to her was well meant; it just happens to have a positive spin off for us.'

In spite of her assurances, Greg wasn't convinced.

'Don't we have a meeting to attend?' said Angela looking at her watch.

'Yes. 4pm,' confirmed Greg.

'OK, that just gives us time to nip through to Paisley so I can apologise to Lambert.'

'Oh, I'll need to hear this!' said Greg.

'No, you don't. This will be a private conversation between two mature police officers who had a difference of opinion, that's all. It's not a big deal.'

'Unless he asks you to apologise loudly enough so the guys in the car park hear it.'

'He's got two chances of that happening, and the most likely one is not a lot. Let's go. It wouldn't do to keep the prick waiting.'

Chapter 21

Greg was a little surprised that Angela managed to apologise in a way that avoided World War III, but somehow she did it. He was curious as to what exactly she said, but she refused to go into details.

The briefing had been advised that the Stewart killing was the work of the serial killer. Those attending also heard various reports, including one from a forensic scientist. The SCAS hadn't come up with anything. Although not stated bluntly, the best chance of catching the person responsible seemed to be either through luck, information from the public, or if the killer made a mistake in a future killing. The thought of having to wait for another murder threw a depressing shroud over the meeting.

Another appeal to the public would be launched, and the television Crimewatch programme would devote an entire instalment to the killings. It was hoped this might jog some memories amongst the viewers and throw up some new leads.

Officers had identified the maker of boots worn by the attacker in two of the murders, but trying to trace buyers would be impossible, as both makes were very common. DNA results had been obtained from a variety of items left at the scenes, but only two had been identified from the database of known offenders. Both people had been traced and ruled out of the inquiry. The conclusion was that the killer was deliberately leaving false clues. However, procedure dictated that nothing could be dismissed out of hand, and everything had to be examined thoroughly. This was resulting in a huge waste of time and was tying up dozens of officers and labs. The meeting was reminded that, contrary to the public's perception from watching programmes like CSI, DNA testing wasn't completed while the investigator drank a cup of coffee. If a particular sample was reckoned to be of higher importance, a result could be obtained between forty-eight and seventy-two hours.

Door-to-door inquiries were continuing. So far nothing of known value had been turned up. CCTV footage of the areas close to the crime scenes was being examined in the hope of identifying a vehicle common to a number of the scenes. The registration numbers of all vehicles were being entered into a computer database and these were being cross-referenced. However, CCTV cameras did not cover the immediate crime scenes, and these scenes seem to have been deliberately chosen by the killer for that precise reason.

A criminal psychologist outlined his findings from his study of the crimes. The killer would be male; between twenty-five and forty, probably white, would have a steady job, and have had a traumatic experience in early life. He thought it likely the killer had been abused by his father as a child. It was likely his parents, or certainly his father, were dead. It was unlikely he would be married or in a stable relationship. There was nothing in the crimes to suggest a sexual motive. The killer was making a statement and needed to be caught for his purpose to be clearly understood, but he would have to be caught and would not give himself up. The killer was taking souvenirs from his victims, but he was not keeping these, he was passing them on to each successive victim. This meant that at any time, the killer would have one such souvenir in his possession. The psychologist reasoned that the killer was doing this to allow

146

police to identify the crimes as belonging to him. This man would be deriving strength for his 'quest' from the media coverage. Also, contrary to popular belief and Hollywood portrayals, serial killers rarely kept cuttings of their media coverage. In summing up, the psychologist stated that this killer would be difficult to catch, but when caught would readily admit to his crimes. He was not the insane person some sections of the media were painting him, quite the contrary; he was an intelligent, well-organised, careful predator on a mission. The psychologist wished them luck in their search for the killer. It was obvious he felt they would need it.

'So, what do you think Sarge?' said Greg.

Angela shrugged. 'Leaving the false clues was obvious from pretty early on, in fact as soon as the DNA results started to come in. The profile is probably pretty accurate but doesn't help much. It'll cut down the number of suspects to a few million. We could check through the files and identify men who were abused as children, but that only includes the cases that were reported. Ruling out guys whose parents were still alive, and guys who are married would narrow it down. But that's all assuming the profile is correct and would still leave us with a huge list.'

'I thought you said that you thought the profile is probably accurate?'

'Yeah, but you need to take that with a pinch of salt. They can only base these profiles on what they know.'

'What do you mean?'

'Well, say over a period of ten years there are twenty murders committed that follow a similar pattern and the police catch twelve of the killers. Let's assume all these killers fall into a particular category, for example, they're all unemployed, around thirty years old, and of below average intelligence. So, the profile will suggest that future killers will follow that general trend. However, what about the eight killers that were never caught? These guys could all be employed in good jobs, around fifty years old and of above average intelligence. So, what's happened to the profile?'

'You're saying the profile can only be based on what we know?'

'Yes, exactly. And can we afford to put all our eggs in one basket? Don't you remember what put the cops off the scent during the hunt for the Yorkshire Ripper?'

'The tape that turned out to be false?' said Greg.

'Precisely. They put their faith in a tape they received where the guy confessing to be the Ripper had a Geordie accent, which Sutcliffe didn't have. And how did they eventually catch Sutcliffe?'

'Luck. They came across a car that had false number plates, and one thing led to another after that.'

'Yes. So, Greg, I am determined that we shall not be sidetracked. We will pursue the inquiry regarding the murder of Stewart until we are absolutely certain it was the work of the *Careful Killer*. Do you agree?'

'Do I have any choice?'

'Not really, so let's get to work and look at the evidence,' said Angela.

'I read somewhere that since the war, Scotland has produced twenty-four per cent of Britain's serial killers,' said Greg, trying to avoid dropping his pile of files as he followed Angela down the steep stone steps. 'Why do you think that is?'

Angela didn't stop, but he saw her shrug. 'It's probably got something to do with the weather,' she said.

She had led Greg to a disused storeroom in the basement of the station. Groping around behind the door, she found the light switch and threw it. Half a dozen light bulbs sparked into life, although one at the back of the room gave a pop and conked out.

'I wonder what they used this for?' asked Greg.

'Probably the rubber hose treatment back in the good old days,' replied Angela.

They blew the worst of the dust off a table and placed the files on it.

'What do we know that's common to all the killings? Let's leave the last one out for now.'

'OK, Sarge. Well, the killer targets males between forty and sixty-five. All have been attacked from behind and strangled with a piece of nylon cord. The bodies have been left where they were killed and a watch has been removed from each victim. This watch has then turned up on the body of the next victim. What appeared at first to be clues were found at the crime scenes, predominately cigarette ends. What DNA results we have had back suggest these have been left as decoys. Fibres were found on some of the victims clothing, but no two victims were found with matching fibres, and none of the fibres have been matched to an item of clothing found anywhere near the scenes. The victims all had a high level of alcohol in their blood. When the crime scenes are plotted on a map, they are all within a twenty-mile radius of Glasgow. Footprints have been found at all but one of the crime scenes. These prints are of a man's boot or shoe, size eleven. Two of the prints so far have been identified to a particular footwear maker, but these are so common that tracing the purchaser is impossible. Although the size has been the same in each case, the prints have all been different. All attacks have been carried out between 9pm and 11.30pm.'

Greg put down his notes. 'I think that about covers it Sarge.'

'Sounds fine to me,' said Angela. 'Right. Let's try and fit what we know of the Stewart killing into the pattern you have established. We'll leave out the location as these differ. Get it?'

Greg nodded.

Angela held up a hand. 'And if we find any deviations from the accepted pattern that can't be explained in a reasonable manner, we'll work on the assumption that this crime has been the work of someone new to the scene. Agreed?'

Greg nodded again.

'Right. Cigarette ends and some ring pulls were found close to the body. Stewart had been strangled. He was killed at approximately 10.30pm. He had been strangled with what appears to have been a piece of nylon cord. His watch was missing, and he was wearing a watch that didn't belong to him. Does all that tie in?'

'Yes Sarge,' agreed Greg.

'OK, so let's continue and look at any deviations from the previous crimes and try and explain them. Let's try and make this the latest in the serial killers list. Firstly, does the watch we found on Stewart belong to the previous victim?'

'Not as far as we can tell,' said Greg. 'My explanation for that is there could be a body we haven't discovered yet.'

'That's a fair point Greg, but all of the bodies have been found within hours of being killed. Is it likely the killer, on that one occasion, hid the body?'

'No, but the murder could have taken place somewhere where people are unlikely to come across the body.'

'But the crimes have all been committed in fairly well populated areas, and on routes used by men returning from various pubs. Can we reasonably believe there is an undiscovered victim out there somewhere?'

'I agree it's unlikely,' said Greg.

'And talking of pubs,' said Angela, 'the autopsy report states that Stewart hadn't been drinking before being killed. Every one of the previous victims had been drinking; at least two of them were quite drunk.'

'So, you think the killer knew these guys had been drinking and that's why they were killed?'

'At least it's a coincidence,' said Angela.

'But no more than that at this stage,' said Greg. Angela shrugged. 'Right. The next point,' she said. 'The medical report has stated that, although nylon cord was used to kill Stewart, the cord was not the same as used to kill the previous victims.'

'OK. Perhaps the killer had used all of the type of cord he had at the start and had to get some new stuff?'

'But we've never found any of the cord used in the killings, is it not possible the same piece of cord has been used every time except in this case?'

Greg shook his head. 'Definitely not. Even if the killer cleaned the cord to use it again, it's unlikely he would have been able to get all the pieces of skin tissue off. No DNA belonging to anyone other than the victims has been found in the strangulation marks. There's been no cross transfer.'

'OK Greg. It's good to see you've been paying attention, but the killer is not likely to keep the cord kicking around. I'd bet he uses a new bit every time.'

Greg hummed and hawed a bit. 'Let's look at it from another angle, Sarge. What if it is the same killer, but he's decided to alter things a bit, so we'd start doing exactly what we're doing now? To divert resources and make it easier for him to continue killing?'

'A fair point, but I don't think so. This killer is building a reputation. He wants us to know these crimes are all his work, hence the business with the watches. It's unlikely he'd deliberately change his formula and possibly weaken his reputation.'

'OK, but the psychologist said that he wants to get caught. When he does, he'll be able to tell us that he varied his style, so he will get the credit.'

'Another fair point. Although I don't think the killer wants to get caught. He'll know that he *needs* to be caught so that his purpose can be known, but we'll call this one a draw. Right, the next point is very important, and to demonstrate this I need you to strangle me.'

'To strangle you? You mean to pretend to strangle you?'

'No. You need to strangle me, at least a bit. Now don't be shy, you'll be the envy of half of our colleagues.'

'What do you want me to do?' said Greg warily.

Angela went into her pocket and pulled out a length of nylon cord.

'Do you have the coroner's pictures of the bodies?'

'Yes.'

'Good. Lay them on the table for the moment. OK, here's the cord, you're the murderer.'

She handed Greg the length of cord and turned her back to him.

'Now, you're, what, five feet eleven or something like that?'

'Exactly that,' said Greg.

'I'm only five feet five, so you'll have to bend your knees a bit when you're doing this. The marks on the victims' necks suggested the killer was approximately the same height as them. OK, now put the cord around my throat and pull it.'

Greg did as he was asked and pulled the cord gently.

'No Greg, you'll need to pull it harder than that.'

Greg pulled the cord harder and Angela stumbled back until her back rested against his chest. He immediately released the cord, and she coughed a bit.

'Do you see what I'm getting at?'

'Yeah, I think so. When you fell back against me it was difficult for me to pull the cord, as my hands were level with my shoulders. I didn't have much purchase.'

'Right, now this time before you pull the cord put a knee into my back, then pull the cord.'

She lined herself up again and Greg tried what she had suggested, but he lost his balance and staggered to the side, letting the cord go as he fell.

'It's too difficult standing on one leg,' explained Greg. 'As soon as you twist to the side, I'm off balance and fall over.'

'OK, let's try it another way. You stand with your back against that wall but try everything else as we've done before. Assuming you don't fall over, I'll try and get my hands back to reach your face. None of the victims had any skin or tissue under their nails, so I assume they weren't able to reach their attacker. Let's find out. Don't let go until I've had a chance to try that.'

They moved to the wall and lined themselves up again. Greg once again put the cord round her neck.

Using the wall at his back for support, he pulled the cord tight and brought his knee up into her back. This time he didn't fall over. Angela reached behind her head grasping at thin air in an attempt to locate Greg, but he easily kept out of range.

'That's it Sarge,' said Greg excitedly, 'I think we've got it now!'

Angela was able to reach the rope, but unable to get any purchase to release the strain. She tried to run her hand along the rope to reach Greg's hands, but she couldn't.

She tried to twist and turn, moving in one direction then the other, but the force exerted by the rope combined with Greg's knee prevented her from having any success.

Then it dawned on Greg that Angela's feet were barely touching the ground and he let go of the rope.

She fell face forward onto the dirty floor.

'Angela!' shouted Greg in a panic.

He dropped the rope and bent to turn her over. As he turned her onto her back he saw at once the bright red mark around her throat.

'Oh Fuck!'

She began to cough and splutter. Tears were running down her face which was bright red. Her mouth was wide open as she gasped for air.

'I'll get help!' said Greg and made to get up, but she waved a hand at him to stop.

Gradually her breathing returned to normal, but she continued to cough. The redness left her face, but it now appeared much whiter than normal. The red mark round her neck looked worse than before.

'Oh Christ, what have I done!' muttered Greg.

'You did what I asked you,' said Angela in a very hoarse voice.

He fetched a folding chair from the back wall, opened it and dusted it down with his handkerchief, then helped Angela into it.

'You said you would try and reach me, and I saw you doing that. I was watching so intently I didn't realise...'

Greg suddenly noticed he was holding one of her hands. He let it go and took a step back.

'Can I get some water please?' said Angela.

Greg hurried off to fetch the water.

She wiped her eyes then took a sip.

'Right,' she got up rather unsteadily to her feet, 'so what have we learned from that?'

'For fuck's sake!' said Greg, 'we're not going to carry on with this are we?'

'I'm OK now,' she said. 'I'm fine.'

'You're not fine! I almost...'

'Greg. It wasn't your fault. You did what I asked you to do. It was my fault. If anything, it worked too well.'

'You're telling me!' said Greg, starting to shake. 'I knew it was a crazy thing to do, but you wouldn't listen! We should get you to a doctor.'

'Greg. I'm OK. There's no need for a doctor.'

Greg walked back and forward for a while as Angela continued to sip her water.

Gradually Greg calmed down.

'Sarge...'

'Greg, if you tell me you're sorry once more *I'll* strangle *you!*'

'I feel how you look,' said Greg, 'I can't stop shaking. I think we should pack it in for today.'

'It's delayed shock,' said Angela, 'it'll pass soon. But I agree, I think we've had enough for today.'

Most of the officers had left for the evening, so they managed to get out of the station without anyone noticing Angela's neck and Greg's shakes.

He gave her a lift home.

'Are you sure you'll be OK Sarge?' he said.

'Yeah, a good night's sleep and I'll be fine.'

'Do you want me to pick you up in the morning?'

'Yes please. Eight thirty as usual?'

'Sure Sarge. Eight thirty.'

She got out of the car.

'And Greg.'

'Yes?'

'Call me Angela. I think we can drop the Sarge thing.'

Angela was lying in bed when the phone rang, again. It was Greg, again. She told him that her breathing was fine, the mark was still there, but was tender rather than sore, and that she was planning to get a good night's sleep except that someone kept phoning her. Pretty much what she had told him the last time he had phoned, all of half an hour ago. This time he took her point.

Greg arrived outside her house at exactly 8.30 the following morning and was relieved when she opened her door and quickly walked to the car. The mark around her neck was clearly visible, although she had her shirt collar pulled up.

'Before you ask, I'm fine. Much better. Did you leave the coroner's pictures in the basement?'

'I'm afraid I did,' said Greg. 'In all the excitement I totally forgot all about them.'

'No problem,' said Angela, 'there's little chance anyone else will have been in there, and we need to finish off from yesterday. In case you're worried, the strangling bit is over.'

'I wasn't really worried,' joked Greg, 'it was you who was being strangled.'

They managed to get into the basement without any problems, and Angela directed Greg to organise the stacked-up tables then she spread out the photos across them.

'Have I got them in the correct chronological order?' she said.

'Yes.' He walked along the line slowly then pointed to the far-left table. 'It started with Tom Kelly in Paisley, then moves through the victims until we reach Robert Stewart. They're all correct.'

'Excellent.' She folded down her collar as she walked to the first set of pictures. 'Now compare the mark on my neck with the first victim.' Greg looked at the pictures then at Angela. 'Almost identical,' he said. She agreed, and then shuffled the first set of pictures.

'Now look at that mark on his back and compare it with this.' She lifted up her shirt and revealed a bruise in the middle of her back, about six inches above her waist.

'Almost identical again,' said Greg. 'Except none of the victims have a tattoo of a butterfly…'

She shot him a *shut-up* glance and he did as the look suggested.

They moved through the victims, finding the same marks on each of them.

'Now let's compare what we've seen with the photos of Stewart,' said Angela. 'First of all, notice that there is no mark on his back.'

'But the coroner reported that Stewart had been hit on the head before being strangled. If he was lying on the ground, there would be no need for the attacker to put a knee in his back.'

'Correct,' said Angela. 'Now look at the marks on his neck.'

Greg did as she asked, glancing back and forth between the photos and his living example.

'They look pretty much the same to me,' he confessed.

'Look closer,' said Angela, shuffling the pictures. 'Look at the pictures of the sides and back of his neck.'

'There are some marks there too, but you don't have those marks.'

'Exactly!' said Angela. 'Now let me tell you why. When the previous victims were strangled, it was done in the same way as we tried last night. By placing the rope around the neck then pulling back like you'd do with a horse's reins and using your knee for leverage. The reason Stewart has different marks is that the murderer placed the cord round his neck, then grabbed the left side of the cord with his right hand, and the right side with his left hand, *then pulled outwards*. The cord made a complete loop round Stewart's neck, hence the extra marks. And because the attacker was pulling outwards, there was no need to use his knee for leverage.'

'Fascinating,' said Greg. 'It all seems to fit. So the cord would have been looped over Stewart's head and then changed hands.'

'And that's exactly the reason for the blow to the head. Stewart would have been at least dazed when the cord was placed round his neck.'

Greg thought about this. 'So, you're saying that this proves Stewart was not attacked by the serial killer?'

'That's exactly what I'm saying. Now your job is to convince me I'm wrong.'

Angela walked over and took a seat where she had sat the previous evening.

'OK,' said Greg. 'Let's see what I can make of all this. Stewart was very tall, over six feet. We believe the attacker is also a big man, but he's unlikely to be taller than Stewart. In this respect Stewart is quite a different victim. This may have made the attacker change his method. He may have been reluctant to take on such a big man, but decided to do so, and to make it easier he cracked him on the head.'

'That's logical,' said Angela. 'But why strangle him in a different way? OK, Stewart was lying on the ground, whereas the other victims were standing up, but why change how you use the cord?'

'I haven't got an answer for that,' admitted Greg, 'but do you think it's really significant?'

'Yeah, I do,' replied Angela. 'While I accept what you said about the relative sizes of the men, I'm asking myself, why choose Stewart?'

'Because he was the first person to come along the path?' suggested Greg.

'So, you reckon the attacker was waiting on a victim?'

'Yes. I think that's likely.'

'OK, if that's the case, what's different about the Motherwell location and the previous ones?'

'He's killed before in parks,' said Greg. 'The hedges provided cover for him to hide in; I don't see any big difference.'

'What was there that he could steady himself on? There are no trees, no wall, nothing substantial for him to lean against. You found out the problems you had getting started with our experiment last night. For a killer who up to now has chosen his locations very carefully to suddenly have to improvise is, I think, pushing things a bit.'

'OK, said Greg, 'I'll accept the possibility that Stewart's killer *might be* a different guy. So, what's our next step?'

'We start to dig into Stewart's background. I've a feeling the killer knew him and used the other murders as cover for this crime. We'll put in a bit of overtime tonight and try and get a closer look at his diary. In the meantime, I'll need to try and disguise this

mark until it goes away. We'll pop into a chemist, unless you happen to have a make-up bag with you?'

Chapter 22

'No, no, no!' The man slammed the computer mouse down on the table. Seven pairs of eyes stared at him, including a pair from behind the reception desk.

He held up a hand in apology and logged off the computer.

He rushed home and retrieved his diary.

Fools!! The papers attribute the Motherwell incident to me, and the police do not deny it!

I will advance my schedule to show them their error. Should I change my plans? No! Why should this imposter inconvenience me! An increased police presence just serves to make my event all the more daring. I just have time to complete my plan for tonight. The weather forecast is favourable. Yes! I'll go for it!

He quickly hid the diary, rushed to his car and drove the short distance to the charity shop he knew had a pair of size eleven boots. The clothing had already been bought, as he didn't think having any of this in his house would pose a great risk were the authorities to check. But the boots were a different matter entirely. The old lady in the shop was preparing to close for the day but was happy to make one last sale. He thanked her politely and drove home. A quick meal, then he laid out everything he would need. Satisfied that he had all he required, he walked into his lounge to watch some television. As he settled down as best he could, he thought again about this imposter killer and how he had reacted in the library. That had been a bad moment, and he scolded himself at showing his annoyance. But he was back in control again and looking forward to his work. He went back into the bedroom and checked everything again carefully. To other people, the procedure might have appeared to be a chore, but he was a professional with pride in his work.

Eventually his departure time arrived, and he quickly got changed then made his way quietly out to the car and drove off. The parking place he had identified for this event was further away from his chosen site than normal, but he would rather risk a slightly longer walk than be spied on by CCTV cameras. When he arrived, a couple of people were walking along the quiet road, so he decided to drive round once more rather than park while they were there. This time the street was clear, so he parked and got out to begin his walk. The two pairs of thick socks he was wearing made walking in the oversize boots a bit easier than before, and soon he reached the park gates. He glanced around to check if there were any other people in the vicinity, then entered the park and took up his position as planned.

The first man to come along the path was walking a dog. The killer held his breath. A dog could screw up his plans. He watched intently as the dog stopped to do a crap. The owner walked past as if he hadn't noticed what his dog was doing. *Dirty bastard*! thought the killer, as he watched the man make no attempt to clean up the mess the dog had made. People like that dog owner disgusted him, they had no consideration for others.

The evening was dry but cold. He moved out of his cover and had a careful look around. Could he have a quick walk to get the circulation going? No, he'd better wait. Give it another thirty minutes. He thought of the media coverage he had been getting. Reporters still talked about him as if he were subhuman. They didn't realise how difficult a job he had. You don't find them hanging about on cold nights doing *their* job! No, they sit in a warm office in front of a computer trying to think up words to describe him to shock their readers. They didn't appreciate his attention to detail, the intricate planning. They had called him mad, and yes, he might be a bit mad to be standing about on a night like this, but he had no other option. He moved back into his cover where the steam from his breath was less obvious as it became entangled in the bushes and evergreen trees.

As the killer waited, less than ten miles away Angela and Greg sat in a car parked in a quiet Motherwell street. Angela lifted a small case from the back seat and opened it.

'What's that?'

'It's a tool used by locksmiths to make a temporary key.'

'Is this official police issue?' asked Greg.

Angela gave him a look.

'Sorry. Silly question,' said Greg. 'Where did you get it?'

'I got this from an old friend of mine who was in the Royal Marines. He used these in his job to get into warehouses and other such places where they didn't want to break the doors down.'

She leaned over to show Greg the contents of the case.

'This rod here is basically the barrel of a key. There is a strip of plasticine fitted to it. This is put into the lock and turned gently. The wards on the keyway on the inside of the lock make a set of indentations in the plasticine. On the other side of the barrel is a set of small holes.' She opened a small section of the case. 'Here's a set of pins of different sizes. The idea is that you select pins to match the size of the indentations and push the pins into these holes on this part of the barrel. What you then get is a skeleton key that will open the lock. Simple really.'

'And this works for any lock?' asked Greg.

'Yes, but you need to know the manufacturer of the particular lock you want to open. There's a different set of tools for each manufacturer. This is a Chubb set which should open any Chubb lock.'

'And you know the Stewart's house has a Chubb lock because you looked when we were there before?'

'Fortunately, yes. Otherwise, I'd have had to bring about a dozen cases.'

'So, we can open the door and get in without breaking anything?'

'Almost,' said Angela. 'We can open the large Chubb lock, but Mrs Stewart also has a small Yale lock. There isn't a set for a Yale lock,' said Angela without waiting for Greg to ask.

'But I imagine you could pick a Yale lock?'

'Yes. But as soon as the door opened the alarm would go off. We need the alarm to go off with the door still locked.'

'So we need to rattle a window to set the alarm off?'

'Exactly. Mrs Stewart will be troubled enough after the death of her husband without an intruder to add to her worries. We're treating her as a suspect at the moment, but it's likely she has nothing to do with her husband's death. You've got to draw the line somewhere.'

Greg was amused that Angela ever drew lines anywhere, but he said nothing.

'Are you sure that rattling a window will set the alarm off?'

'Yeah. Assuming the sensitivity's set OK.'

'And if it's not? In fact, what if it's not even switched on?'

'Then we might have to actually break the window. I'm only kidding Greg, I told you no breaking would be involved. Right, let's do this exactly as we planned it. Let me open the big lock then we'll get to work on the window. We'll walk up to the wall, you stand with your back against it, and then let me climb up on you.'

'I'm a bit uncomfortable with this,' admitted Greg.

'I'm not very heavy, you'll be OK.'

'I didn't mean that I'm worried about your weight!'

'I know, I'm winding you up. Come on, don't be a wimp! What have I told you?'

'You said that if for any reason this doesn't work out, you'd take full responsibility.'

He followed her through the gates and up to the front of the house.

Greg stood nervously while Angela fiddled with the large lock.

'What's keeping you?' whispered Greg.

'Give me a break, I've never done this before. Shit! I've dropped one of the pins.'

She knelt down and started to scrabble around on the path. 'You don't have a metal detector in your pocket, do you? No, forget it, I've found it.'

She carefully put her built up key into the lock and turned. Greg heard the heavy lock click open.

'Right, give me a leg up.'

Greg did as asked and lifted Angela up to the window. She gave it a slight rattle. Nothing. She rattled it a bit harder. Still nothing. Greg was sure the noise was certain to attract the attention of a neighbour, and his initial reservations were giving way to dread.

'I'll need to get onto your shoulders,' whispered Angela. Without waiting on his agreement, she stepped up, almost scraping one of his ears off with her shoe.

She rattled the window again. Nothing.

'One last go,' she whispered.

'I don't know why you're whispering,' said Greg, 'you're already making enough noise to wake the dead!'

She ignored him and gave the window an almighty clatter.

The piercing alarm startled Greg and he gave an involuntary jump which resulted in Angela falling off his shoulders and onto the ground.

'Come on!' she said getting to her feet quickly.

He followed her as they hurried back down the path, out of the gates and back to their car.

Angela started to dust herself down. 'Come here,' she said.

Greg did as he was told, and Angela brushed at his shoulders.

'It might look a bit strange you having footprints on your shoulders. There, that's better.'

Greg opened the car and they got in. Angela pushed her lock kit under the seat and out of sight.

'Aren't we going to radio the station?' said Greg.

'Give it a minute,' she replied. 'If the alarm is switched off, Mrs Stewart's still at home.'

For what seemed like ages, they sat and listened to the racket. Lights were switched on in some of the neighbouring houses, and further up the street one curious man left his gate and started to walk towards them.

'Make the call, Greg.'

Arthur Watt had finished his job on the backshift and was walking home wearily. It was only another twenty-three days until he retired, and he couldn't wait. The past two or three years had been heavy going. When he was younger, the job had been easy. Back then he had been able to throw the boxes and crates about as if they were child's toys, but now it was physically draining. As if the job didn't take enough out of him, he then had to walk a mile to get home. But he had no option, and anyway, he wouldn't have to do it for much longer. His wife's need for their car was greater, as the elderly people relied on her. She would leave her job as a district nurse at the same time as him, and they would move south to be close to their son and his family. Hopefully, they would get the price they wanted for their house, and then, combining that with their savings, they should be reasonably well off. The small flat they had their eye on would suit them down to the ground. The last thing on his mind as he took a shortcut through the park was the serial killer.

'So, you're both with the CID?' asked the uniformed policeman.

Angela took out her warrant card and showed it to him. 'I didn't get that from a cereal packet,' said Angela, 'and the quicker you accept that the quicker we can get on with this.'

'We can't just break in,' said a uniformed policeman. 'We need to contact the owner.'

'I believe the owner is away staying with relatives,' said Angela. 'The woman who lives here is the wife of former Chief Inspector Stewart, the man who was murdered a few days ago. This attempted break in may be linked to that crime. We need to check it out.'

'But we've checked all the doors and windows, nothing is open. The alarm probably scared away whoever was here. And that's assuming someone was here, and the alarm wasn't set off by a bird banging into the window or something.'

'And what about the upstairs windows?'

The policeman looked up at the building.

'How are we going to get way up there?' he said.

'I don't know,' said Angela, 'but a burglar might have managed it. Can we take the chance that someone might be inside the house right now? What if we...what if *you* leave, then it turns out that a burglary has been committed?'

The policeman looked at his partner for inspiration.

'Listen,' said Angela, 'There's a chance the door is only secured by the Yale lock. I could probably get that open without causing any damage. If we can get in, we can check out the house. If it's clear, the Detective Constable and I will stay there while you check with the neighbours to find out if any of them happen to know the alarm code. How about that?'

'You're the boss,' said the police constable, happy to pass the responsibility on to the superior officer.

Angela walked up to the door and fiddled about with something she had taken from her pocket.

A few moments later she opened the door.

'Let us go in first,' said one of the uniformed policemen.

Angela stood aside to let him and his partner pass.

'We'll check downstairs first.'

They fumbled about a bit until they found the light switches.

Angela and Greg followed a distance behind as the officers moved from room to room.

'Remember to check the windows,' said Angela as the officers finishing checking the downstairs rooms and started up the stairs. 'We'll wait in the corridor in case an intruder gets past you.'

She nodded to Greg and he stood outside the study while Angela went inside. She quickly opened the desk, then took out the diary and started to flick through it.

There were some faint thumps and bangs audible even above the racket the alarm was making as the officers searched upstairs.

Angela scribbled down some information in her notebook as she continued to leaf through the diary.

'They're coming back down,' whispered Greg.

Angela left the diary open and walked quickly to the door.

'No sign of anything up there, Sarge,' said one officer. 'All the windows are secure.'

'Good,' said Angela. 'We'll wait here until you speak to the neighbours. If we get no joy with them then I'll try and get Mrs Stewart on the phone.'

The officers nodded their agreement and set off to speak to neighbours.

Greg moved to stand at the open front door and Angela went back to checking the diary. After taking another few notes, she returned the diary to the drawer and then switched on Stewart's computer.

She had just switched it off when the officers returned.

'A Mr Waddell who lived two doors up knows the code,' said the first officer looking pleased with himself. 'Apparently he and Mrs Stewart had the foresight to tell each other their codes in case exactly this would happen when one of them was away.'

The officer punched in the code and the alarm went off.

They reset it and left the house, thanking the officers for their help and returned to their car.

'Where to now?' asked Greg.

Angela took the strange barrel out of the case she had pushed under her seat. 'We wait a minute or two, and then I go back and lock the Chubb. We really don't want to trouble Mrs Stewart with all this.'

Chapter 23

'Have you heard the news?' said Greg as Angela got into the car the following morning.

'Yeah, I heard it on the radio. The media are already saying it's another murder carried out by the serial killer.'

They entered the station and Angela found a brief report in an envelope on her desk. It was the results of running the registration number through the database.

'The car's registered to a Ms Elizabeth Reid Her address is given as 23 Roberts Street, Hull.'

'I wonder what she as doing so far from home?' said Greg.

'Whatever she's doing,' said Angela still looking at the report, 'she won't be going home soon, at least not in that car. It's been written off in an accident.'

'And the owner?'

'It doesn't say,' said Angela, 'but you're going to find out, OK?'

She handed the report to Greg, and he set off to make inquiries.

'The driver of the car when it was involved in the accident was Elizabeth Dixon, the car owner,' said Greg when he returned from his inquiries.

'She was admitted to the Monklands Hospital, transferred to the Queen Elizabeth then released yesterday. She's staying with her brother and I have the address here in Airdrie.'

'Excellent,' said Angela, 'I think we should pay her a visit.'

'There's one more thing I found out,' said Greg. 'The traffic police are treating the crash as suspicious.'

Angela raised her eyebrows. 'Now that *is* interesting. Come on Greg! The game's afoot!'

Greg shook his head sadly.

'What is it?' said Angela.

'Oh nothing,' said the detective.

'I've always wanted to say that, so don't spoil my moment.'

'OK Sherlock,' said Greg.

'Let's try and get a word with one of the officer's looking into the car accident.'

Angela took out her phone and made a call.

'Bill Fletcher is one of the guys dealing with the crash, and he's here at the station just now,' said Angela.

'I heard that I had almost been assigned to him.'

'But you got me instead,' said Angela.

'Yes.'

'Did I detect a note of disappointment in your voice?'

'No, I tried to answer as emotionless as I could so you would detect *nothing* in my voice.'

'Then you didn't quite manage it, Greg.'

'Hi Bill, it's good of you to wait until we arrived.'

'No problem,' said DS Fletcher, 'I've a few calls to make, but nothing that can't keep.'

Bill led the way through the back to a small, dingy office.

'So, you're interested in our car accident?'

'We suspect this vehicle might be linked to the murder in Motherwell,' said Angela, 'The suspicious nature of the accident may have a bearing on our crime.'

'I see,' said Fletcher, 'well, I'll tell you as much as we know. We're not one hundred per cent sure what happened, but we do suspect foul play. He spread some pictures of the car out across the desk .'

'It got quite a clatter,' remarked Greg.

'Not half,' said Fletcher, 'the woman was lucky to get out alive.'

'What speed do you believe the car was doing?' asked Angela.

'Probably under twenty miles an hour,' said Fletcher, 'but the lorry that smashed into it was doing over thirty. That's why most of the damage is on the passenger side. The lorry tried to swerve and caught the car on the rear passenger side, spinning it round. Had the car entered the junction a second earlier or the lorry not swerved, then it would have hit the car fully side on.'

Angela nodded. 'So, what makes you suspect foul play?'

'The car brakes failed going down the hill,' he explained. 'One of the brake pipes was snapped completely in two.'

'Could this not have happened in the accident?' asked Greg.

'No. We found a trail of brake fluid starting from where the car had been parked and running down the hill. By the time the car reached the junction it would have had no brakes at all. The trail is fairly fine at the start, and then there is a larger quantity of fluid on the road, about where the driver would have tried to apply the brakes.'

'Could the pipe simply have failed through corrosion?'

'No, both ends of the pipe were in very good condition.'

'And I imagine there were no signs of any fluid in the road leading up to where the car was parked?'

'Exactly,' confirmed Fletcher.

'I can see why you're classing it as suspicious,' said Angela. 'What's the story with the driver?'

'A woman in her late twenties, lives in Hull, up here visiting her brother. From a local respectable family, nothing amiss there that we can find. So far we've not turned up any witnesses who claimed to have seen anyone suspicious near the car. We have no evidence of either the brother or sister having any enemies, although the brother did report having a brick thrown through his window some time before the accident, but the uniformed guys put this down to drunken yobs.'

'So, you're at a bit of a loss to explain it?' said Angela.

'I'm afraid we are at the moment. Our traffic boys are looking into it and we're getting the car examined in greater detail, but it wasn't a fatal crash, so it's not been given a high priority. We should hear something back in a few days.'

'Well Bill,' said Angela. 'Thanks for bringing us up to speed.'

'Any thoughts Greg?' said Angela as they walked to their car.

Greg sighed. 'This is like a jigsaw puzzle except we don't know if all the pieces are from the same puzzle and also have no idea what picture we're trying to make.'

'An interesting analogy Greg. But I was hoping for something a bit more positive.'

'Mr Reid? Mr Brian Reid?'

'Yes?'

'I'm Detective Sergeant Porter and this is Detective Constable Anderson, we wonder if we might have a word with your sister, Elizabeth?'

'Come in,' said Brian, standing aside to let them pass. 'Is it about the accident?'

'Partly, yes,' said Angela.

'As you'll know,' said Brian, 'my sister has been very ill. She's still not a hundred per cent, so please take your time with the questions.'

They stopped and let Brian lead the way into the lounge. 'Elizabeth, these are police officers who want to ask some questions about your accident.'

Elizabeth was sitting in the armchair fully dressed, but she was wearing no make-up and her hair hadn't been combed. Brian indicated that the officers should sit down.

'Our questions have more to do with the car than the actual accident,' said Angela. 'We're interested in the movements of the car in the days before the accident. To be precise, we believe the car was parked close to a house in Motherwell. The house belonging to a Mr and Mrs Stewart.'

'I was driving the car on that day,' said Brian. 'My car was in the garage for repairs and I borrowed Elizabeth's car.'

'I see,' said Angela, 'and can I ask what business you had at the Stewart's house?'

'I went to talk to Mr Stewart. I wanted to ask him something about an incident that had happened some time ago, when he was still in the Police Force.'

'Can you be more specific?' said Greg.

'Our father was killed a number of years previously, and I wanted to ask Mr Stewart if he could throw any light on the incident.'

'And could Mr Stewart help you?'

'No, not really.'

'And was that the only time you spoke to him?'

'Yes.'

'You didn't speak to him two days after your first visit?'

'No. I drove round to his house, but I didn't think there was anyone at home.'

'Did you knock on the door?'

'No. I waited to see if anyone was around. I was a bit nervous to meet with him again. I didn't want him to think I was being a nuisance.'

'You mentioned an accident in which your father was killed. How long ago was this accident?'

'It was more than ten years ago.'

'Forgive me, Mr Reid, but why after all this time did you think Mr Stewart would be able to help you?'

'Because he did it! That bastard was responsible!'

They all looked at Elizabeth.

'I'm sorry,' said Brian, 'my sister's still suffering from the effects of her accident.'

'Don't make excuses for me!' shouted Elizabeth. 'Have you found out what caused my accident?' she said, looking at Angela and Greg. 'No, of course not! You'll be too busy chasing whoever killed that lying bastard! He got what he deserved, better than he deserved. I hope he rots in hell!'

Brian signalled to the officers to follow him and they got to their feet.

'That's right!' continued Elizabeth. 'Fuck off the pair of you!'

In the hallway, Brian again made excuses for his sister.

'That's OK, Mr Stewart,' said Angela. 'We will probably need to speak to you again, but perhaps it might be better the next time if your sister wasn't present, at least not until she makes a full recovery.'

'Are they gone?' asked Elizabeth.

'Yes. Did you have to make a scene?'

'It'll give them something to think about,' said Elizabeth, now perfectly calm. 'If need be, we can just say I was a bit loopy due to all the drugs I'm on.'

'I wish you had warned me,' said Brian.

'I didn't think of it until they started asking questions. Would you rather have had to go into all the details?'

'I'll have to the next time.'

'Yeah, but by then we'll have worked out what you should say. And I don't think they'll want to speak to me in the near future.'

'That was...different,' said Greg. 'What did you think?'

'Reid's explanation is believable to a point. He could have been asking Stewart for his help, that's what Maureen Stewart said. But why wait ten years? And what about the sister's outburst?'

'Do you want me to dig out the details of their father's accident?'

'Yeah. It wouldn't do any harm in having a look at what there is. We might find something that explains the sister's attitude. Just to be on the safe side, check when Elizabeth had the accident and when she was released from the hospital. I would guess she was in there when Stewart was killed, but we'd better make sure.'

'Are you thinking that one of the Reid's may have been involved?'

'I don't know. The sister's outburst shows she wasn't too keen on Stewart, and her hatred appears to stem from the accident of ten years ago.'

'Where to now?'

'We'll go back to the station and see if we have Stewart's phone records through yet.'

'Have you made anything of the diary?'

'I was waiting until we had the phone records. As I thought after my first look, there are few entries where Stewart wrote a name. The phone records might help us a bit.'

'It's interesting that this latest killing has come so soon after Stewart's.'

'Yeah,' agreed Angela, 'it certainly is. And I think I know why.'

'The Boss wants to see you.' Detective Sergeant Logan gave Angela the news as soon as she and Greg returned to the station. As she walked towards Russell's office, Logan made a throat cutting gesture to Greg and smiled.

'So, you want to see me about...'

'About this early edition evening paper.' The chief lifted a newspaper from the side of his desk and opened it. He put on his glasses and began to read aloud.

'As the manhunt for the serial killer continues to throw up few clues, the police continue to withhold information from the press. The only comment reporters could gain from a detective leaving the station this afternoon was...*fuck off*.'

The chief took off his glasses and looked at Angela. 'Of course the paper doesn't actually print *fuck off*, it has the letter *f* followed by two stars then the letter *k* then *off*, but I assume that's the expression they meant to convey.'

'But Chief, lots of detectives left the station, what makes you think they're talking about me?'

The Chief put his glasses back on and read some more.

'The *female* detective then barged past waiting reporters to her car and left.' He took his glasses off again. 'Now, how many female detectives are stationed here?'

Angela tried to think.

'I'll save you the trouble of doing mental arithmetic, Detective Sergeant, the total is one. And that one is you.'

Angela opened her mouth to speak, but the Chief held up a hand to stop her.

'I know the press can be a nuisance at times, Angela, and I know they're now jumping to conclusions at the drop of a hat, but we need them on our side. It wouldn't be the first time that an enterprising reporter turned up something useful for us, so we need to work with them, not have them turn against us. And this sort of comment not only harms our relationship with the press, but it also has a negative effect on the public reading it.'

Angela was only half listening to what the Chief was saying, she was thinking about ripping the head off the reporter responsible for the report.

'So, please, think before speaking in future. *No comment* would be much better. That's still only two words and wouldn't take you any longer to say it.'

Angela was dismissed and got up to leave. *No comment* means no comment, she thought to herself; it's meaningless, but *fuck off* means fuck off, that's much better!

The Chief watched her back as she left and gave a slight smile. He put his glasses back on and picked up the paper. 'Police continue to be baffled as to the identity of the man who is terrorising the West of Scotland,' he read. 'It is feared the man could strike again at any time and the police seem powerless to stop him.' He took his glasses off and threw the paper in the bin. *Fuck off,* he thought to himself.

'How'd it go?' asked Greg.

'Greg, would you imagine, even for a moment, that if a newspaper reporter asked you for a comment and you told him to *fuck off* that he'd print it? No, forget I asked. You'd probably not tell him to *fuck off* in the first place.'

She hurried off and Greg followed, as usual, trying to catch up.

'I might,' said Greg to her back, 'if he really annoyed me. I wouldn't worry about it.'

Angela stopped so quickly that Greg almost bumped into her.

'Greg. Do I look worried?'

'Well, you look a bit...stressed.'

'So what if I am?' Her eyes glowered. 'People are dying out there and we're no closer to nailing this bastard! We should all be more than a bit stressed!'

'OK, OK. Calm down. Don't take it out on me!'

'Well, right at this moment you're standing right in front of me and that's why you're getting it.'

With that she spun round and rushed off.

Greg was sleeping soundly when his phone rang. He fumbled around for the receiver and the bedside light.

'Hello?' he said, trying to wipe the sleep from his eyes.

'Greg, it's Angela.'

'Hello, what's up?' He reached for his clock, fearing he had slept in. 'Christ, it's 2am! What's happened?'

'Nothing's happened. I want to tell you a story.'

He was about to ask if it couldn't wait until the morning, then he realised that phoning him at 2am meant that it couldn't. 'OK,' he said.

'When I was a young beat constable, I was assigned to work with Detective Sergeant John Harrison. He was in his late forties and was very pissed off at having to work with a junior officer. The fact that I was a woman made matters worse. We had our fights, but eventually we managed to get along. Better than that, I think he began to look on me as a daughter. He had had a daughter, but she had been killed in a car accident when she was eight or nine. In turn I looked on him as a father figure. We worked well together and he taught me a lot: ow to read witnesses and suspects, when to be firm and when to be soft. He had a real instinct for that, and he encouraged me to develop one of my own. He was as tough as nails but had a soft centre and he cared about people. One day just before Christmas he was killed in the line of duty. Not like the movies, nothing as glamorous as a shootout or a car chase. No, he fell through a rotten wooden floor in a dirty, disgusting building and broke his neck.' She stopped talking, but Greg said nothing. When she started to speak again, she spoke almost in a whisper and Greg had to strain to hear her.

'We'd been after a drug dealer, a real low life. This guy had been trying to peddle drugs outside a school. He'd set himself up in an ice cream van to attract the kids, and then he'd try and sell them drugs.

'We wanted to find out where he had stashed his pile, and wanted to catch him with the whole load, not just a few bits and pieces. We followed him to an old, abandoned hotel outside of town, then up to the third landing and that's where John fell through the floor. He turned round to speak to me, and then simply disappeared in a cloud of dust. The last thing he said to me was *be careful Angela*.

'The dealer heard the crash and ran to see what was going on. He looked through the hole and saw John lying on the floor below. Then he started to laugh. He had taken drugs himself and was out of it, and he laughed and laughed and laughed. If I had managed to get my hands on him I'd have killed him. But I couldn't.

'Anyway, we found the dealer's hidden stash and he was put away. He was a pathetic individual. If it hadn't been for the fact that he was dealing to kids, I could have pitied him, but his arrest had indirectly cost the life of the finest officer I have ever known. I grew up that day, Greg. And I coped, but it was difficult, very difficult.' She stopped talking again.

'Goodnight Greg.' Then she hung up.

Greg held the receiver for a few moments, placed it gently in its cradle, then lay down to go back to sleep.

Thirty seconds later he sat up, put the light on, picked up the phone and dialled a number.

'Hello?' said Angela in a shaky voice.

'Angela, it's Greg. You're wrong.'

'Oh Greg, can't this wait until the morning?'

'No. You woke *me* up, remember? If I wait until the morning, I won't have the balls to tell you.'

'Tell me what?'

'To tell you that you're wrong.'

'Wrong about what?'

'Everything! For someone who has the reputation of being always in control and possessing great intuition, you're being pretty dumb.'

'Greg. I don't know what you're talking about, and we really need to get some sleep...'

'Angela! You're going to listen to me or I'm going to come round to your house and bang on your door until either you let me in, or I get arrested. John Harrison would be ashamed of you. You said that you grew up the day John died, but you didn't. You *stopped* growing then. You went into your shell. Oh, I know that's not the way it appears, but that's because you cover it up. You know what to look for in others, and you paint a picture of yourself for others to see what you want them to see. But it's not really you.'

'Have you finished?'

'No, I'm only just warming up. You tease and torment me, not because you want to, but to keep me away. You don't want me to see you as anything other than my superior officer. You let your guard down when you asked me to call you Angela, and I bet you're regretting it. Perhaps you think I might develop personal feelings for you - well don't flatter yourself Angela, but even if I did, that's life. You don't socialise with people because you don't want them to see a human side. Someone who maybe gets drunk, and who maybe makes a fool of herself now and again. But shit happens to people every day. People die, and family and friends grieve, and then they move on. John lost a daughter tragically, but he moved on. You're still staring down that hole John fell through, and the quicker you leave it behind in the past where it belongs the better. I'm not telling you to forget about it, you'll never forget about it, but you need to move on. Right. I'm finished now, so goodnight.'

He put the phone down before she could reply and lay down to go to sleep.

On Monday morning he sat in the car outside her house nervously waiting her arrival. He didn't look at her as she got in and headed for the station as soon as she had closed her door.

He followed their usual route. There was none of the usual banter, only silence. They stopped at traffic lights that were showing red.

'*Don't flatter yourself, Angela,*' she said, quoting Greg from the early phone call. 'Are you that good a catch?' She continued to look straight ahead.

'Fucking right,' said Greg, starting to pick away now that the lights were at green. And that was the only time the phone calls were mentioned by either of them.

Chapter 24

They arrived at the station to find that a briefing had been called.

'I'll keep this brief,' began the Chief. Someone behind Greg muttered that *that* would be a first.

'We have reason to believe that the murder of former Chief Inspector Stewart in Motherwell was not the work of the serial killer. We believe this was carried out by a copycat.'

There were various mumblings and mutterings among the assembled officers.

'Although many aspects of that crime are similar, we are working on the assumption that this is coincidental. There are enough crucial discrepancies to make us believe that it was not the work of the man we are hunting. A press release will be issued shortly.' He glanced at Angela. 'Any officer questioned by the press should refer the reporter to our press office. The only acceptable response apart from this is *no comment*. I will take a very dim view should any aspect of this briefing appear in any section of the media before the official press release has been issued.'

'I need to go and see the Boss,' said Angela after the meeting had finished.

'I don't think that's a good idea,' said Greg.

'Why? What do you think I want to see him about?'

'Well, I assume you've taken exception to his comments about the press because you thought he was having a dig at you.'

'He *was* having a go at me, but that's not why I want to see him.'

'Oh,' said Greg.

'No, it's about something quite different, and I want you to come with me.'

'Angela? Please do me a favour.'

'What do you want?'

'Just this once, please knock before you go in.'

She did as Greg requested and knocked on the Chief's door. They waited outside until he called for them to enter.

'I hope this won't take long,' said the Chief, shuffling files on his desk, 'I'm due at HQ to get my own briefing.'

'It's about the press release,' said Angela, taking a seat without being invited. The Chief nodded for Greg to take a seat.

'What about it?'

'I think it's a bad idea to let the press know that we are ruling the Stewart killing out as being the work of the serial killer.'

'Why do you think that?' said the Chief as he continued his file shuffling.

'I've no doubt Stewart wasn't killed by the guy we're chasing, but I don't think it will help to let him know that we know that. Quite the opposite in fact, I think it might help us more if we stress that we think he *did* kill Stewart.'

Russell left the files alone and sat back in his chair.

'OK, you have my complete attention. Give me your reasons.'

'We're assuming that this guy is narcistic; he's full of his own importance and is trying to make a point. We won't know what his point is until he's caught, but he does have his reasons for what he's doing. The taking of a watch or something personal to one victim then leaving on the body of his next tells us that he is branding his victims. I think he was really pissed off when he was credited with a murder he didn't commit. I think that's why the last one happened so soon after Stewart, the killer wanted to set the record straight. He didn't want someone else getting the publicity he saw as his alone.'

'So, what would you suggest we do?' asked the Chief.

'We should continue to make the press think that we believe Stewart was a serial killer victim.'

'And what would we gain from that?' said Russell.

'Many serial offenders take pleasure in the attention they receive. Arsonists will quite often hang around and watch the fire services tackle their handiwork. They get off on that. Many killers write to the police, taunting them. They need to be close to the centre of the activity. It adds to their feeling of superiority. I'd bet he's desperate to see us rushing about chasing him and getting nowhere. For all we know he could be attending some of the press conferences.'

'Surely he wouldn't risk that?' interrupted Greg.

'No,' replied the Chief. 'Angela's correct on that score. In fact, we've been checking the credentials of everyone who attends these briefings. Everyone has checked out OK.'

'We now have another victim,' continued Angela, 'one we know to be the work of the serial killer. He'll be expecting us to admit that we made a mistake with Stewart. That will add to his feeling of superiority. If we don't admit we were wrong, he'll need to take steps to convince us.'

'If we go along with what you suggest,' said the Chief, 'he could kill again to give us another example.'

'I don't think so,' said Angela. 'He's already tried that. I think he'll try something a bit more personal. Something to convince us that the killing of Stewart was different. There's no doubt he'll kill again, but without being too cold about it, whether it's next week or next month doesn't really matter. We badly need a break in this case. We need him to do something different. He's calling all the shots and we need to take some of the control away from him.'

The Chief looked at his watch then stood up.

'I really need to get to the briefing,' he said, 'but I'll think about what you've said. I'm not saying I'm convinced, and anyway, it's people a lot higher than me who need to be convinced. I need to decide if I would appear a right jackass mentioning it to them. But I do appreciate you giving me your thoughts. One thing you are one hundred per cent correct about is control. We somehow need to get the control of the situation away from him, but whether your suggestion is the way to do this, I'm not sure.'

'I thought that went quite well,' said Greg when they had left the Chief's office. 'At least he didn't say that he thought you were an absolute nutter.'

'And what do you think?'

'What I think doesn't really matter; it's not me you have to convince.'

'But I need to know if you're with me on this.'

'Well, I'm your partner, so I'll do whatever...'

'Greg! Stop fuckin' about! What do you think?'

'I'm not convinced,' admitted Greg. 'I think you might be right about him wanting to get closer to what's going on, but I don't know if this is the way to force his hand into doing that.'

'I'm not convinced myself,' agreed Angela, 'but we really need a glimmer of light at the end of the tunnel. Barring a stroke of good luck, I can't see what'll get us closer to this guy.'

'So, what now?'

'It's time for some good old fashioned police work. I'll start to work through Stewart's phone records while you dig out what you can on the accident involving the Reid family.'

Greg returned to the office two hours later where Angela was still poring over her notes.

'How's it going?' asked Greg.

'Bo...ring,' she said, carelessly tossing her pencil onto the desk. 'I hope you've had a more rewarding time than me. By the way, don't you think it was considerate of me to give you the more interesting task and to keep the tedious job for myself?'

'Perhaps we could put it another way,' said Greg. 'You sent me out into the pissing rain while you stayed here sitting on your arse.'

'Wrong, Greg! In the first place, I didn't know it was raining, and secondly, *lady* superior officers, don't have arses, we have bottoms. And I had to stay here in case the Boss returned from his briefing and decided to give me a medal.'

'I would think that's unlikely.'

'You're probably correct, but one never knows. So, enthral me with what you've discovered.'

'Before I do that, do you fancy getting some coffee or something?'

'Great idea. We'll take it in the canteen, I'm sick of the view from this desk.'

She gathered up her notebook and set off with Greg in the direction of the canteen.

'I bought you lunch the other day,' she said, 'so you can buy the coffees. I'll just nip out for a quick fag.'

She returned just as Greg had sat down with his tray at a table.

Greg outlined what he had discovered about the Reid accident while they took their coffee.

Angela listened intently.

'So, the father was killed at the scene and the daughter was put on life support? The inquiry declared that it had been an accident and the file was closed?'

Greg confirmed that had been the case.

'What about in the years since the accident?' she said.

'I thought you might ask,' said Greg, 'so I dug around a bit more. The mother died from a drug overdose about a year after the accident. Elizabeth, the woman who was less than friendly with us, took the decision to turn off her sister's life support.'

'So Brian and Elizabeth Reid lost their parents and sister as a result of an accident that involved a police car,' said Angela. 'It's difficult to imagine what going through that would be like. You said Chief Inspector Stewart was a passenger in the police car, so he had first-hand knowledge about the accident. But did you find anything to explain why Brian Reid would want to speak to him after all this time?'

'Nothing at all,' said Greg. 'On the face of it, it was simply a tragic accident. Perhaps they've harboured a grudge against Stewart and for some reason it's taken this length of time to reach the surface?'

'Anything's possible, but I wonder if something's happened to set this off. What did you find out about Brian and Elizabeth?'

Greg quickly detailed what background he had uncovered, education, employment records, all rather mundane stuff.

'Keep your notes, Greg, when we find out a bit more we might need to refer to them again. Now, what did you find out about the policeman who was driving the car at the time of the accident?'

'He was Constable Turner, Sergeant Turner when he retired through ill health. Still alive, no current employment. Again, nothing that jumps out as being significant.'

Angela was deep in thought. 'He was promoted after the accident?'

'Yes. Two years later. Do you find that strange?'

'Yeah. A bit.'

'But I suppose if he was completely exonerated over the accident, there's no reason why he shouldn't have been promoted. His seems to have been a good officer.'

'I'd have thought it unusual to promote someone to Sergeant so close to his retirement.'

'But he retired through ill health, perhaps his health problem wasn't known at the time of him making sergeant?'

'It's possible, but I'm still surprised at his promotion. You know the way things work, exonerated or not, in many peoples' minds there's no smoke without fire. I'd have thought the stigma of being involved in a fatal accident might have stuck with him.'

'That would have been unfair, don't you think?'

Angela shrugged. 'That's life, I'm afraid. OK, that'll do for now. I've a feeling there's a link somewhere we've not found yet, but that's a good job, Greg. Now let me tell you what I've discovered from the phone record.'

'Interesting?' said Greg.

Angela shrugged again. 'Perhaps,' she said, 'it certainly throws up some leads for us to follow. Whether they'll go anywhere or not remains to be seen.'

She opened her file and notebook.

'First the bad news. Stewart did receive a call just before going out on the night he was murdered, but the caller number was barred.'

'That's suspicious,' said Greg.

'Could be,' agreed Angela, 'but some people tend to do that as a matter of habit, especially if they don't want the person they're calling to return the call. It was the only barred number Stewart received a call from in the past six months, so either the caller didn't normally block their number, or that was the only call they made to Stewart. There are some numbers that Stewart called frequently. One is their son. Two others are significant, I think; both incoming and outgoing, one to a landline and the other a mobile. The landline is registered to a security firm, Collins Securities. The mobile is the personal phone of Steve Collins, the boss of the firm. Mrs Stewart said her husband was doing some part time work, so I'd guess we now know what this is.....Greg, what're you doing?'

As she had been speaking, Greg was scrambling over his notes.

'I'm sorry,' he said, 'but that name rings a bell. Wait a minute. Yes, here it is.'

He flicked over his notebook to a page where he had underlined some names.

'How's about this for a coincidence?' he said, grinning from ear to ear. 'There was a man in the back of the police car at the time of the accident that killed Mr Reid. The man was on his way to the station to be interviewed as a witness. The man was a Steven Collins.'

'Now that *is* interesting,' said Angela. 'Greg, I think you've just earned yourself another veggie burger.'

'I think I'll pass on that,' said Greg, 'but I think I'll see what I can find out about Mr Steven Collins.'

'Greg, you read my mind. Go to it, my boy. I'll go back and see if Russell has returned with my medal.'

Russell had returned, but without Angela's medal. However, he did want to see her.

'I thought over what you had said, Angela, and decided to put it to the meeting if no one had any better suggestions. Well my suggestion caused quite a stir. Almost everyone was against it at the start. But the Chief Super decided that we should talk it over, look at the pros and cons. He kept asking for alternatives, but no one could come up with anything. Eventually I think he wore everyone down. The bottom line is that we've revised the press statement. This'll cover the latest developments in the hunt for the serial killer and it won't mention the Stewart murder at all. We won't confirm or deny that his killing is linked to the serial killer. If any questions are asked of the press office, they'll sit on the fence.'

'Thank you, Boss,' said Angela.

'Oh, don't thank me Angela. We're taking a big chance here.'

Angela rose to leave.

'There's one more thing,' said the Chief. 'We've had a call from Mrs Stewart, the wife of Robert Stewart. I understand you talked to her a few days ago?'

'Yes, I did.'

'Well, she phoned asking if there had been any developments with the investigation into her husband's death. It is fortunate, under the circumstances, that you went to speak to her. I want you and Constable Anderson to talk to her again. Remember one thing. Officially this is still part of the hunt for the serial killer.'

Angela was dismissed and returned to where Greg was waiting.

He seemed more eager to tell her his news than to hear about her interview with the Chief.

'Steven Collins is an interesting guy,' said Greg when they had settled once more in the canteen. 'At the time of the accident, he was providing information regarding a mob, handling stolen goods.' Greg stopped to brush some crumbs left by the previous occupier of the table onto a napkin which he then deposited in a bin.

'Doesn't sound very interesting to me,' said Angela, while smiling at Greg's obvious displeasure at the state of their table.

'Then how does it sound if I tell you that he now runs one of the major security companies in the area, and the company has been investigated more times than we've had hot dinners. Accusations of bribery, theft, intimidation and God know how many other things. And that's only his company. The people whose warehouses he guards have also been investigated and raided on numerous occasions.'

'But no convictions?'

'Not only no convictions of anyone employed by the company, but no cases ever brought to trial.'

'And this is the company Stewart was working for?'

'It appears so, yes.'

'Well, that is interesting. I think we should do a bit more digging into Steve Collins' business dealings.'

'I'm not finished,' said Greg. 'There's one more thing I think you'll find interesting.' He produced a sheet of paper from his pocket. 'I did a bit of research to see what I could find out about the other ex-policeman, Peter Turner. I didn't find much; his wife is dead and he took early retirement because he has a heart problem. He has one son, Roy. Roy started work quite recently for Business Software Limited, a small company based in Chapelhall. They have a web site, and I had a quick look at it.' Greg handed the sheet of paper he had been holding to Angela.

'That's a printout of their Sales personnel.'

'Brian Reid!' said Angela.

'Correct,' said Greg. 'Now what is it you always say about coincidences?'

Chapter 25

‘So, do we have a possible motive for the Stewart killing?’ said Angela.

‘He didn’t get along with his son, Richard, so we can’t rule him out. Steve Collins appears to have been a business associate, so he must be on the list. I don’t know if Elizabeth Dixon figurers on the list. The fact that Stewart was involved in the accident that killed her father suggests it might be worth looking into that. Brian Reid could be involved along with his sister. The fact that Brian Reid works with Roy Turner could be more than a coincidence. We haven’t ruled out Maureen Stewart, although we have no reason to suspect her.’

‘OK, so we have a list of half a dozen that are worth investigating.’

‘That’s it, at the moment,’ said Greg.

‘We should find out Richard’s whereabouts on the night his father was killed. If it turns out he is up here just now, then there would be no harm in having a chat with him. We’ve spoken to the Reids, but I’d say we need to dig around a bit more before speaking to them again. I think we should leave Steve Collins for the present, as I reckon he’ll be a difficult character to deal with. So, by a process of elimination I think we should have words with Peter Turner. He may be able to give us some more background on Stewart.’

'Do you want me to phone Maureen Stewart and ask if she's remembered anything else about the time before the killing that might be useful to us? I could work her son into the conversation and find out if he's staying with her.'

'Brilliant Greg! It's moments like these that remind me why I took you under my wing.'

Greg had found out that Richard had travelled to Motherwell with his mother but had now returned home. However, he would be back for the funeral which was to take place on Friday. They had driven to Peter Turner's house, found that he was at home, and been shown into the lounge.

'We're investigating the murder of Robert Stewart and believe you had known him,' began Angela.

'Yes, that's correct,' confirmed Turner.

'Did you have much contact with Mr Stewart after you retired?'

'I spoke to him occasionally, just to catch up on old times, but hadn't actually seen him in more than a year.'

'I wouldn't have thought a Sergeant would have had much direct contact with a Chief Inspector?' said Angela.

'I think he liked to have some contact with the lower ranks just to help keep his feet on the ground.'

'And when was the last time you saw him?'

'I can't remember the exact date,' said Turner, 'but it was at a retirement function for a couple of officers we had worked with. I didn't manage to attend his retirement do as I wasn't very well at the time.'

'But you say you last saw him about a year ago?' asked Greg.

'Yes, that's right.'

'And when was the last time you spoke to him?'

'It would have been perhaps a week before he died,' said Turner.

'And was there a particular reason for your call?'

'No, not really. I just thought that I hadn't spoken to him for some time and felt I shouldn't put it off any longer.'

'That was quite fortunate, wasn't it?' said Angela.

'I don't understand what you mean by fortunate?'

'Well, to call him so close to his death. It was just as well you didn't leave your call much longer.'

'Yes, I suppose so.'

'We believe Chief Inspector Stewart recommended you for promotion to Sergeant?'

'Well, he was on the panel and had suggested to me that I should sit the exam, so I suppose you could say that he pushed me towards it.'

'And you were promoted just a few years before you retired?'

'Yes.'

'Have you any idea why he chose to promote you?'

'He didn't promote me, he was part of a panel that promoted me,' said Peter Turner, his eyes narrowing as he suspected there was more to the line of questioning than immediately obvious.

'OK. Do you know why he suggested that you try for promotion at such a late stage in your career?'

'I didn't know it was a late stage in my career. I had always thought about promotion and probably just needed a bit of encouragement.'

'What can you tell us about Brian Reid?'

'Brian? Brian works with my son, that's how I met him. Roy introduced us.'

'And you know his sister Elizabeth?'

'I know *of* her,' said Turner, 'I've never actually met her.'

'I imagine you'll know about her accident?'

'Yes. A terrible thing. She's lucky to be alive. But I'm wondering, what has this to do with Robbie Stewart's murder?'

'Oh, we're just gathering some background information. Trying to build up a picture of his movements before he met his death.'

'I'm afraid I can't help you there. I don't get out as much as I used to, and, as I've said, I haven't seen Robbie Stewart for about a year.'

'One more question. Can you tell us where you were on the evening of January 31st?'

'Yes, that was last Monday. I remember that date well as I had to go into hospital for tests on that day. My son dropped me off first thing in the morning and picked me up again late afternoon on the following day. I'm waiting to have a heart valve operation, and they wanted to try out some different drugs in the run up to the op.'

'What did you think?' said Angela when they had returned to their car.

Greg shrugged. 'His recollection of the phone call ties in with Stewart's phone records. He didn't volunteer any information on the accident that killed Reid's father. I thought you might have asked him about that?'

'I had planned to,' said Angela. 'But I changed my mind. I think we should do a bit of research into Steve Collins and Stewart's involvement with him. I'm regretting not knowing about the Collins-Stewart link when we were in the Stewart house looking at the diary.'

Greg drove off, and as usual kept well within the speed limits.

'He seemed to get a bit uneasy when we asked him about his promotion,' said Angela.

'I thought that, too,' agreed Greg. 'Do you suspect there's more to it than meets the eye?'

'Oh, I don't know,' said Angela. 'Anything connected with Stewart has a bit of a fishy smell to it, but nothing we can put our finger on. Hopefully we'll turn up something in his papers.'

'If he has any,' said Greg.

Maureen Stewart invited them in as if they were old friends. They declined her offer of coffee and settled into a brown leather settee in her spacious lounge. It crossed Angela's mind that the house had a particular smell to it. A smell that was very common in houses belonging to older people. Perhaps it was the type of furniture polish they used.

'Are you getting anywhere?' asked Maureen Stewart.

'The honest answer is no, Mrs Stewart, we haven't uncovered a motive for your husband's murder and as yet we have no obvious suspects.'

Angela paused. She had repeatedly turned over in her mind how best to approach Maureen Stewart. Although still technically a suspect in the death of her husband, Angela had pretty much ruled her out. The Detective Sergeant decided to lay her cards on the table. 'Mrs Stewart, we've ruled out the serial killer as a suspect, although we are not revealing that to the press just now and I must ask you not to tell them that, should they ask you. We believe the killer was a copycat. This copycat may have chosen your husband at random, but I'm not convinced about that.'

'I see,' said Mrs Stewart. 'Well, thank you for your honesty, and I can promise you I will not be saying anything to the press. I was expecting you to say things like *our inquiries are continuing,* or *we are pursuing various lines of inquiry.* All things which mean absolutely nothing.'

'Mrs Stewart, we need your help. We believe it is quite possible an associate of your husband may be responsible for his death. At the very least we need to eliminate people from our inquiry.'

'Yes, I can understand that,' said Maureen Stewart looking straight at Angela. 'Can I ask, have I been eliminated yet?'

Greg shifted uneasily in his chair.

Angela stared straight back at Mrs Stewart. 'No, you haven't.'

'So you're sitting there, telling an ex- chief inspector of police's widow that you still consider her as a suspect in his murder?'

'Yes, I am.'

Mrs Stewart leaned forward in her matching leather armchair.

'Good. That's exactly the way it should be. Now, what can I do to help you, or at least do to help remove myself from your suspects list?'

Greg let out a silent sigh of relief.

'We're interested in your husband's business associates, Mrs Stewart, we would like to try and rule them out as suspects if we can. To do that it would be very helpful if we could have a look at any business papers your husband may have kept.'

'If he has any business documents they'll be in his study. Unfortunately, his study is rather large and one thing it has in abundance is piles of paper. What these are, I've really no idea; I stopped cleaning his room years ago. He always claimed that after I had cleaned, he could never find anything. This was rubbish of course. Anyway, after I stopped cleaning, he still kept misplacing things. His pride stopped him admitting this, but it suited me fine, because that was one less room I had to keep clean and tidy.'

'Would you mind if we looked through some of his things?'

'Not at all, take all the time you like. I have to go out to attend to a few things, but you are welcome to stay here while I'm gone.

I'll show you where things are in the kitchen in case you want a cup of tea or coffee. I believe he keeps a diary in one of his desk drawers. Then there's our computer. I call it *our* computer, but I only ever use it for sending emails to some friends. But I know Robbie used it for work. It doesn't have a password.'

They started to search through the piles of papers in the study and Mrs Stewart left to attend to her business.

'Would you have thought that Stewart was into home baking?' asked Greg.

Angela turned to look at him and he was holding up a cookery book with the picture of a strawberry something or other on the cover. Greg started to flick through it. 'Angela, have a look at this. Dates have been written beside some of the recipes, and the most recent I've noticed was only two months ago.'

'Let's have a look at it,' said Angela.

She flicked through the pages.

'I see what you mean. I'm sure this is his writing. See, it's the same as the writing in the diary.'

Greg looked between the recipe book and the diary.

'It looks the same to me,' he said.

'Now this gets interesting,' said Angela. 'Notice that where he has written a date, he has also underlined something in the recipe. Look here. He's written a date then underlined the word *dough*. He's also written the figure *205* beside it.'

'That could be the temperature.'

'Hmmm, then what about this one. He's underlined *bread* and written *400*. I'd have thought that that heat would have been more of a cremation than a cooking temperature. Not that I know much about cooking, I'm more of a micro waver myself.'

She flicked through some more pages.

'Here he's just written a date and underlined a word. He's underlined the word *head* from *1 head of fennel*. And in this one, he's underlined *branch* from *1 branch of celery*. Again, there's a date but no figures unlike the previous ones we looked at. In this one he's underlined a figure *150ml*.'

'I can't figure it out,' said Greg.

'Neither can I,' said Angela, 'where did you find this?'

'It was on the bookshelf.'

'Did you bring that rather effeminate briefcase with you?'

'I brought my laptop in its bag, if that's what you're referring to,' said Greg.

'Good. Go get it and put the recipe book in the bag. That book is your homework for tonight. In the morning you can explain to me what it all means.'

'Yes Miss,' said Greg sarcastically.

Angela turned on the computer.

'Anything interesting?' asked Greg.

'Not really,' said Angela. 'He doesn't have any folders entitled *bribes* or anything like that. Do you have a memory stick with you?'

'Why don't we just ask her to take the computer with us?'

'Not at this stage,' said Angela. 'I'll be happy just to get a copy of his address book and his emails.'

'I could copy them on my laptop,' said Greg.

'Excellent,' said Angela, 'you do that, and I'll have a look around.'

Chapter 26

'I'm sure they'll be back,' said Peter Turner.

'Yes, so am I,' agreed Brian.

'Perhaps we should just come clean and tell them the whole story?' suggested Roy. 'I'm sure that's what Elizabeth wants.'

'She doesn't always get what she wants,' said Brian, 'I'll bring her round.'

'But things have moved on a bit,' said Peter, 'if it was only my screw up from years ago then fine, but you're forgetting about Elizabeth's accident, Mrs White, the Scott family. Somebody, somewhere could be getting away with murder and the longer we take in talking to the police then the more chance they have of never being caught.'

'Look, we don't know about these other incidents, even Elizabeth's accident might have been just that, a freak accident.'

'Roy, you're being naive. Somebody's behind this and we're not equipped to find out who it is.'

'OK, what do you suggest we do?'

'We tell the police everything we know, starting with the covered-up accident from years ago,' said Peter Turner.

'Then you'll probably go to jail,' said Brian bluntly.

'Better that than someone else getting injured or killed. How do we know these incidents have stopped? This could be the lull before the storm.'

'The note that came through my window said *leave it or else*. We don't know who these people are. Going to the police is hardly leaving it.'

'I think we need to bring Elizabeth into this,' said Peter thoughtfully. 'We're sitting here discussing things she should have a say in. After all, it was her who ended up in the hospital. Stewart is gone, and he's taken his story to the grave with him. I know you're pissed off about that, Brian, but there's nothing we can do.'

'For all we know it could be the same guys who knocked off Stewart,' said Brian. 'I know the police line is that it was the work of the serial killer, but we don't know that for sure.'

'Did you tell the police about me and Elizabeth?' Roy asked his father.

'No.'

'I told the guys from Airdrie,' said Brian.

'Then that'll be one reason they'll come back,' said Roy. 'As soon as they compare notes with the guys who interviewed Brian, they'll want to speak to us all.' He turned to his dad, 'You should have told them.'

'I didn't tell them any lies,' said Turner, 'if there's one thing I've learned from years of police work it's not to volunteer information if you can until you've had a chance to figure out where that leaves you. If they do come back and ask the right questions, I'll give them the right answers.'

'How would it be if we tell anyone who asks everything except the details of the original accident?'

They considered Brian's suggestion.

'So, what reason would you and Elizabeth have for snooping around Stewart and the other people?'

'Exactly the reason we did, Roy, to get to the truth of the accident. We'll tell them we felt there was more to it than was reported. We'll say we asked your dad, and he wouldn't help us, so we looked elsewhere for help. That's basically the truth, or certainly as close as we can get without revealing the whole story. These facts will let them properly investigate all the weird things that've been happening.'

'But they'll be missing one vital piece of information,' said Peter Turner, 'they won't know that Stewart knew you had sussed him. And Stewart knowing might be the key to everything that's happened.'

'We'll have to take that chance,' said Brian, 'I can't think of how else to handle it. But I'm sure we'll be asked a lot more questions. Trying to come up with another story that we'll all stick to won't be easy.'

'The one dodgy link in the chain is Elizabeth,' said Roy. 'We've no right to ask you to try and get her to go along with this.'

'OK, said Brian, 'let's work on the assumption that we'll proceed the way I've described. I'll go and talk to Elizabeth, even if I can persuade her to say nothing and sit on the fence our story should hold together. I'll give you a ring and tell you what she decides to do so at least you won't be making complete fools of yourselves if the police talk to you again.'

'OK,' started Brian, then paused while he gathered his thoughts. 'Dad was killed in an *accident*, no intent whatsoever. It shouldn't have happened, and possibly wouldn't have happened if Stewart hadn't been driving, but he was, and Dad and Caroline died. You've been with Roy; you know what's he's like. He's like his dad, a really nice guy. Roy did nothing to our father and Caroline. Peter Turner did, and he's suffered the torment for years.'

Brian saw Elizabeth open her mouth to speak. 'I know,' said Brian quickly before Elizabeth could interrupt, 'his suffering is nothing like ours, but he *has* suffered. Our quest is likely to have cost Betty White her life and would have taken the lives of Terry and Pamela Scott's family were it not for a stroke of good luck. I almost lost *you* for God's sake! There's something going on here and we need to get to the bottom of it before anyone else suffers. It's way beyond a ten-year-old accident. I could go out and get killed tomorrow in another 'accident'. Would that be OK as long as you nail Turner? We need to let it go. *You* need to let it go, Elizabeth. *Please*, I beg you.'

'I want to speak to Peter Turner,' said Elizabeth quietly.

'Peter, this is my sister Elizabeth.'

'Please sit down,' said Peter Turner.

Elizabeth did as he asked. Brian left them alone and went to sit in his car.

'Ever since I met Brian I knew I'd meet you one day,' said Turner. 'I've tried to rehearse what I'd say to you, but nothing sounded...adequate.'

He reached over and lifted a photograph from the mantelpiece, then handed it to Elizabeth.

'That's my late wife. She knew nothing about the real circum-stances of the accident. I deceived her along with almost everyone else. I convinced myself I was doing it for her and Roy. Now I talk to my wife every day and ask for her forgiveness. I don't hear her reply, but I hope she's forgiven me. But I know if she was here, she'd tell me that I should be asking for the forgiveness of you and Brian. There's no reason why you should forgive me. I didn't even have the guts to tell Brian until he accused me. Even after all this time I couldn't take responsibility for what I did. I supposed

I hoped I'd take my secret to the grave with me. Brian will have told you about our plan. Well, I've been thinking about it since he left, and I'm not going along with it. I'm going to tell the police the whole story.'

He stopped talking and took a sip of water from a glass that had been sitting on a small coffee table beside his chair.

'Yes, for the first time in my life since this whole sordid affair I'm going to take responsibility for what I've done. Perhaps after I do that your father and sister will start to forgive me, too.'

Elizabeth stood up to replace the photograph, and then sat back down again.

'I think you misjudge my family, Mr Turner. I'm sure they've forgiven you long ago. It's me and Brian who've wanted revenge. I came here wanting to hate you, to confront the monster who destroyed our family. I've listened to what you've had to say and waited for the anger to build up inside me. But it didn't happen. Perhaps it's easier to hate someone from a distance; again, I don't know. Keep to the plan you discussed with Brian and Roy. It's not revenge I want now, it's justice, and it's not for me, it's for Betty White and the Scotts.'

Chapter 27

Angela looked out of her window and then checked her watch. It was almost 8.40 and no sign of Greg. She picked up her phone to ring him, but before she could dial his number the phone rang.

'Angela, it's Greg. I've had a puncture. The wheel's being changed right now, and I'll be there as soon as I can.'

'OK Greg. Have you remembered your homework?'

'Yes Miss. See you soon.'

He arrived about twenty minutes later and Angela joined him in the car.

'You're looking a bit flustered,' remarked Angela.

Greg held up his dirty hands. 'I couldn't get the bloody wheel nuts off! Then I split the wheel brace. It was one of those cheap ones you get with the car. Fortunately, a passing motorist stopped and gave me a loan of hers. She had an expanding wheel brace.'

'*Hers*? I see. Rescued by a woman.'

'Yes. And she was very nice. A young woman with dark hair, big blue eyes, a nice smile and wearing a very subtle and distinctive perfume.'

'Are you trying to make me jealous, Greg?'

'No, why would I want to do that?'

'Because she had an expanding wheel brace, and you think I don't.'

'I didn't even know you had a car.'

'I don't, but I still might have an expanding wheel brace. I'm buying the car in instalments.'

'So, you don't have a car?'

'Well, I kind of have a car.'

'You've either got a car or you haven't. Which is it?'

'I have a car, but it's in bits at the moment.'

'Did you have an accident?'

'No, it just decided to dismantle itself one night in the garage to crave attention.'

'So you had an accident?'

'No. I burned the clutch out. So how did you get on with your homework?'

'Well, although I say so myself, I think I'll be able to bring a smile to your face.'

'Lots of guys have tried and failed, Greg, but take your best shot.'

'The numbers Stewart has underlined are always written beside words like *bread* or *dough*, so, corny as it may sound, I think this refers to money. I wasn't sure what the dates would mean, but I checked them against the diary notes you gave me. Some are close, but I don't think they're close enough to be significant. I then compared them with arrest records, but the first few didn't match, so I gave that up. I then checked them against the file on this security company run by Collins, and bingo! The dates tied in perfectly with raids the police made on premises his company was guarding. Even the words Stewart had underlined were significant. When he underlined *head*, the raid took place at the head office. When he underlined *branch*, the raid took place at one of the warehouses he had on his books. There were some other words underlined which seemed to suggest which specific warehouse, but I didn't have time to cross check all of these. What do you think?'

'Obviously we'll double check what you're telling me, but if what you say is correct then you have definitely rung my bell Greg. That would suggest Stewart was informing Collins of the impending raids, and probably being paid for doing so.'

'Collins himself is quite an interesting character,' continued Greg. 'It seems that he started out as a legitimate businessman. He had a furniture store that was doing quite well for a time, and then business dipped. Cash flow became a problem, so he started double swiping credit cards where people used these for big purchases. When the buyers got their statements in from the card companies, they contacted Collins. He immediately apologised and refunded the second payments.'

'Meaning that he had an extra amount of money in his bank for a month gaining interest,' said Angela.

'Exactly. This seemed to go quite well for a time, but business didn't pick up, and eventually he couldn't manage to refund the payments. He managed to get friends to bail him out so he avoided a conviction.'

'Had he been convicted he'd have spent a couple of years in the pokey. That's one of the things that's always pissed me off about our justice system, Greg. A guy swindling money gets jailed, but thugs who go about beating people up get community service and fines. It's true what they say, the system values property over people.'

'They also say there are more criminals in business than in jail,' said Greg.

'That's also very true. You should see the pissy wee portion of chips my local chippy gives you. If that's not robbery I don't know what is! OK, once we've double-checked the dates, we'll dig a bit deeper into these warehouses. We'll try and get some idea of what the police thought they would find in these raids. Oh, and I think we should check with Stewart's bank. If he's been getting paid by Collins, we should be able to find deposits of cash.'

They spent the morning poring over files and the computer databases. Angela double-checked the dates from the recipe book against police activity while Greg found out what he could about the failed raids on the warehouses.

'You're very quiet, Greg,' said Angela.

'I was just thinking about Maureen Stewart and wondering how she'll react to finding out her husband was a crook, or at least helping crooks.'

Angela put down her pen and leaned back in her chair.

'Well we're not at that stage yet. If we don't find any evidence that she had knowledge of Stewart's activities, we'll hold off as long as we can before telling her. It's good to be sensitive to these things Greg, but only as long as it doesn't get in the way of the investigation.'

Greg nodded and went back to scanning the database.

'Oh, there's one bit of good news,' said Greg. 'I asked for anything the local guys down south had on Richard Stewart, just on the off chance. We got lucky there. It turns out he was stopped for speeding on the night of his father's murder. He was breathalysed as a matter of routine. He passed it OK, but this all took place around 8.30 in the evening, so there's no way he could have been up here a few hours later.'

'OK, Greg. So that rules out a trip to the seaside.'

By lunchtime, Angela had confirmed what Greg had discovered the previous night, the dates matched almost perfectly.

'All the raids involved Trading Standards,' said Greg. 'They were hoping to find counterfeit clothing, DVDs, CDs, fags, all that sort of stuff. But there were also some of the Drug Squad boys involved.'

'And they found nothing?' asked Angela.

'A few bits and pieces,' confirmed Greg. 'Most of the stuff in the warehouses was legit, but they did find a few fake designer bags and some DVDs. The raids had been planned at least a few days in advance. Our boys had to liaise with the Trading Standards so we weren't able to hit the warehouses at the drop of a hat. It would have been difficult to have kept the dates of the raids secret. Certainly someone in Stewart's position would have been able to find out without much trouble.'

'So what's bothering you?' asked Angela, seeing Greg's troubled look.

'I just can't figure out why someone involved with the warehouses would want to bump off Stewart. OK, he wouldn't be as much help to them being retired, but he still met with them, so I assume he was passing on some information. It seems a huge jump from counterfeit goods to murder.'

'Stewart might have wanted more money,' said Angela, 'or he may have been threatening to disclose what he knew of their operation.'

'Why would he do that?'

'No idea,' said Angela. 'But we've got to consider every possibility.'

'But still,' said Greg. 'To commit a *murder.*'

'There could be a lot of money involved,' said Angela, 'plus jail sentences. All we have at the moment is a possible motive.'

'Do you think we should speak to Collins?'

'No. We'd be fishing. And the last thing we want is to let him know that we suspect him of anything.'

'Stewart may not have been acting alone,' said Greg. 'Collins may still find out that we're snooping about.'

'And that's exactly why we're not going to tell anyone what we're doing,' said Angela. 'Let's go and get some lunch.'

They returned to the station bringing their lunch with them. Angela was happy to get a burger and coke from a nearby cafe, but Greg insisted on going somewhere else for something more to his taste. They had dropped into a branch of Stewart's bank and, after identifying themselves, were allowed to get a limited list of transactions. Angela was flicking through these while Greg ate his lunch. Angela's lunch was long gone as she ate it while waiting on Greg being served in Subway.

'I've been thinking about the method of strangling,' said Greg. 'If the assailant had to lean against a tree or wall or whatever, there could be traces of his clothing on whatever he rested against. Do you think the crime scene investigators will have thought to check them out?'

'If they didn't, it'll be too late to do it now. They did find fibres on most of the victims' clothing. Remember what the French forensic scientist Edmond Locard said, *every contact leaves a trace*, although he probably said it in French. We could ask him, but we'd need a Ouija board since he died in 1966.'

'There's something that puzzles me,' said Greg suddenly.

'Go on.'

'Something crossed my mind while I'm going through these bank records. There have been no cash deposits of any significance at all. There have also been no large withdrawals. I was in their kitchen and I'd say it is pretty expensive and quite modern. Then there's their cars, both pretty new. I can find no listing of any car loans or any other kind of loans.'

'I checked up on those. There were no finance arrangements taken out on either of them.'

'So, either they paid cash, or the money has come from Mrs Stewart's bank account?'

'Well, this is a joint account, but that's not to say they didn't have other bank accounts. This is the one Stewart's pension is paid into, so I'd have thought this was the main account.'

'We'll need a warrant to see other accounts and in greater detail. Let's leave that for the present.'

'Do you think Turner might be involved in whatever Stewart did?'

'It's possible,' replied Angela, 'but there's no comparison between the two as far as money goes, at least not on the surface. It might be an idea to visit Turner again and mention Collins to him, just to get his reaction. On the way over, we could drop into the hospital and check that Turner was there when he says he was.'

This time Angela drove. She had driven round the hospital car park once or twice and failed to find a space, so she dropped Greg off to ask questions while she continued to look for a place to park. She was on her fourth or fifth circuit when Greg came back out.

'Peter Turner was undergoing tests at the hospital on the Monday and Tuesday, just as he told us.'

'OK,' said Angela, 'there was no harm in asking. Let's go and talk to him.'

She drove the few miles out of town to Turner's home in the nearby village.

'You don't look too surprised to see us again, Mr Turner?' said Angela.

'No, I've been expecting you to call back. Do you want tea or coffee this time?'

'Why not,' said Angela, 'after all, this is just a friendly chat between colleagues.'

Peter Turner went into his kitchen to prepare the drinks and Angela and Greg looked around the room.

Greg made a gesture of rubbing his fingers together that Angela correctly took to mean money. She shook her head.

'How are you managing on your pension?' shouted Angela.

'Oh, not too bad,' said Peter. 'I don't need a lot of money. I stopped smoking and don't drink, so things are pretty much OK. My mortgage was paid off before I retired, and I haven't had a holiday since my wife died, so I get by and even manage to put a little away as well. I can't complain.'

He returned from the kitchen with a tray carrying their drinks and also some biscuits.

'I've never met a cop yet who didn't eat biscuits,' he explained.

'Well, this man here'll be your first,' said Angela indicating that she meant Greg. 'He's a vegetarian.'

'Ah,' said Turner, as if that explained why Greg didn't eat biscuits. Just to spite her, Greg took one.

They sat and drank their coffee and made some small talk.

'You must have met quite a number of villains in your time,' said Angela.

'Oh, I met my share.'

'People like Steve Collins for example.'

'Yeah, Collins was a past master at the great escape.'

'He was the witness you had in your car on the night of the accident, wasn't he?' said Angela.

214

'Yes. In all the commotion we had forgotten about him being in the car.'

'And he's never been in trouble since,' said Angela.

'Well, he's never been caught,' said Turner. 'That's not quite the same thing.'

'He runs a security company now I believe,' said Angela.

'That's what he calls it, yes,' confirmed Turner.

'And what would you call it?' said Greg.

'He employs crooks to guard warehouses storing crooked stuff belonging to other crooks,' said Peter Turner. 'Perhaps Crooks Incorporated would be more appropriate?'

'I wouldn't let him hear you saying that, Mr Turner; he may have you up on slander charges.'

Turner laughed. 'Oh, I haven't seen him for years and I intend to keep it that way. Let me give you a little advice detectives. If you plan to go up against Collins, watch your backs. He's big time now.'

'Sounds a really serious guy,' said Angela, 'I wouldn't have thought counterfeit goods would have elevated him to the status of a crime boss.'

'Counterfeit goods?' said Turner laughing. 'Yes, that'll be what the files say.'

Angela and Greg glanced at each other.

'Detectives, the authorities may have raided warehouses under Steve Collin's protection and said they were looking for counterfeit goods, but that's only part of it. Oh, his cronies still deal in them all right, but he's moved up in the world since the early days. Oh, no. Steve Collins is thought to be one of the main drug dealers in Scotland. Not the traditional drugs like heroin, but the new designer drugs.'

'I've never heard Collins name being mentioned in connection with any major drug bust,' said Angela.

'Oh, Collins is way above getting his hands dirty. On paper, he simply runs a firm that provides security for a number of warehouses, but the suspicion is that he's much more involved than that. Taking him down would be like tackling a Mafia crime family, much too big a job for local law enforcement. But now and again they felt they should rattle his cage a bit, just to let him know they're there.'

'Scanning through the records of the raids, a fair number of goods were seized. Yet Collins has never been charged,' said Greg.

'In the first place, the raids were on premises he had been hired to guard. As I've said, he doesn't have any other ties to these places. The crooks he employs as security know when to look the other way. And the people running the warehouses knew when raids were planned, and which warehouse would be hit. Collins used these places to store his drugs, and it was an easy matter to transfer his stock to other premises when he knew a raid was planned. And the good thing from his point of view about pills is that you can pack a hell of a lot of them into a few boxes.'

'So, the raid would take place, some goods would be seized, and everyone would go home happy?'

'That's pretty much it as far as I know. A few small-time guys would be up on charges, but nothing would be traced back to Collins.'

Greg had been sitting with his mouth open as Turner told his story. Now he found his voice. 'If you knew this, why didn't you tell someone?'

'Who would I tell?'

'Your superior officer of course!'

'Yes, tell the inspector and so on. Except it wouldn't go any further than the chief inspector.'

'Why?' said Greg.

'Because it was the chief inspector who told you,' said Angela. 'Chief Inspector Stewart told you what was going on, didn't he?'

'Not is so many words,' said Turner, 'but he managed to paint a picture for me. At first the raids worked out OK, and I had no reason to suspect anything. But then there were whispers, talk about how unlucky the drug boys were. The authorities knew by the amount of stuff on the streets that they were only clipping off the tip of the iceberg. Stewart told me that the drug raids would fail because higher powers wanted to lull Collins into a false sense of security. He never actually explained who the higher powers were. He suggested that they wanted to find out where Collins was getting the drugs from. Was he importing them, or was there a factory set up somewhere in the UK? Basically, to find the source. He suggested he was going along with Collins under orders from higher up.'

'And you believed him?'

Turner shrugged. 'What would you do? A superior officer confides in you that he is working under orders that appear to subvert police activity, but he's doing this for a greater goal than the short-term gain through seizing counterfeit goods. The suspicion was that either through loose talk or a bent copper somewhere, Collins was getting word that the raids were going to take place. If the raids had been stopped, Collins would know that the police knew there was a leak. Keeping the raids going was meant to lull him into a false sense of security, at least until such times as the leak could be identified and plugged. Then there would be a major raid and the whole business tied up. Remember, the records show that the raids were after counterfeit goods, not drugs. In those days, few people knew much about designer drugs. Then otherwise healthy young people started dying and people began to take a lot more notice. I was one of the few, perhaps the only, copper to be given the nod as to the greater plan. So, what would you do? Go above him to the super? The chief super? Or even to the chief constable? And tell them what? That you had been keeping quiet about this for years on the advice of your chief inspector, but wanted confirmation that you hadn't been played as a fool? You could do that, sure, but what if Stewart was genuine? What if the leak was from someone above him? The whole operation would be blown to bits. And if I had been spun a line and the copper immediately above the chief inspector confronted Stewart? It'd be your word against Stewart's.'

'And Stewart kept working for them after he retired?'

'I've no idea.'

'That's quite a story Mr Turner.'

'Yes, I suppose it is. You're both probably sitting there wondering how I managed to keep quiet, but you weren't there. I've condensed years into a few minutes, and Stewart could read people; he could certainly read me. Even as I was telling you the story, I was wondering why I didn't do something, but it all happened so gradually. Before I knew it, I was trapped. I suppose that's how people become alcoholics. They don't just waken up one day an alcoholic. It creeps up on them. Have you seen the film *One Flew Over the Cuckoo's Nest*? I remember the Indian Chief talking about his father who had been an alcoholic. He said his father drank out of a bottle, and then one day the bottle started drinking out of him, something like that. I've always remembered that scene, very powerful. And that's the way it was for me.'

'Quite a story,' said Greg when they were back in the car. 'What should we do?'

'About Turner? Nothing. We need to concentrate on what we're going to do about the whole Collins thing. We're in danger of getting side-tracked here, Greg. Remember we're investigating Stewart's murder. Anything else will have to be put aside until we solve the murder.'

'Do you think Collins may have had Stewart murdered? Perhaps he was asking for more money or threatening to spill the beans.'

'He certainly would have more beans to spill than we first thought,' said Angela, 'assuming of course that Turner isn't dreaming the whole thing up.'

'Perhaps Stewart had outlived his usefulness?'

'Perhaps, but murder is a pretty drastic step.'

'Well, back to my original question; what do we do now?'

'There's one thing that puzzles me, Greg. How did Collins get his claws into Stewart in the first place? That's the one thing Turner didn't tell us, and I reckon even if we had asked, he still wouldn't have told us. My instincts tell me it happened around the time of the Reid accident. I think it's the key to the whole weird plot. Think about it. Collins, Stewart and Turner all together with members of the Reid family at that one point in time. And now, years later, we have the same characters involved again.'

Chapter 28

'Hello?' said Greg.

'Are you awake?' said Angela.

'Well, I am now. What's up?'

'Get dressed and pick me up as soon as you can. There's been another murder.'

They arrived at Centenary Park which was ablaze with blue flashing lights. Numerous police vehicles and an ambulance were abandoned, rather than parked, on the grass. People wearing white overalls, gloves and hats looked ghostly as they shuffled about, lit by numerous arc lamps making the area look like a scene from *Close Encounters of the Third Kind*. A makeshift plastic tent had been set up as a protection against the elements over what Greg and Angela correctly assumed to be the immediate crime scene.

'I thought you would want to view the body,' said Superintendent Black who had been waiting on their arrival. Angela and Greg nodded and were shown along the path the forensic team had cleared.

'I'll leave you to it,' said Black.

Inside the tent, the body was illuminated by more arc lights. Police photographers seemed to have all the pictures they needed and were packing up their gear.

'Have you taken any snaps of the crowd?' asked Angela.

The photographer glanced over at the dozen or so people and assured her that he had.

Angela spoke to one of the forensic staff and asked him to check the trees close to the body for traces of clothing.

'Oh shit!' said Greg softly.

'Have you never seen a body before?' asked Angela.

'Yes, but not like that,' said Greg. He nodded at the man lying on his back, his arms up in the air and his hands frozen in a desperate attempt to free his throat of the restriction that was killing him. His unseeing eyes bulged in their sockets and his tongue protruding from his mouth was swollen and angry looking. One or two of the uniformed cops exchanged a sly grin at Greg's reaction.

'Cadaveric spasm,' said Angela, pointing at the corpse.

'Correct,' said a voice behind them which caused Greg to jump. 'Instant rigor mortis sometimes seen on a corpse where the dead person has been using his muscles with great exertion while dying. An excellent example.'

'And you are?' asked Angela.

'Doctor McIntyre.'

'I'm DS Porter and this is DC Anderson. Do you have an estimate of the time of death?'

'I'd say between four and five hours ago.'

'Sometime between ten and eleven?' said Greg.

Angela moved carefully to take a closer look at the body. Greg gingerly shuffled up behind her.

'Can you tell the cause of death at this stage doc?' asked Angela while still looking at the body.

'Clearly it was a violent death and going by the marks on his neck I'd put my money on strangulation.'

'Anything else doctor?'

The doctor pursed his lips. 'There are no other obvious injuries. No loss of blood I can detect, and the clothing doesn't appear to have been disturbed. There is a distinct smell of alcohol, but whether or not the victim was drunk is a question only the post-mortem will answer. A male in his late 50s or early 60s I'd say, but I can't be of any more help at the moment I'm afraid.'

Angela thanked McIntyre then indicated for Greg to move away from the scene. They retraced their steps carefully until clear of the body.

'I reckon the killer had been hanging about waiting on a victim,' said Angela.

She moved away from the bushes and Greg followed.

'Where's the super?' asked Angela to a group of officers.

'He left,' said a detective. 'He told me to answer any questions you might have, and he would speak to you in the morning. I'm DS Mullins; I was the first CID man on the scene.'

'Who found the body?' said Angela.

'An old lady out looking for her cat.'

'She lives in Centenary Avenue, across there.' He waved vaguely. 'I think she's a bit confused'

'Where's she now?' asked Greg.

'They took her to the Monklands in a state of shock. Poor soul. She lives alone and they're trying to contact some of her relatives. Some of the uniformed boys are looking for her cat.'

Greg burst out laughing. 'Sorry, but we've a murdered man lying here, and some officers are looking for a cat?'

'We've tried asking the old lady questions, but she keeps going on about her cat. It's the shock. The doctors reckon that if we find her cat and assure her that it's fine, she'll calm down a bit and be able to tell us more about finding the body.'

'Couldn't you just *tell* her you've found her cat?' asked Greg.

'We thought of that, but she's not totally stupid. She wants to *see* the cat. She gave us a very detailed description of it which won't really be necessary unless it's discovered some means of taking its collar off. But we humoured her.'

'Well humour me for a bit,' said Angela. She nodded at the small group of people being held back behind police tape. 'Any witnesses?'

'No. Just curious members of the public, and the press of course. That reminds me, do you want to say anything to the media?'

'Me? Absolutely not! Did the super not speak to them?'

'Very briefly. He basically said *no comment* but in a superintendent sort of way. But I think they're hoping to get a bit more than that.'

'I bet they are!' said Angela, 'but not from me they won't! Do you know anything about the victim?'

'Not yet. He had no wallet or any form of identification on him, but he has between twenty and thirty pounds in his pocket, so that would tend to rule out robbery as a motive.'

Angela nodded and began to walk back to their car.

'Can we remove the body now?' asked the detective.

'If your guys have finished, yes. Try and get him identified as soon as possible. Someone may be sitting at home waiting on him.'

'Back home?' said Greg when they were back in the car.

Angela nodded.

'Centenary Park,' said Greg. 'That's a nice name.'

'Airdrie became a burgh in 1821,' said Angela. 'The park was built in 1921 on the 100th anniversary, hence the name.'

'I find it strange and slightly disturbing that you know that,' said Greg.

'My father was born and brought up in Airdrie,' explained Angela, 'and was very proud of the town. He was also very proud of what he knew of its history and took great delight in boring his family with his knowledge on every opportunity. Unless, of course, someone mentioned football. Then he would start on a potted history of Airdrieonians. But you're from Edinburgh, so you'll not know anything about football.'

Greg decided not to rise to the bait, especially as he did indeed know little about football, as rugby was his game.

'So what have we learned?' asked Greg.

Angela frowned. 'Not a lot, I suppose, except to confirm that our guy is patient and dedicated.'

'I wouldn't have thought *dedicated* was an appropriate word,' said Greg.

'No? So, what word would you use to describe someone who is prepared to hang about for ages in this weather waiting to carry out his task?'

'I'd have said demented was more appropriate.'

Greg flicked on the wipers to clear the light rain that had now started to fall. He tried setting the wipers to clear the windscreen continuously, but they made a very annoying squeaking sound, so he contented himself with flicking them on and off.

'I've fucked up, Greg,' said Angela softly.

'How do you mean?'

'I advised the boss not to tell the press that Stewart wasn't killed by the serial killer. I hoped this might provoke the killer to do something stupid. But it seems to have provoked him in a different way.'

'That's not your fault,' said Greg. 'You're not responsible for what this nutter does!'

'No. I've misjudged this guy.'

During the rest of the journey Angela only gave minimal answers to anything Greg asked.

Greg dropped her off and left for home to get some sleep. Angela changed into her nightclothes, poured herself a glass of wine and slumped into her reclining chair. She hoped she would drop off to sleep but knew that she wouldn't. There was too much running through her mind.

Another triumph! But there's no time to rest on my laurels, there's still so much work to do. I imagine they'll eventually catch that guy who did the Motherwell job. Oh, how pissed they'll be when they find they have a copycat!

But could this character try to take credit for the events he wasn't involved in? Even if he did, the police surely won't be stupid enough to believe him.

No, that won't happen, there's no need to give it another thought.

But I have a plan. It's risky, but I know I'll carry it off as expertly as I have all my previous tasks. My one concern is that the authorities are so slow on the uptake they may not realise how I'm playing with them. If that turns out to be the case, then I'll just have to give them a nudge. I really should be using my time more productively, but they need to be set straight.

It's strange how things work out. While I will eventually get the credit for saving so many, I hope my dear mother will be seen as the real martyr to this cause. Through her suffering many, many others will be freed from their tormentors. It's from her memory that I draw my strength.

The newspapers have decided who I am; they think they know everything about me except my name. Or at least that's what they think. And they are so wrong, and that makes this journal essential in educating them. They think they know what drives me, but they know nothing.

The first thing that needs to be corrected is that the acts themselves don't give me any pleasure, that's very important. As the life drains out of my victims, I do feel some regret. I would be sub-human if I didn't. But my focus must be on the bigger picture. Always the bigger picture. Nothing must detract from that.

'You look like shit,' said Greg when he picked her up at the usual time. 'Didn't you get any sleep?'

'Not much,' admitted Angela.

'I've been thinking about the advice I gave the chief,' she said.

'Are you still blaming yourself for what happened last night?' said Greg.

'Yes and no,' said Angela. 'I misjudged what this guy would do, but I think we acted in the best interests of the case. It took me a while last night, or rather this morning, to come to that conclusion, but that's what I think. We need to break this case somehow, and so far, the guy's been lucky. I took a chance, and it didn't work out.'

'You didn't take the chance,' said Greg, 'that was the chief's decision. You advised him and he followed your advice. There was every chance the guy who was murdered last night would have been killed no matter what advice you gave. It may have happened later than last night, or to a different guy, but there's no doubt it would have happened to someone, sometime.'

Angela's mobile rang and she answered it.

'The chief wants to see me,' said Angela.

They arrived at the station just after 9am. Angela went into the chief's office while Greg got himself a cup of coffee.

'I wanted to see you before you got started this morning Angela. It's about last night. Our ploy seems to have backfired.'

Angela sat down and noticed that DI Lambert was sitting at the back of the Boss's office. His presence made her uncomfortable.

'Do we know that it's the work of the serial killer?' she asked.

'Not a hundred per cent as yet, but we're pretty sure it is. But I wanted to speak to you about the decision to treat the Stewart case as not the killer's work.'

Angela opened her mouth to speak but the chief stopped her.

'DI Lambert here has raised some concerns over our approach.'

Angela glanced at Lambert and he smiled smugly. She wanted to smack him in the mouth but resisted the temptation.

'OK John. Let's hear what you think.' The Boss sat back in his chair and folded his arms.

'I should point out, Sir, that many of our colleagues share my opinions.' (*Safety in numbers, thought Angela.*)

'So, the strategy isn't your own?' asked the Boss.

'Oh no, Sir. It's my idea. But I've floated it among members of the team, and I find general agreement.'

The Boss nodded but said nothing.

'It's common knowledge that the idea not to identify the Stewart killing as the work of another person came from DS Porter. I'm afraid the tragic events of last night have shown this idea to be foolhardy at least, and negligent in the extreme. Rather than goad this killer, I believe we need to pander to his ego. Make him think he's achieved something. Hopefully that would take the edge of his lust to kill and give us the time we need to assess all the evidence. DS Porter's approach seems to be to encourage him to kill as many times as it takes for him to make a mistake and therefore be caught.'

Russell had been watching Angela intently during Lambert's remarks, and he sensed that she was about to explode.

'I see,' said the Boss, holding up a hand to prevent Angela from speaking.

'The idea to suppress our belief that Stewart was not killed by the serial killer was indeed Angela's idea. But I didn't know that it was common knowledge?'

'Yes sir, I'm afraid it is. We know that DS Porter had been reprimanded over speaking to the press, and we put two and two together.'

'And I'm afraid you added two and two and came up with five or six,' said the Boss. 'I did reprimand Angela for speaking out of turn to the press, but her remarks had nothing at all to do with the Stewart killing.'

'Oh,' said Lambert. 'We assumed...'

'Never assume, DI Lambert. Assumptions can form the basis of investigation or inquiry, but assumptions must be tested at a very early stage to see if they hold up in the light of the evidence. In this case, I'm afraid your assumption is very wide of the mark. The *foolhardy or criminally negligent* idea you mentioned was actually put into play by my superiors on my recommendation.' He paused and stared at Lambert to allow his statement to sink in. 'The tactic was not the result of remarks Angela made to the press. Do you really think I would allow an operation to be taken down a different course from that which was intended by an officer making remarks to the press?'

'If you put it that way, sir, I suppose...'

'But you have thrown up some interesting points, John. It would appear that my next case conference should emphasise who is making the decisions in this investigation, especially if there are many other officers who are under the same misapprehension as you. Now, do you have any other points to raise?'

Angela resisted the temptation to look at Lambert as he rose to leave the office.

'It was the correct decision, Angela,' said the Boss when Lambert had closed the door. 'I'm quite convinced of that, and I'll defend that decision if I'm asked to. What the chief constable did may have resulted in another murder being committed sooner rather than later, but it was worth taking the chance. If anyone outside these buildings knew that they might think we're playing with people's lives, but we're trying to save lives. We're trying everything we know to catch this murderer. I wanted to tell you this face to face before you continue with your investigations.'

'What you've told me, Chief, was almost exactly what Constable Anderson told me on the way here.'

'Really? Perhaps I should promote him.' He smiled briefly. 'The press release later will say that this is the seventh murder. We're keeping to the line that Stewart's killing was part of the series.'

Angela smiled at the Boss and got up to leave.

'One other thing Angela,' said the Boss as she opened his door. 'I didn't bring John in here to give you something to gloat about. I needed to nip the whispering in the bud and that's what I did. I could have spoken to John without you being present, but I wanted you to hear his view. The last thing I want is to increase the divisions in this investigation. Officers will not always agree on the way forward, but I need everyone to be quite clear about who decides that way.'

'So?' said Greg when she left the Chief's office.

'I am gradually revising my initial opinion of our gaffer,' said Angela. 'Let's examine what evidence we have from this morning's crime. I'm afraid we'll have to put the Stewart murder on the back burner for now.'

The rest of the day was spent reviewing the early morning murder. The victim had now been identified as James Bryce, a fifty-eight-year-old car mechanic who had recently become a grandfather. His relatives had been informed. Everything was a replica of the previous crimes. The watch found on the body had belonged to the victim killed before Stewart.

Uniformed officers were conducting door-to-door inquiries in the area around Centenary Park, and an appeal had been put out for motorists driving in the area to report anything unusual they had noticed. There was some coverage by CCTV cameras of the hospital area, but nothing of the park. What footage that existed was being viewed by officers. The lady who found the latest body had been reunited with her cat, and she had provided some information, but nothing that seemed to suggest any leads to the killer.

Public appeals usually brought in a mixed bag of attention seekers and people who believed they had relevant information, particularly in high profile cases. Everything had to be checked and recorded and this all took a considerable amount of time. Petty criminals in the murder areas were having a field day. It was almost as if the CID had taken a vacation all at the same time.

Angela stood sipping a cup of coffee at the door leading to the open plan CID area.

'You know Greg,' she said, 'it would be easier looking for a needle in a haystack, and at least we know what a needle looks like. These guys and dozens like them have been sifting through stacks of evidence and come up with nothing that seems relevant. We all need a break, even a small one, to give us some encouragement.'

'Are you getting discouraged?' asked Greg.

'I don't get discouraged,' said Angela, 'I just get very pissed off, and my current level of pissedoffedness is pretty high.'

'You might be interested in this,' said Greg.

'What is it?'

'It's the evening paper.'

Angela looked at her watch. 'At 4 in the afternoon?'

Greg shrugged. Angela took the paper from him and walked to her desk with Greg following. She spread the paper out over the various files scattered on the desk and read the front page.

'That's interesting,' she said, pointing to a particular paragraph.

'Is that the bit where they report that a police psychologist basically says the killer is a cowardly wimp?'

'A fair summary Greg. Not only is the chief sticking to the line that Stewart was a serial killer victim, but he's upped the stakes. He's pretty much throwing down a gauntlet to this guy.'

'How'll we know if the guy picks it up?'

'A very good question, Greg, a very good question indeed.'

'And the answer is?'

'We're dependent on a very vigilant and intuitive officer having his or her wits about them. We're also dependent on the killer being pissed off at the Stewart killing, and deciding to try and set the record straight. He's tried that already with two killings, but we haven't taken his lead. It's a question of does he let it go at that, or does he try something else. I just hope he tries another approach and doesn't start to bury us under a pile of bodies. Anyway, I think we'll call it a night Greg.'

'Are you still planning to go to the Stewart funeral tomorrow?'

'Yeah. Partly out of respect for Maureen Stewart and partly to have a look at who else turns up.'

'Do you think Turner will be there?'

'He said he would be going, but I'm more interested in seeing if Collins turns up.'

'And how will we recognise him if he does?'

'Peter Turner hopes he can help us out in that respect.'

'Didn't he say that he hadn't seen Collins for a while?'

'He did say that, but he'll have a better idea of what he looks like than we do. We don't even have a mug shot of Collins to help us.'

Motherwell Cathedral was packed out, with people standing in the aisles and even some outside. The police officers had been there fairly early and had taken seats towards the back of the cathedral. However, as it became clear there wouldn't be enough room for everyone who wanted to attend, they moved to stand at the back and gave up their seats to an elderly couple. Many of the mourners wore police uniforms, and the Fire Service and Ambulance Service were also represented.

'It'll be a big thing to disillusion so many people,' whispered Greg.

Angela nodded but said nothing. She continued to run her eyes systematically along the rows of people trying to identify someone who fitted Turner's description of Collins.

'I haven't seen anyone who matches the description of Collins,' said Angela quietly. 'We'll try and nip out before the handshakes start. Perhaps we'll spot him among the mourners as they leave.'

The service ended, and Greg and Angela managed to manoeuvre their way out to where the lane was packed with cars. The drizzle of half rain, half sleet, which had come on just as the service started had now stopped and hazy winter sunshine bathed the mourners as they left the cathedral.

'Now that's a surprise,' said Greg. Angela followed his stare and spotted Brian and Elizabeth Reid standing at the side of the large wooden doors beside an older man.

'There's Peter Turner,' said Angela. 'I assume the younger man with him is his son.'

Peter Turner noticed the two police officers but made no move to come towards them. He nodded discretely in their direction, and then walked towards two men standing on their own just off the small path to the left of the cathedral doors.

'What's he doing?' said Greg.

'I think he's asking that guy for a light,' said Angela.

'I didn't know Turner smoked,' said Greg.

'No, neither did I,' said Angela. 'I'm sure he said that he'd stopped smoking.'

The man Turner had spoken to nodded to his friend who dipped a hand in his pocket and produced a lighter. Turner accepted a light, thanked him, and then returned to where his son was waiting.

'Let's try and get a closer look at that obliging character,' said Angela.

'I think that guy's too young to be Collins,' suggested Greg. 'Wait a minute. The older man with him. He fits the description.'

Angela moved quickly across a small grassy area to get slightly ahead of the two men.

'I'd bet that's him!' she said as Greg caught up with her.

The man in question was now walking quite quickly with his companion along the waiting line of cars.

'I'll follow him and see where he goes,' she said to Greg. 'You keep an eye on the Turners until they leave. Meet me back at the car.'

'Peter Turner walked back to his son and handed him the cigarette. Then they left without talking to either of the Reid's as far as I could see,' said Greg when he joined Angela at their car.

'Collins and his companion got into a Mercedes with a driver who had been waiting on them. Both got into the back of the car and it left. I got the registration number.'

'OK,' said Greg. 'Quite a worthwhile morning.'

'Should we try and have a few words with Stewart's son while he's up here?' asked Greg.

'That was my plan, but I'm not sure now. I think we'll keep him on the back burner until we hit a dead end, especially as his speeding incident pretty much rules him out.' Angela took out her phone and started pressing some buttons.

'Who were you calling earlier?' asked Greg.

'No one,' said Angela. She handed her phone to Greg. 'Now we have an up-to-date picture of our Mr Collins.'

That evening, Brian and Elizabeth Reid met up with Roy at his father's house.

They had stopped off and bought some fish and chips on their way out of town.

'Was he sure?' asked Peter Turner as he unwrapped the steaming food.

'He couldn't be a hundred per cent, but he felt pretty sure it was him,' answered Brian as he waited on his sausage supper being found amongst the pile of food. He grabbed the one can of full fat Coke in case someone beat him to it.

'But it wasn't Collins?' said Peter. 'The neighbour...what was his name?'

'Derek Nelson.'

'Yes, he's sure the gas man who called on Betty White wasn't Collins?'

'No definitely not,' said Brian, 'he was certain. He said it was the other guy, the guy who gave you the light. And you've no idea who that guy was?'

'I've never seen him before as far as I can recall. But that appears to be another piece of the jigsaw in place.'

'So, we need to find out who he is,' said Brian, taking a bite of a battered sausage after dipping it in brown sauce.

'And I'll bet he doesn't work for any gas company.'

Chapter 29

'What're you looking at Greg?' asked Angela.

'It's the reports you asked for from the stations where people had offered information on the serial killings. I don't think you've made any new friends with your request.'

'If I wanted to make new friends, I'd start a Facebook page. Why are they bitching? They would've had to log every visit anyway, so what's the big deal?'

'Well, they needed to extract the info from the logs and compile separate lists because you specifically said you didn't want to wade through piles of crap.'

'OK, I'll send them chocolates or flowers or something. Anyway, did you have any joy?'

'It depends on what you mean by joy. They've certainly done as you asked.' He waved some sheets in the air. 'Here's details of everyone who phoned or called the stations to offer information on the Stewart killing. It's amounting to dozens, and these are only the people they dealt with in the past two weeks.'

'Does anything jump out?'

'Let's see. Two callers said they had seen aliens in the area, another reported strange lights but didn't actually see the aliens. One was sure he saw someone resembling Lord Lucan in the park, although for some reason his appearance hadn't changed since he was last seen in 1974. We've had a few confessions from regulars who confess to everything.'

'Fascinating, Greg, now is there anything useful clutched in your hand?'

'I'm not sure, I've still quite a number to go through.'

Angela put out her hand. 'I don't see why you should have all the fun; give me a pile and I'll help you.'

She suggested that they make three bundles, one for *totally ridiculous*, the second for *highly unlikely*, and the third for *possibilities*.'

'In which bundle will I put Lord Lucan and the aliens?' asked Greg.

'I know where I'll put them if you don't get on with it,' said Angela.

Many of the reports included more detail than Angela expected. Unfortunately, none that she saw gave her any glimmer of hope. As she placed her twelfth report on the *unlikely* pile, she glanced at the empty space that was the *possibilities* pile.

'If we go through the lot and we still have no possibilities,' said Angela, 'we'll go through the middle pile again in case we've missed something.'

'Oh, I'm looking forward to that,' said Greg.

Another fifteen minutes passed, then Angela suddenly stood up. 'This is doing my nut in; I'm going for some coffee. Do you want some?'

Greg nodded, not wanting to leave the current report he was reading.

Angela sneaked out for a cigarette, and then returned with the coffees. As she placed them on the desk, she noticed the *possibilities* pile had one report in it.

'Did you put that there to wind me up?' she asked.

'I was going to put it in the *unlikely* pile,' said Greg, 'but there was something about it I thought was strange.'

Angela picked it up and read it.

'It's quite detailed,' she said, and then read some of the report out loud. 'A middle-aged man was hanging around the park gates at approximately 10pm. He was well built and above average height, the witness estimated around 6' 3". He was wearing a dark coloured jacket and had what appeared to be a waterproof cap on his head although it wasn't raining. He was also wearing dark gloves. The witness reported that the man checked his watch frequently, and repeatedly took something out of his pocket and checked it, although the witness had no idea what this was. The man walked back and forward a few times and walked with a large gait.' She looked at Greg. 'We know it's likely the attacker wore gloves, and trace fibres were found from a dark jacket. A man the height as described may well need size eleven shoes. But it's all pretty inconclusive.'

'Read on a bit,' said Greg. 'The officer knew that the estimated height of the serial killer is under 6' and that psychologists estimate his age as younger than middle aged, so she tried to thank the witness for his time and conclude the interview.'

'But the guy became agitated and accused her of not taking him seriously. Now why would he do that?' said Angela after reading more of the report. 'Are you thinking that the witness appeared quite desperate to be taken seriously?'

Greg nodded.

'Well,' said Angela, 'it's possible but...' She froze in mid-sentence.

'What is it?' asked Greg.

'Did you see the name of the witness? Gary Ridgway.'

'What of it?' said Greg. 'Does the name mean something to you?'

'OK, so the name Gary Ridgway means nothing to you?'

'It rings a bell.'

'As well it should, as he's one of America's most notorious serial killers active during the 80s and 90s.'

'OK, but in my defence, I should point out that he's already been caught, so I'm unlikely to find his file coming across my desk; he lived in America, so again his case is unlikely to concern me.'

'These sound more like excuses to me, but never mind; it's no surprise the name wasn't recognised. Plus, it could be a coincidence. Have you checked the address this guy gave?'

'I'll do it right now,' said Greg turning to his computer. 'Yes, it's a legitimate address in Leeds as the witness said.'

Angela moved round to look at Greg's monitor.

'I'll bet you as much money as you have in your pocket that there is no Gary Ridgway living at that address. 25, Cromwell Street was the address where Fred and Rosemary West raped and murdered their victims. Except their house was in Gloucester and it's since been demolished. We need to speak to the officer...'

'WPC Fraser,' said Greg. 'She's based in Rutherglen.'

'We need to speak to WPC Fraser as soon as we can. She could have been taking a statement from the serial killer and didn't know it.'

'Will we go to her or get her to come to us?'

'We'll drive through to speak to her. Give the station a ring, Greg, and find out when she's on duty.'

Ninety minutes later Greg and Angela were sitting in a small interview room with WPC Fraser.

'I remember him well,' said the young officer. 'He was very polite and sounded quite positive about what he was telling me. Then he flew into a temper when I tried to conclude the interview. I knew I had another person waiting, and what he was telling me didn't tie in with the guidance I had regarding the suspect. I know that mentioning the temper bit in my report makes me look bad. But I was told to record everything that happened during these interviews and that's what I did.'

'What's your first name, constable?' asked Angela.

'Wendy.'

'Well, Wendy, you did exactly the right thing. If you hadn't noted down the bit about the temper, it would have been easy to skip over the report.'

'And you think it might be significant?' asked WPC Fraser.

'It may be very significant,' said Angela, smiling. 'Now can you describe the man you spoke to?'

'He'd be about 5' 9" tall, medium build. I'd say late twenties or early thirties. White skinned, fair hair, a bit long, bushy side-burns, a moustache and thick-framed glasses. He was well dressed and politely spoken. From his accent I'd say he was probably from around this area.'

'Could the hair, sideburns and moustache have been false?' asked Angela.

'It's possible,' said Wendy, looking a bit confused. 'I didn't look at him all that closely, I was busy writing down what he was telling me.'

'Did he say what he had been doing in the area?' asked Greg.

'Yes, I asked him that. He said he lived in England but had been up here on business and had been visiting a contact at home as he didn't have time in his schedule to meet that person in an office.'

'Do you know where he was meeting the contact?'

'He said he had used his Satnav to find a postcode and wasn't sure of the street. He said the number was 10 and he thought the street was Rillington Street, or something like that. The address sounded familiar for some reason.'

Angela smiled. 'Did he say who the contact was that he was visiting?'

'He said he was visiting Jim Reginald.'

'Do you know much about serial killers, Wendy? I don't mean the current case, but historic killers?'

'Not really, no.'

'It's a pity,' said Angela. 'In July 1953, John Reginald Christie was hanged for killing four people, including his wife Ethel. He buried his victims at his house at 10 Rillington Place, London.'

'Oh,' said WPC Fraser. 'So, you don't think this man witnessed anything? He was just in here as a sick wind up?'

'No, it wasn't a sick wind up, Wendy. There's every chance you spoke to the killer we're all chasing.'

'So, I screwed up?'

'I wouldn't say that. Had you been more aware of serial killers you may have sussed what was going on, but he probably saw that you were a young officer and decided to take a chance. Don't feel bad about it; if you hadn't written your notes as thoroughly as you did, we wouldn't be having this conversation. What you've told us may well help us in breaking this case, although we still have a long way to go.'

'You were very soft with her,' said Greg when they were on their way back to Airdrie.

'Did you expect me to bawl her out because she failed to suss out the guy?'

'Well, yes, to be blunt. She sat and interviewed the killer. He gave her lots of clues and she didn't catch on.'

'I'll admit an older officer may have cottoned on to something not being right, but she feels bad enough without me shouting at her.'

'What makes you think she feels bad?'

'Her eyes, Greg. I saw it in her eyes. I thought you'd see that. Don't you always notice pretty young women's eyes? Or don't you go for women in uniform?'

Greg decided to ignore the hook. 'So, you think it was our guy?'

'I'm sure of it.'

'So, apart from the serial killer calmly walking into a police station and giving a statement, what do we know now that we didn't know before?'

'Well, you tell me Greg.'

'We know something about the guy's appearance, even although I think you're correct about the disguise. He sounds local. The psychologist seems to have it correct with the age and skin colour, and that's about it I think.'

'Oh no, Greg. We know something much more important than that. We know that the guy reads the papers and can be provoked. He was called a wimp and he's pulled this off to show that he isn't. If he can be provoked once, he can be provoked again, as long as we don't make it too obvious.'

'Are you hopeful we'll find out more about him?'

'You mean after examining the CCTV footage from the area around the station?'

'Yeah, that and possible fingerprints.'

Angela frowned. 'There's no doubt we'll have some footage of the guy walking to the station. That should enable us to confirm what Fraser said about his height and build. I'm pretty sure our guy will have made sure he parked his car somewhere well away from CCTV cameras, so we're unlikely to get lucky regarding the car he drove, assuming of course that he did use a car. WPC Fraser told us that he didn't have anything to drink during his interview and didn't touch anything such as a pen while he was in the station. He will have touched door handles, but so will lots of other people, so I'm not holding out any hope we'll get useful fingerprints. But, as I said, we've got to try. You never know. This bastard's got to make a mistake sometime.'

'Does it piss you off that he went to the station?'

'Funnily enough, not really. It shows that we can take some control back. That might be useful to know later.'

They arrived back at Airdrie and Angela was eager to speak to Russell, He was in transit to a meeting, but she managed to reach him on the phone while Greg reviewed the latest information from forensics on the serial killings.

'The Chief takes the same view as me regarding the witness. He reckons we have at last found a way to exert some sort of control over this guy. The question is, where do we go from here. Anything new?'

'Yes, replied Greg. 'I can't remember all the scientific mumbo-jumbo, but they now seem fairly sure our guy isn't a size eleven.'

'Well, that ties in with what WPC Fraser told us. I've sent an initial report on the guy's physical appearance to the central office and they'll pass it on to the officers who're checking through the funeral pictures. It might help them narrow down the search a bit. You're looking very thoughtful Greg.'

'I've got an idea,' said the DC slowly, 'but it might be a bit crazy to say nothing of expensive and time consuming.'

'OK, so you've given me three good reasons why we shouldn't do it before you've even given me a clue as to what your idea's all about. Not exactly the best way to approach a subject.'

'It's the shoes,' said Greg, 'they've all been different and they've all shown signs of wear. We're now fairly confident the guy doesn't take that size, so where did he get them? Even if he knows someone who takes that size, is that person likely to have half a dozen spare pairs to give away? And would the killer even ask for them?'

'Ok, Greg, that all makes sense to me. Now it's time for the crazy, expensive and time-consuming bits.'

'I reckon the most obvious place to pick up shoes like that are in charity shops, jumble sales and car boot sales,' Greg was becoming enthusiastic now. 'I'd rule out jumble sales and car boot sales as you don't find many of them held in winter. That leaves charity shops, and he may well be buying clothing from these places as well. Anyway, getting back to the shoes. I don't think our guy will have a supply of these sitting in his house. Too risky in case we're a bit smarter than he thinks we are and decide to raid his place. I reckon he buys them as he needs them. What if we ask all charity shops in a certain area to withdraw all size eleven shoes and boots from sale, apart from a few selected outlets? We could place some officers in these shops still stocking the large size to watch for anyone buying them and try and get some detail about the person. What do you think?'

'So, we ask all charity shops to withdraw these shoes from sale? Let's say there's half a dozen charity shops in every town and there are, at a guess, sixty or seventy towns, perhaps more in the Glasgow area. That means we have to contact almost five hundred shops and ask for their co-operation. We then have to place officers six days a week in the handful of shops we select and hope our guy wanders in looking for shoes. Is that your plan?'

'Pretty much, yes.' His initial enthusiasm was beginning to wane.

'You know, Greg, sometimes you can be quite brilliant. Come on! I'm going to see if I can gatecrash the meeting and have a quick word with the Chief.'

Fools! I'm surprised they manage to catch litterbugs, never mind murderers! You would think they would have learned something after the Yorkshire Ripper balls up. They've already decided exactly the type of person they're looking for and dismiss anything that doesn't fit their profile.

OK, I gave them a bogus description, but it really annoyed me that my information was rubbished out of hand. They really shouldn't do that. Especially as their profile will be based on false clues I left for them. Perhaps this journal will set them straight.

Chapter 30

'So, do we put it to a vote?' asked Roy.

'I don't think we need to,' said Brian. 'No one has come up with an alternative.'

Roy looked around the room and everyone nodded.

'Fine,' said Peter Turner, 'I'll phone the DS who came to see me.'

'We just need to decide how much to tell her,' said Roy.

Peter Turner looked at Elizabeth. 'We tell them everything,' she said. 'Everything except what we know about the accident that started this whole thing. We just say that we were trying to get information about it from you and Stewart and leave it at that.'

'Are you sure?' said Peter.

'Yes, I'm sure,' replied Elizabeth.

Peter Turner picked up the phone and dialled the number Angela had given him.

'Had you anything planned for today?' asked Angela.

'Not really,' said Greg.

'No. Me, neither. We're quite a sad pair when you come to think of it, aren't we? I mean, here we are on a Saturday, going to talk to people we could easily have put off until Monday. Have you come back to earth after Russell approved your plan?'

'Yes. At first, he looked at me as if he thought I was mad. Then he looked more thoughtful. He reckoned it would be possible to ask the headquarters of all the charity companies to contact their individual branches, so that wouldn't involve a lot of police time. He suggested we find which stores have CCTV and use them to stock the shoes. That would avoid the need to station officers in these shops.'

'So he's going to think about it?'

'Yes. He said he'd get back to me when he had a chance to consider it over the weekend.'

'Sounds promising.'

'Getting back to today's business, have you any idea what they want to tell us?' asked Greg.

'No. I said some days ago that all these people being together again after the accident of a decade ago isn't a coincidence. I reckon we're going to hear something useful.'

'To solve the Stewart case?'

'Perhaps not to solve it, but to give us a better idea where we should be looking.'

Greg parked as close as he could to Turner's house, and they walked round the corner and up the slight incline to the old wooden gate.

'Let them do most of the talking, Greg.'

Turner opened the door before they knocked and showed them into the lounge.

'I've just made some coffee,' said Peter, 'would you like some?'

They accepted and he went into the kitchen to prepare it.

'Before we start,' said Elizabeth, 'I want to apologise for what I said the last time I saw you. I wasn't quite myself then.'

'That's OK,' said Angela, 'you had been through a lot. How are you feeling now?'

'Much better, thanks.'

They continued to make small talk until Peter returned with the coffees.

'We've elected Brian as the main spokesperson,' said Peter.

'Whenever you're ready Mr Reid, we'll try not to interrupt until you've finished.'

Brian thought for a moment, and then started to talk. 'Elizabeth and myself have never really got over what happened years ago. We both tried to forget about it, but...well, I suppose it wouldn't be too strong to say that I became obsessed with some aspects of the accident. When Roy started working at my company that set things off again. So, we decided to try and find out if we could shed new light on what happened. Just to satisfy ourselves and to try and help us move on.'

Angela and Greg both nodded.

'Elizabeth and I first spoke to an old neighbour called Betty White. She had been at the scene of the accident on that day. Unfortunately, she couldn't add anything to what we already knew. I had become friendly with Roy, and he introduced me to his dad. I didn't mention to Roy who I was as I didn't know what he knew about that event years ago. I then spoke to Peter alone, but he couldn't help me, so I then spoke to Chief Inspector Stewart. I knew there had been another person in the police car that killed our dad, but I didn't know who he was. Elizabeth and I went back to see Betty White and we found out that she was dead. She had apparently fallen down the stairs and broken her neck, but after speaking to a neighbour of hers we thought her death was a bit suspicious. Roy found out who I was and that I had spoken to his dad. He wasn't very happy and thought that reopening old wounds was affecting his dad's health. This was probably true, as Peter had had another heart attack and was in hospital. The following evening, a brick was thrown through my window. I called the police and reported the incident, but what I didn't tell them was that a note was attached to the brick. This note.'

Brian took the piece of paper from his pocket and handed it to Angela. She opened it, read it, and then passed it to Greg.

'I had a bit of an argument with Elizabeth and she told me she was heading down south to where she lived. On the way down, she was going to drop in and see Terry and Pamela Scott. Elizabeth had found out at Betty White's funeral that Terry might know something about the accident. Elizabeth spoke to them, but again they couldn't tell her anything useful. Instead of going back home, Elizabeth met up with Roy, without Roy knowing who she was. I had no idea this was going on. Anyway, a week or so later there was a fire in the Scott's house. The family survived, but the fire was treated as suspicious. The next thing was the crash in which Elizabeth's brakes failed or were tampered with. Then while Elizabeth was in hospital, Stewart was murdered. And that's about it.'

Angela took a drink of her coffee and leaned back in her chair. 'From the way you've told us the story, I assume you believe all these incidents are linked in some way?' said Angela.

'Yes,' said Brian.

'Why should they be linked?' asked Angela. 'What do you think it is that someone is trying to prevent you finding out?'

'I've no idea,' said Brian. 'I don't even know if it has anything to do with the accident of years ago. But there's one other thing that's very important. Before Betty White's death, a neighbour of hers had seen a gasman leave Betty's house. It was clear that this description didn't fit Stewart or anyone else we knew. The neighbour, Derek Nelson, agreed to come with us to the Stewart funeral. Peter recognised Steve Collins, the witness he and Stewart had in their car on the day of the accident, and pointed him out to us by asking him for a light. Collins didn't have a light, but his companion did, and Nelson was sure he was the gas man he had seen at Betty's house.'

All eyes turned to Angela.

'I can understand why you've reached the conclusions you have,' she said, 'but your assumptions may be baseless. Assuming the fire and your sister's car crash weren't accidents, I'm looking for a motive in all this. OK, Brian and Elizabeth were digging around trying to find out anything they could about the accident involving the police car years ago. So? Why would someone want to stop that? And not just want to stop it, but to go to the lengths of killing people?' She sat back in her chair shaking her head. 'You two would have to be making real pains in the arses of yourselves to get someone so pissed off. And even then, why target the people you were speaking to? Why not target the pair of you?'

'But my accident,' said Elizabeth, 'wasn't that someone trying to stop me digging around?'

'OK,' said Angela, 'I'll give you that one.'

Greg was obviously keen to join in, so Angela gestured for him to speak.

'Let's assume, for the moment, that the incidents are related,' he said. 'I've also been trying to think of a motive. What did someone think the White woman and the Scott's would have to tell you that would be so damaging to them that it provoked such extreme action? I just don't get it.'

'So, you're not going to do anything?' asked Peter Turner.

'I wouldn't say that,' said Angela. 'You've voiced your concerns regarding serious incidents. But, as far as we know, the fire at the Scott's house and Elizabeth's crash are already being treated as suspicious. We can report your concerns about the death of Betty White and ask for that to be revisited. The witness you've told us about, the chap called Nelson, we can certainly speak to him and then talk to the guy who was with Collins at the Stewart funeral. But as for linking these crimes together, it's all a bit circumstantial. Unless there's something else you haven't told us?'

Angela looked at Greg and he took her cue. 'I agree. I still don't see a possible motive for such drastic action.'

'How about if I tell you that Stewart, and not me, was driving at the time of the police car accident, and that he was drunk? '

Brian tried to interrupt, but Turner carried on. 'And that after the accident, Collins, who as Brian, said was in the car, had Stewart in his back pocket and continually got the heads up when police raids were planned on the premises he was employed to guard. Would any of that give you a motive?'

'Don't listen to him!' said Brian, 'he doesn't know what he's talking about! He's just trying to make a case for this business to be investigated.'

'Yeah,' added Elizabeth, 'he's been under a lot of stress lately.'

'Mr Turner,' said Angela when the others had stopped blustering. 'What you've told us is very serious and alarming. You're saying that a serious incident from many years ago was covered up by a senior officer. In addition, the same officer seriously hampered numerous police investigations into other serious crimes.'

'Yes,' said Peter quietly, 'that's exactly what I'm telling you.'

'And you're not just telling us this story to persuade us to investigate the recent incidents?'

'No,' said Peter. 'If you prefer, I can go along to a station and make a formal statement.'

'What you've told us could be the missing piece of the jigsaw,' said Angela thoughtfully.

Peter Turner sat back in his chair with his eyes closed while Brian and Roy started pacing around the room. Elizabeth sat with her hand on her brow.

'Are you feeling all right, Mr Turner?' asked Greg.

'I haven't felt better in a long time,' answered the ex-policeman, the relief evident in his voice.

Angela nodded. 'Well folks, I reckon that's it, unless there's anything else you want to tell us?'

No one said anything, so Angela continued. 'We'll take this note and check it out.'

'So what do you think?' said Greg when he and Angela had left the house and were back in their car.

'We now have a possible motive for Stewart being killed. Remember, the Reid's started to dig around while Robbie Stewart was alive. We know that Stewart knew they were digging, and he knew what they were digging for, assuming we believe Peter. If Robbie Stewart told Steve Collins about the Reid's doing a bit of snooping, Collins may well have been concerned about his hold over Stewart being discovered. Stewart won't have been going about setting fires and throwing bricks through windows, but some of Collins' cronies could have been involved.' She took the note Brian had given her out of her pocket. 'We'll check this out, but I'm pretty sure it's not Stewart's handwriting.'

'But why would Collins kill Stewart?' asked Greg. 'After all he'd done for Collins?'

'Killing the goose that laid the golden egg, you mean?'

'Yes.'

'Well, Stewart had retired. Perhaps he was no longer of use, or certainly his use would have been limited. The Reids seemed to be finding people who they thought could help them, but Stewart, and to a lesser extent Turner, were the two people who could confirm everything.'

'But say that Stewart had admitted what he'd been doing,' said Greg. 'How would that affect Collins?'

'Do you realise how much shit would be stirred if Stewart admitted his part in the accident? There'd be all sorts of investigations. His involvement with Collins would almost certainly come out. Then the digging into Collins background and activities would really step up a gear. Collins is likely to have big associates. How would they feel about a thorough investigation into Collins? It'd be like a rock thrown into a pool, God knows how far the ripples would travel and who they would affect. No. I reckon it's possible Collins decided to cut his losses.'

'But why not get rid of the Reids? Why Stewart?'

'Well, there appears to have been an attempt on Elizabeth, although I think that was a case of mistaken identity. Remember that Stewart noted down the registration number, but Brian Reid had been driving the car that day. I reckon Stewart was the more obvious target as he is one of the people who could confirm everything.'

'This is a real can of worms,' said Greg, shaking his head.

'It certainly is, but I'm going to get to the bottom of it one way or another. I hate anything to do with drugs!'

'I hope you're not going to turn this into a personal vendetta, Angela?'

'I don't know what you mean?'

'Yes, you do. Your former partner, John Harrison. I hope you don't see this as a way to avenge what happened to him?'

Angela didn't reply and Greg didn't push it.

'There's a report on your desk you might be interested in,' said another detective when Angela and Greg arrived at Airdrie Police Station on the following Monday morning.

'What is it?' asked Angela, but the officer just shrugged and wandered off.

She sat down at her desk and opened the manila envelope.

'What do you think about this?' she said, handing the report to Greg when he arrived with their obligatory morning coffee.

'Burglary,' he said reading the heading, 'what's that got to do with us?'

'Read on,' said Angela.

'Oh.'

'Yes, oh. Grab your coat Greg. We're going to check this out.'

A uniformed officer was on duty outside the Stewart house when Angela and Greg arrived. They identified themselves and went into the building.

'So, Mrs Stewart's not at home?' asked Greg.

'No, she's down at her son's place, but she'll be on her way back up by now.'

'Shouldn't we wait on her? She'll have a better idea if anything's missing.'

'True, but I'm not really interested in what's missing. I'm more interested in where the burglar's been searching.'

They went into the lounge. The furniture was exactly as they remembered it, but the drawers in a display cabinet were open, and various items lay around on the floor.

'Greg, you have a look upstairs.'

Greg went to do as he was asked, and Angela walked into Stewart's study. His bookshelves were empty, the books being scattered around on the floor. The drawers had been removed from his desk and their contents also strewn around the floor.

'It doesn't look as if they went upstairs,' said Greg arriving to join her. 'Jeez, they've certainly made a mess of this place.'

'Do you notice anything missing, Greg?'

'Yes, the computer.' Greg pointed to the space on the desk where the computer had sat.

'But they've left the monitor,' said Angela. 'They've also left a couple of watches, including one which looks to be gold. Does that suggest anything to you Greg?'

'Yes, they came looking for the computer, and it wasn't any ordinary burglary.'

'Exactly. We'll know more when Maureen Stewart has had a chance to assess things for herself, but I'd guess the thief got what he was looking for. Or at least he thinks he did.'

'The recipe book?'

'Spot on again Greg. Anyway, I have a devious little plan hatching in my brain. Did you ask for updates on the Scott house fire and Elizabeth's car accident when you came in this morning?'

'I did, and I was promised that I'd have the info by lunchtime.'

As promised, Greg had the information he'd been seeking by 1pm.

'We're no further forward on Elizabeth's accident. There were no witnesses and we have no suspects. The Scott fire is being treated as arson. A gas pipe had been fractured, but the fire started before the gas could build up to result in an explosion. It seems to have been quite a freak set of circumstances, but lucky for the Scotts, if you consider having your house burned down as lucky. Again, no witnesses and no suspects. I also checked into the Betty White death, but there was nothing to suggest foul play.'

'I need to run something by you Greg. Don't jump in and protest until I've finished.'

'I'm not sure I like the sound of this,' said Greg, 'but try me anyway.'

'Not here, Greg, let's go out for lunch.'

Lunch consisted of the usual fast-food takeaway eaten in the car. Angela waited until they had finished eating before she started explaining her thoughts to Greg.

'Let's start off by assuming Brian Reid's correct. Stewart got the wind up, told Collins, and Collins decided to get rid of Brian's informants. Stewart was then killed, for reasons as yet unknown, and shortly after his house was broken into by someone looking for something. They took his computer, and by this time have probably searched through it. Unless some of the stuff means more to them than it does to us, they'll have found very little. But what would they be looking for? We have the recipe book which seems to tell us quite a bit about Stewart's dealings with, we assume, Steve Collins. Does Collins know that Stewart kept a form of records of their dealings? I surmise that he did. Probably Stewart told him this as a form of insurance policy. So, they won't have found this. They won't know that it definitely exists, and they wouldn't know that it was kept in his house. He could have lodged it with his bank or his lawyers. They may suspect that Stewart has recorded their dealings in great detail, but as we know, he didn't. I suspect that Stewart's recipe book was no more than a form of diary, or a bookkeeping record. Anyone finding it wouldn't have a clue what it was all about. He did it this way to ensure that if anything happened to him, there wouldn't be major repercussions that would affect his wife. How does all that sound to you?'

'Pretty reasonable,' said Greg, 'there's nothing in what you've said that would have me protesting, but I expect that bit's still to come.'

'Spot on again Greg. Put yourself in Steve Collin's place for the moment. You're sitting in your office, and you get a phone call, or even better, an email. This message says something along the lines of, I've got Stewart's book and you can have it for X amount of money. What would you do?'

'I'd be tempted to pay out if the book is genuine.'

'OK, let's confirm that it's genuine by including brief details, say a few dates and payments.'

'Then I'd arrange to meet whoever had the book and pay to get it. So, you're suggesting we send Collins an email and set him up?'

'No. That would be viewed as a sting operation. Anyway, I think he'd be suspicious of a stranger making contact. I reckon it would have to be someone he suspects might know the relevance of what the book contains. Someone like Peter Turner, for example.'

'You don't mean Peter Turner *for example*, you mean Peter Turner *full stop*. This is crazy! There's no way we can get a member of the public wrapped up in this, even if he is an ex-policeman. It's totally irresponsible.'

'If you listen to my colleagues, *totally irresponsible's* my middle names. It's a good plan, Greg.'

'Oh yes, it sounds great, but you've overlooked one small point. What's to stop Turner having made copies of the book before handing it over? Collins may have arranged for the murder of two people and the attempted murder of others - do you think he would draw the line at Turner?'

'I never said the plan didn't have risks.'

'Didn't have risks! I thought you didn't watch movies? This is straight out of one, and the kind of one that ends up in a very messy and nasty ending. If Turner got injured or killed, do you think our Boss would pat us on the back and say never mind guys, you tried your best?'

'So, you're not too keen on my plan?'

'It's a good plan, for a movie.' Greg gave an exasperated sigh. He thought for a few moments and then continued in a rather resigned tone of voice. 'We're out of our depth. We should take this higher up.'

'O.K, Greg, perhaps you're right. Let's get back to the station. I'll think about it a bit more then decide whether to take it to the Boss.'

Greg breathed a sigh of relief and started the car.

On the journey back Angela turned over in her head what Greg had said. She had already made up her mind, even though she'd told Greg she would think it over. This plan wasn't going to the Boss. Her instincts told her that Peter, Roy, Brian and Elizabeth would do something about Collins. It would be very rash and ill advised, but people did that sort of thing when family members were threatened. Taking her plan to the Boss might have two outcomes. It might be ruled out completely, or it might be given further consideration. In either of these two scenarios, time would be a factor. And Angela didn't reckon that they had time on their hands. Her big problem was Greg. He felt they were out of their depth, and he could be correct. There was no way she could order him to go along with her plan, and if she told him she was going ahead with it, she didn't rule out him reporting this to the Boss. She glanced at him as he concentrated on his driving. He looked very young, very inexperienced. She felt that if she really wanted his help, he would give it to her. But blowing her career was one thing, blowing his was quite a different matter. No, she was on her own with this one.

Angela spent most of Sunday morning thinking. She now had her own car back after the clutch repair, so she didn't need Greg to pick her up anymore, but she hadn't told him that.

'Mr Turner? It's Angela Porter here. I'm sorry to bother you again, especially on a Sunday, but I was wondering if I might have another word with you? It's not official, in fact it's very unofficial.'

She drove through to Glenmavis and took Stewart's diary with her.

'I didn't know if you just wanted to speak to me or all of us together,' said Peter. 'I can get the others to come round if that's what you want?'

'No, it was you I wanted to speak to. After we have our talk you can choose to tell the others or not, that's up to you.'

Peter made some coffee and sat a cup down in front of her.

'I'm not sure whether to expect an official visit sometime soon,' he said, 'but I did get the impression this wouldn't be in the near future.'

'As far as I'm concerned,' said Angela, 'it won't be at all.'

'And does your young DC share that view?'

'To be perfectly honest, no, he doesn't. But he won't do anything without telling me first.'

'He struck me as a very honest copper,' said Peter, 'not that you don't. But you strike me as being...well, how shall I put it? Yes, more worldly. Robbie Stewart is dead, and for all I know I might not be far behind him. I think you've weighed up the effect that dragging us through the mud would have on the living, and I don't think you like the look of how that balances out.'

'But at the same time, a crime is a crime, Mr Turner. And a policeman committing a crime is more of a crime in my book.'

'I agree completely, but I reckon your superiors will be more... again, how shall I put it...yes, politically aware.'

Angela laughed. 'If you're saying that I'm not politically aware, then you've got me there. I know they may well be reluctant to expose the Force to ridicule. I've no doubt they'd somehow manage to put a positive spin on it.'

'No doubt, Detective Sergeant, but I don't think that's the reason for your visit today.'

'Please call me Angela, and yes, you're right. I came here to ask if you're willing to help me trap Steve Collins?'

Turner took a deep breath. 'Would I be correct in assuming this would have nothing to do with official police business?'

'That'd be correct.'

'And am I correct in assuming your plan might even border on being illegal?'

'Correct again.'

'And no doubt there would be an element of danger involved?'

'I'm fairly sure that would be the case, yes.'

'So why do it?'

'What do you mean?'

'My question's simple. Why would a young officer risk her career and put herself in danger rather than use official means to catch a bad guy?'

'Because official means might take some time, and I suspect other people might get hurt during the wait. Perhaps even Mr Collins himself, not that I'm in any way upset at that thought.'

'I see.' Peter Turner looked at her carefully, and then glanced at the book she had sitting on her lap.

'And where does the strawberry flan enter your plan?'

Angela opened the book. 'This is a book we found in Robbie Stewart's house. We're pretty sure it contains details of payments made to him as rewards for information he passed on about raids on the warehouses. Stewart's house was burgled, and his computer stolen, but I think this is what the burglars were after.'

'So, what do you intend to do with it?'

'I want you to offer to sell it to Steve Collins.'

Chapter 31

'We are hoping later today to be able to confirm that the various charity outlets are going to assist us. The branches with CCTV will continue to stock the footwear. This may seem like a shot in the dark, but I view it as being proactive rather than reactive. Thank you.' Russell concluded his brief statement.

'Well done Greg,' said Angela quietly.

Greg didn't reply, but there was no doubt how he felt. He hadn't been mentioned by name as the originator of the plan, but that didn't matter. The people who mattered would know where the idea came from, but more importantly, Angela knew.

They walked back to their desks, collected their things and set off once again for Motherwell, having confirmed that Maureen Stewart was back home.

'So, you're fairly sure nothing of value is missing, Mrs Stewart, apart from the computer.'

'Yes. I've tidied up and I can't think of anything else. I seem to have been quite lucky. I imagine whoever broke in must have been disturbed. I have a fair bit of cash in a drawer upstairs, money my husband kept around for minor emergencies. We tried not to touch our bank account if we could avoid it, and fortunately my husband was paid in cash for the work he did. Oh, he did tell the tax people in case you think we've been dishonest.'

Angela smiled at Maureen Stewart's openness.

'Have you any idea who did this?' asked the old lady.

'I'm afraid not,' said Angela, 'we think it likely someone knew you were away from home and took the opportunity to break in. I very much doubt if they'll come back.'

Maureen Stewart didn't look convinced. 'I don't know,' she said, 'I really don't know if I feel comfortable living here. It might have been all right if Robbie was here, but now...'

She looked around the room and Angela suddenly felt really sorry for her. She wanted to tell Mrs Stewart that everything would be fine, that they had a prime suspect for her husband's murder, and that the same person broke into her house. She also wanted to tell her that this person would soon be in jail, but she couldn't. As she tried to console the woman, Angela mentally added another to her list of reasons as to why Collins should be put away.

Peter Turner sat staring at his computer screen. The small cursor blinked innocently, waiting on him taking some action. But he just sat and stared at the screen. The brief message announced Collin's agreement to meet with him. There was no mention of the book or the price. To a casual observer, the message could be anything, old friends meeting up, business associates getting together, even relatives planning a chat over coffee. But to Peter Turner it meant possibly putting an end to the waking nightmare he had been going through for over ten years. He stared at the screen for another few minutes, and then switched on his small printer. After it booted up, he told it to print two copies of the message. After some whirring and clicking, two sheets of paper were fed through the machine. He reached down to retrieve them and read the short message again. The email had been sent as a separate message; it had not been sent as a reply to the one he sent to the address provided by Angela. It simply stated – *re your suggested meeting, venue and time suits fine, see you there.* And that was all, no names either at the start or finish. Well, he told himself, you've done it now! That one-line message told him that there was no going back. His first instinct was to tell Roy, Brian and Elizabeth. Instead, he reached for his phone and dialled Angela's number.

'He's agreed,' was all he said when she answered.

'Greg,' said Angela, 'I'm going to take a day off tomorrow.'

'Why?' asked the younger detective.

'I've some family business I need to take care of.'

Greg almost said, *'you've got a family?'* but stopped himself just in time.

'Don't look at me like that,' she said.

'Like what?'

'As if I've just eaten the last veggie burger that exists on the planet.'

'It's just...well, you've never taken a day off since I've been working with you.'

'Greg, I've only worked with you for a few months. You say that as if I've just buggered up my chances of a long service medal. It's one day. You'll be fine. And you can drive about at your snail's pace without me nagging you. You can eat anything and anytime you want, you don't need to go out of your way to pick me up and you can organise your desk the way you like it and not have me throwing files and bits of paper all over it just to mess it up.'

'Do you do that?'

'Yes, sometimes, just for fun. Anyway, I won't be in tomorrow, you can solve a couple of cases all on your own.'

'I hope it's nothing serious?'

Angela looked at her partner and realised he was really quite concerned.

'It's no big deal, I just need to attend to a few things. I need to see a lawyer about something really boring and I can't see him at the weekend, so I've made an appointment for tomorrow. Nothing to worry about.'

'I'm not being nosey; it's just that you're so involved in the Stewart case, it's not like you...'

'Greg, whatever else we may think about what we do, you need to remember that this is only a job. When we walk out of these doors at night, the job's over for the day.'

Greg nodded, but now he was really worried. If the business Angela had to attend to resulted in her referring to what they were working on as *only a job,* then her business was a lot more serious than she was making out.

There had been a number of questions regarding the charity shop plan at the evening briefing. All these staff had been instructed not to talk about the operation at home or with friends. The Chief realised that this was placing a lot of faith in members of the public, but he had little option but to trust these people. He betrayed signs of the stress everyone was working under by becoming a bit aggressive with one officer who asked if he had thought about the possibility of the killer actually working in a charity shop. It was clear that many officers had reservations about the plan, and when the meeting broke up there were more mutterings than normal.

As soon as Greg had dropped her off at her home, Angela got changed, and then set off for Peter Turner's house in her car.

'Are you sure your son won't drop in?' she asked the ex-policeman.

'No, he's working late tonight, and his normal drop-in day is a Wednesday.'

'Well, hopefully it'll be all over by then and you'll be able to give him some good news.'

Peter gave her a copy of the email message which she read, then put it in her pocket.

'I think he'll expect there to be more information in the book than I've told him,' said Peter,

'I'm sure he will,' said Angela, 'but there's nothing we can do about that. At least listing some of the dates and sums in your email to Collins appear to have convinced him that you do have something he wants. He'll probably just check to see that you're not handing him any old rubbish. How're you feeling about to-morrow?'

'Well, it's too late to go back now, which is maybe just as well. Do you think he'll suspect that he's being set up?'

'I really don't know,' confessed Angela. 'If it was a complete stranger who had contacted him, then I'd imagine he would. But he knows you. I'm assuming he'll think that Stewart kept you pretty well informed as to what he was up to. You just need to stress to him that what you really want is for you, your son and friends to be left alone. My guess is that Collins has taken the action he has out of desperation rather than a desire to hurt people.'

'I hope you're right.'

'OK.' Angela took a pen out of her pocket. 'Have you seen anything like this before?'

'It looks like a pen.'

'It is, and it even writes, but it's a video camera which gives one hour of recording from a full charge. It has a USB connection so that the video and audio can be downloaded into a computer.'

Peter took it from her. 'Very clever. So, I just clip this into my pocket and forget about it?'

'As long as you remember to switch it on, yes, that's all you have to do.'

'I assume you borrowed this from the station?'

'No. I bought it mail order through play.com. I've made sure that it's fully charged, and I don't reckon your meeting with Collins will take very long, but it's important you get him to say something about Stewart and any of the others. Have you worked out what you're going to say?'

'Yeah, I've been going over it in my mind. I just hope I don't make it too obvious.'

'OK. Now remember, I'll be there before you're due to arrive and I'll keep an eye on you throughout your meeting with Collins. If I see anything I'm not happy about I'll jump in. So, don't worry, there's no way Collins would try to harm you in public. As soon as I see your meeting breaking up, I'll follow you back to your car and then back here. We'll download what the camera has picked up, then see what we've got.'

'Will the video be admissible in court?'

'Even if we couldn't use the recording in court, we'll have information that will allow us to investigate specific events.'

Peter Turner double-checked everything again. He had the book, the pen, his phone and his car keys. He checked his watch. 10.15. That gave him plenty of time to get into town and to get parked. Fortunately, it was dry outside, although still cold. But he knew the Robert Hamilton had patio style heaters, so he would be able to sit outside where it was very public. Angela planned to watch him from the British Heart Foundation shop across the road.

He checked his jacket pockets for the last time and opened his front door.

'Hello Peter. I thought it might be better to meet somewhere a bit more private.'

Before he could react, Collins and a friend had pushed him back inside his house and closed the door.

'Ah, this'll be the book,' said Collins taking the recipe book from Peter. Collin's companion pushed the ex-policeman down into a seat.

'Now let's see,' said Collins opening the book.

Peter watched as Collins flicked through the pages. He stopped now and again to read some bits and pieces. The other man watched Peter intently as they both waited.

'Not quite as detailed as you suggested,' said Collins still browsing, 'but interesting all the same.'

He closed the book. 'Now, where have you put the copies?'

'I haven't made copies,' said Peter, 'I just want to get rid of the thing.'

'I see,' said Collins. 'You asked for quite a lot of money for this book, and it occurred to me that you might want more money at some point in the future.'

Peter shook his head while Collins stared at him.

'You're not looking very well, Peter. Would you like a glass of water?'

'I've got a heart problem,' said Peter, 'perhaps I need to take a pill.'

'OK,' said Collins. He looked at his companion. 'Go get Mr Turner a glass of water.'

Collin's companion nodded and went looking for the kitchen. Peter reached into his top jacket pocket and pulled out a small section of bubble wrap containing two pills. As he did this, he caught the pen with his hand, and it fell onto the floor.

Collins bent to pick it up. He glanced at it, clicked it a few times, and then handed it back to Turner.

Peter carefully returned it to his top pocket just as Collin's companion returned with a glass of water. He handed it to the ex-policeman who had taken one pill out of its housing. He put the pill in his mouth and took a drink of water.

Collins opened the book again and flicked through some pages. 'I recognise the handwriting as belonging to the late chief inspector, but I wonder just what someone would make of the entries? They don't really tell the reader very much, do they?'

Collins looked at the rear cover of the book. 'I'll tell you what I'll do, Peter. The sticker tells me that the book cost £13.99.' He put his hand in his pocket. 'I'll give you twenty quid for it, which is pretty generous as it's second hand and someone has written all over it.' He burst out laughing.

'How does that sound to you?'

'The money's not important, I just want you to stop hurting my friends.'

Collins put on a surprised look. 'I've never hurt anyone, Peter. I'm sure if you cared to supply me with dates and times, I could convince you that I was nowhere near where these incidents took place.'

'You know what I mean,' said Peter, 'I'm not stupid.'

'Yes, I know you're not. But I'm a businessman. And business is good. I had a working relationship with the late Mr Stewart, a very profitable one for both of us, and I couldn't allow that relationship to be put in danger.'

'So, you killed Betty White and set fire to the Scott's house?'

'No, I didn't. It was your friends who caused these regrettable incidents – Brian and Elizabeth Reid. I'm surprised you didn't take steps to stop them, bearing in mind your involvement in their father's accident. I did you a favour.'

'You haven't done anything for me,' said Peter bitterly, 'don't try and turn this on its head and pretend you're the wronged party. You did what you could to protect Stewart, and in turn, protect your arrangement.'

Collins nodded. 'Yes, that was my primary concern, I'll admit it. But you can't tell me that you didn't benefit. That would be hypocritical. All these years of keeping quiet, then all of a sudden it looks as if your big secret might be about to come out because two people couldn't let bygones be bygones. I don't understand this revenge thing at all. And where has it got them?'

'They know what happened,' said Peter softly.

'So, you told them?' said Collins. 'Are they going to get you hauled off to jail?'

Peter shook his head.

'No?' said Collins, 'so where does that leave them? I don't understand it at all.'

Angela checked her watch. The shop assistant eyed her suspiciously as Angela picked up a copy of *Gardening for Beginners* for the fourth time and flicked through it without even as much as a glance at what was written on the pages. Something had gone wrong. She could understand one of them being late, but not both. Putting the book down, she hurried out of the shop. It crossed her mind to phone Turner, but she decided against it. If he had been held up for any reason he would have phoned her. If he didn't phone it was because he couldn't, and that thought worried her. She covered the remaining fifty yards to her car at a jogging pace and set off for Glenmavis.

Within ten minutes she had entered the village, and she slowed down partly due to the narrow roads, and partly to have a look around. Peter's car was parked outside his house. She drove slowly down the slight incline and round the sharp right-hand corner. Parked thirty yards from the corner was a familiar black Mercedes with the driver sitting in the car. She drove past and continued along the road. When she reached the main road through the village, she accelerated past the small group of shops and up the hill to the church on the corner. Taking a right and then another right she was heading back down towards Turner's house. She managed to find a parking place, switched off the engine and got out. As she walked quickly down the hill towards the ex-policeman's house, she tried to recall the layout of his home. She knew the kitchen was at the back of the house, but she had no idea if he was likely to have left this door unlocked. Fumbling in her pocket, she was relieved to find she still had the small tool she had used to open the Yale lock on Maureen Stewart's door. The rows of terraced houses were separated by communal closes, and she quickly made her way through the one adjoining Turner's place. The back door was solid and had no glass panels to allow a view inside. She unlocked the door and inched it open very slowly. As the door opened enough to allow her to enter, she could hear voices coming from the lounge. She stepped forward as quietly as she could and strained to identify the voices she could hear. Then, with a sickening thud, something struck her on the back of the head, the floor rushed up to meet her, and then nothing.

Why did people make so much noise when she was trying to sleep? Why did the room keep on moving? Why was someone trying to steal her jacket? Why was this bed so uncomfortable?

'She's a cop,' said Collin's companion, as he handed his boss the warrant card he had removed from Angela's jacket pocket.

'Ah. We now have a problem Peter.'

Peter Turner opened his mouth to say something, then realised it would be a waste of time.

'You'll have to believe me when I tell you that I regret what I'm going to have to do. Until your detective friend arrived, I was going to take the book and leave. It would all have been over, but now, well, this complicates things quite a bit. However, I need to put business first, so here's my plan, and feel free to point out any flaws you may find in it. You and Stewart made an arrangement years ago after the tragic accident. This worked fine until the Reids started to stir things up. To make matters worse, the police investigating a house fire and a near fatal car crash began to ask you questions. It reached the stage where this young lady detective had almost worked everything out. She came here today to question you again, and you realised that the game was up. In desperation, you knocked her out and set fire to the house. You left her here and went off planning your suicide. You didn't fancy dying in a fire and wanted to go out less painfully. A bit melodramatic perhaps, but the best I can come up with at short notice. How does that sound?'

'And what about her?' said Peter nodding towards Angela.

'That's really up to her. If she wakes up and manages to get out of the house, then good on her. She doesn't know who hit her, and I'd imagine she'll think it was you.'

'So, you want me to stick my head in an oven or something?'

'That's one detail I haven't worked out yet, so I'm afraid you'll have to come with us until I do.'

'You want me to calmly walk out of here with you knowing what you plan to do with me?'

'Yes. If you want your son to be safe. I'll promise you that if you come with us, I'll leave your son alone.'

'Why should I believe you?'

'And why should I want to risk more than I have already by having one more person killed? I suppose the bottom line is that if you don't agree to come with us, we can knock you out and leave you here with her and then go after your son. If you do as I want, your son will be safe. It's up to you.'

'So, I'm planning to commit suicide, but I don't think to leave a note for my son?'

'I imagine not everyone leaves a note.'

'I'll write you a note now. If you promise not to harm my son, or the Reids, and let the policewoman go.'

'I'm afraid not. The woman cop will have to take her chances in the fire. As for the others, well...'

'Won't a note make my suicide more convincing?'

Collins looked at Turner, trying to work out if the ex-policeman was up to something.

'OK,' he said eventually, 'write it now.'

Turner walked slowly over to his computer and took a sheet of paper out of the printer. He took the pen out of his pocket and wrote a short note, then handed it to Collins.

'No,' said Collins, 'it wouldn't do for my fingerprints to be on it, just put it on the table.'

Turner placed the note and pen on the table and Collins leaned over to read it. Satisfied, he straightened up. 'Now we wouldn't want that to get destroyed in the fire, so I think we should leave it outside." Turner picked up the pen and paper,

"OK, have you got your car keys?'

'Why?'

'Because you're going to follow us. It'd be a funny suicide if you were found miles away and your car was parked outside your door. Now let's go out the back. Bill start the fire in the lounge.'

'What'll I use?' asked Bill.

'Use your initiative, there must be something flammable kicking about.'

Bill rummaged about in the kitchen, and found some paint stripper which he took into the lounge and started to splash around on the carpet and chairs. He then lit a match and dropped this onto the floor. Satisfied that the fire had caught, he walked back into the kitchen to where Collins and Turner were waiting by the back door. They left, closing the door behind them, and indicated that Turner should put the note on the path.

'Put that brick on top of it in case it blows away,' said Collins.

Peter did as he was asked and placed the note and pen on the ground, and then placed the brick on top of the piece of paper.

'We're heading to Chapelhall, Bill will go with you in case you get lost.'

Collins walked round to his Mercedes where his driver was waiting on him.

'OK John,' he said as he got into the car, 'Let's go back to the office, and keep an eye in your mirror to check that Bill and Turner are still behind us.'

Inside the house, the fire had spread to the chairs and other furniture. Folds of thick black smoke rolled along the ceiling. The wooden furniture crackled and sparked angrily as the flames crept towards the kitchen where Angela was lying semi-conscious. The fire paused when it reached the stone kitchen floor, but the flames leapt up the doorjambs and prepared to make the jump to the ceiling. The wood fittings continued to crackle as the varnish bubbled and spat. Ugly black drops of molten plastic started to drip onto the floor where they burned briefly adding more acrid smoke to the billowing mass.

The last thought Angela remembered having before she lapsed into another bout of unconsciousness was that she was going to die.

Then she opened her eyes and saw Greg. She blinked as she tried to focus and wondered what was pressing on her face. She reached up a shaky hand to touch the oxygen mask, but Greg gently moved it back to her side. 'You're going to be fine,' he said. She felt herself rising into the air and floating past the side of the building. Strange aliens wearing brightly coloured clothing waddled past. Everywhere there was a hissing noise. Blue lights bounced off the walls as she passed, still floating with Greg at her side. She tried again to lift a hand but couldn't as someone was holding it. She felt that she was burning up, every part of her body felt as if it was on fire, everywhere except her nose and mouth where the cool oxygen washed over it. For a brief moment she felt that she was going downhill, and then she levelled out again. Suddenly there was a clanking noise, and a white blanket replaced the sky. No, it wasn't a blanket, it was shiny and smooth. Then she was moving. Not the jerky movements of before, but a smoother movement. Hands seemed to be all over her. A face she didn't know leaned over and shone an annoying light in her eyes. She felt a slight prick in her arm and tried to look to see what was going on, but the leaning figure gently turned her head to look straight up, then the light was shining in her eyes again. She could feel something tight across her legs and chest. Not uncomfortably tight, just enough to stop her moving. As if she would want to! No, she just wanted everyone to go away and let her sleep. She glanced to the side and saw Greg. He was sitting very close to her and looked to be very sad. She wondered why he was sad but decided she should sleep. She could ask him later. She wanted to push her hair back out of her eyes, but just as the thought came into her head, someone did it for her. She tried to say thanks, but her voice didn't seem to be working.

Chapter 32

'Listen, I've told you I'm fine, so why don't you all fuck off and leave me alone! I'm leaving right now! If I need to sign something, give me it and I'll sign it, but I'm going out that fuckin' door right now!'

'I think she's feeling better,' said DS McLean.

'I'd say so,' agreed Greg.

'And you work with her?' asked the DS.

Greg nodded in the affirmative.

'Oh, I bet that's *loads* of fun,' said the grinning McLean. 'How're you feeling?'

'So, help me Greg, if you ask me that once more I'll kill you. I feel fine except for a thumping sore head, a smoker's cough without the pleasure of the fags, and a barbecued face. To say nothing about being really pissed off!'

'I'm pretty pissed off myself. So much for a day off to take care of family business. Angela, I need you to tell me what's going on?'

She stopped just outside the hospital doors. 'Greg, did I imagine it, or were you with me in the ambulance?'

'I was with you, yes.'

'So, we were both in the ambulance?' Greg nodded. 'Then how the fuck are we to get out of here?'

'I got one of the uniformed boys to drive my car here,' explained Greg. 'Did you get your head X-rayed, or did you storm out before they got round to that?'

'I'm not that stupid, Greg, I did get my head examined and there was nothing wrong. Or at least that's what they'll find when they look at the pictures.'

'So, you had an X-ray, but left before knowing if it showed up anything?'

'That's pretty much what happened, yes.'

'So, you could be running about with a blood clot slowly building up in your brain?'

'Greg, don't be so dramatic. I had a bump on the head, that's all. If they find something, they know how to get in touch with me.'

'Oh that's fine then. But there's no way you're driving, and if you suddenly drop dead and I don't get a chance to say this, then assume I'll be saying *I told you so.*'

'Fine. Right, we need to get over to Collin's office as soon as we can. We need some guys to meet us at Chapelhall. But we don't want them to go in with all lights blazing or we could end up with a hostage situation. I'll explain everything on the way.'

'So, you pretended to need a day off to go through with some crazy plan you and Turner dreamed up?'

'Yeah, that's basically it.'

'But you couldn't tell me?'

'I didn't want you to get involved for your own good, Greg. So how come you did get involved?'

'I followed you.'

'You followed me?'

'Yes. I phoned the garage after you said you were taking a day off and Billy said he had returned the car to you. I parked around the corner from your place after I dropped you off and followed you when you went to Turner's house. I've been following you all day. I'm not surprised you burnt the clutch out; you really should pull away more gently.'

'You're a sneaky bastard!'

'Yes, fortunately for you. I could point out that one of the times you picked up the gardening book you were holding it upside down. Perhaps you could keep that in mind for the next time you're under cover.'

Angela quickly outlined what had been going on and ended with saying that Collins planned to arrange the suicide of Peter Turner.

'So that explains the note I have in my pocket,' said Greg. He took out the note and handed it to Angela.

'You didn't see a pen, by any chance?'

Greg took out Angela's pen and handed it to her.

'Brilliant! Now do you have your laptop with you?'

'It's on the back seat,' said Greg.

Angela reached over to retrieve it. 'You know that you shouldn't leave valuable objects in view like that, Greg; it encourages thieves.'

'And you shouldn't take on bad guys on your own, it encourages them to try and kill you.'

She tried to reply but had a coughing fit. Eventually she recovered, and opened Greg's laptop. She took a small USB cable from her pocket and connected the pen to the computer.

'Come on, come on,' she said between coughs as the computer attempted to download from the video pen.

Suddenly the screen displayed a picture of Steve Collins. The picture was pretty good, and the audio even better. *And why should*

I want to risk more than I have by having one more person killed? I
suppose the bottom line is that if you don't agree to come with us, we
can knock you out and leave you here with her and then go after your
son. If you do as I want, your son will be safe. It's up to you.

Angela stopped the display. 'Fuckin' brilliant!' she said. 'The
best thirty quid I've ever spent.' She unplugged the pen and gave
it a kiss. 'Now if we can just get to Peter before Collins does something else stupid. Greg…'

'I know, I'll drive a bit faster.'

They arrived at Chapelhall just as darkness began to fall. Angela looked at her watch. 'Christ, he's had five or six hours, I didn't
realise it was so late.'

Greg drove slowly round the small industrial estate. As he
turned to the right, they saw two police patrol cars and another
unmarked car parked at the side of the road.

'Ok, pull in beside the patrol cars.'

Greg pulled over, stopped the car, and they identified themselves
to the waiting officers.

'The car we were asked to look out for is parked at the back of
the building,' said a uniformed constable.

'Are there any windows at the back?' asked Angela.

'There's a few, but they're blacked out and have mesh gratings
over them,' said the policeman. 'It's a pretty old building, I actually thought it had been condemned.'

'Good. Right, take one of the patrol cars round the back and
park as close to the car as you can get without being visible. If
anyone comes out of the building towards the car, grab them.'

She turned to two of the detectives who had arrived in the un-
marked car. 'You two go with them. I don't know how many people

will come out, but I doubt it'll be more than three or four, and one of them'll be a good guy. The good guy's called Peter Turner, he's...'

'I know him,' said one of the detectives.

'Great,' said Angela, 'I don't care what happens to any of the others, the main thing is to get Turner and keep him safe. If you can grab the others, fine, but you must get Turner.'

'Are the other guys likely to be armed?' asked one of the detectives.

'I really don't know,' admitted Angela, 'but be careful just in case. The rest of you come with me.' Angela, Greg, two detectives and the four uniformed officers made their way towards the entrance to the building.

'You've really got to believe me, Peter, when I tell you that if there was another way out of this situation, I'd take it. As I've said before, I'm a businessman.'

'You're a drug dealer,' said Peter.

'And drugs are big business. Some of our wealthiest companies are drug companies. What makes me so different?'

'You really want me to answer that? Next you'll be telling me of the many benefits your poison brings to the people taking it.'

'It all depends on what you mean by benefits. Is cannabis any more harmful than tobacco? Many experts think not, so why is cannabis banned but not tobacco? I'll tell you why. Because the government makes money from tobacco. Oh sure, they preach on about the damage it does to your health, and they use this as a regular excuse to increase the tax on cigarettes. Why don't they ban tobacco if they're so worried about our health? The reason they don't want us taking cannabis is because they don't make any money from it. The drugs I sell aren't addictive, they simply help people to have a good time.'

'They kill people,' said Peter coldly.

'Cars kill people; almost anything can kill people if used incorrectly. The people who take my drugs know what they're doing, or if they don't, they shouldn't be taking them. You walk into any A & E department on any weekend and you'll see the effect alcohol has on people. But do we ban that? Of course not, it all comes down again to money.'

'Tobacco and alcohol are legal, your drugs aren't.'

'But you're wrong there. All of my drugs are legal, or they are to start with. The UK along with Germany, Canada and some other places bans a drug when it becomes a concern. Other places, such as Australia, ban drugs based on their chemical structure only, which means that millions of possible drugs are banned even before they're created. But these laws won't cover drugs that have no structural similarity to any known controlled drug. My philosophy is to introduce to the market a new drug before the authorities has a chance to ban it. When a ban is enacted, I move onto another drug.'

'So, you think all that makes you a straight up citizen?'

'It makes me a businessman. There's a demand and I supply it. What could be simpler?'

'All that might be very well, and the courts may take a lenient view, but everything changed when you started to kill people.'

'I already told you that I had no direct.....'

'Oh for fuck's sake! Much more of this sanctimonious crap and you won't need to fake my suicide, I'll gladly volunteer!'

Collins smiled thinly. 'You're a brave man. Anyway, my point is that I had to protect my business and that of my associates.'

Angela, Greg and the other officers opened the front door and moved quietly inside the building.

'What a dump,' whispered Greg, 'are you sure Collins operates from here?'

'He's taken over a small set of offices a mile or so away. Those're being renovated. This is his old place.'

'Old place? You're not kidding,' said Greg, glancing around.

The ground floor appeared at one time to have been a small manufacturing area. There were spaces where machinery once stood, and tatty yellow lane markings on the stone floor. A metal staircase led up to another smaller level which had a gantry where people could have looked out over the machinery below. Towards the back of this upper tier was what appeared to be a small office area. The only light inside the building was coming from the office.

Two sides of the building had very few windows, and none of these was less than ten feet or so above the ground. The other two walls appeared to have no windows at all.

The group paused until their eyes became accustomed to the gloom.

'You two stay here,' whispered Angela to the two detectives.

Angela led the way and started to climb the steps. She stopped when she heard a loud creaking noise behind her. Glancing behind, she saw that one of the uniformed officers had grabbed the thin metal handrail to aid him in climbing the stairs. They stopped and listened, expecting to see someone appear at the top of the stairs checking to find out what was causing the noise. But no one appeared.

They started to climb again. It was very dark inside the building, but they didn't want to use torches in case this alerted the people in the office above. They made slow progress, as every time they looked up to see where they were going, their eyes would adjust to the light coming from the offices. When they looked down at the steps, they had to wait until their eyes grew accustomed to the darkness before they could proceed.

Suddenly there was a clatter as the constable at the rear of the small group lost his footing and fell forward onto the next steps. Angela heard a softly muttered *shit*. They waited again, all anxiously watching the light shining from the office and expecting it to grow in intensity as someone came to check on the noise. Again, there was nothing.

After what seemed like an age, they reached the top of the steps. Every step they took was accompanied by a worrying creaking sound, but eventually they reached the door of the office. Angela signalled them to stop, and she put her ear to the door.

She held up two fingers to indicate that she could hear two voices.

'Greg,' she whispered to her young partner. 'You wait out here in case someone makes a run for it.'

Greg nodded.

Angela reached for the door handle and slowly and carefully pushed it downwards. Then she took a deep breath and pushed the door open. She rushed into the room followed by the other four officers.

'Police!' she shouted, 'stay where you are!' The officers blinked momentarily as their eyes grew accustomed to the light.

Steve Collins was sitting behind a large wooden desk, leaning back in a swivel chair. Sitting on a chair on the other side of the desk was Peter Turner, and ten feet away against the back wall sat Collins' two companions. Bill made to stand up, but before he could organise himself, one of the officers rushed over and pushed him back down into the chair. Collin's driver made no move but sat with his mouth open glancing between Collins and the uniformed officer who had moved to stand beside him.

'Are you OK, Peter?' said Angela.

Turner looked up at her, smiled, then nodded. 'I'm surprised to see you,' he said, 'are *you* OK?'

'I've been better,' said Angela, 'but I'm improving all the time, especially now we have this dirt bag.'

Collins raised his eyebrows. 'Are you referring to me, officer?' he said.

'I'll give you one thing, Collins, you're a pretty cool customer under the circumstances.'

'And what circumstances are you referring to?' asked Collins.

'Well, let me see now; off the top of my head I'd say murder, attempted murder, kidnapping, arson, drug dealing. We'll be checking your car to see if it's got an MOT and insurance, but that can wait.'

'That's quite a list, officer, but I think you've made a mistake. I don't know who I'm supposed to have murdered or attempted to murder, but as regard kidnapping, I assume you're referring to Peter here. If so, I should point out that Peter drove here in his own car, which makes kidnapping a bit difficult to prove. I think it's all been a bit of a misunderstanding.'

'I'm sure Peter will tell a different story,' said Angela

'That may be, but I'm sure my colleagues will back me up.'

'And you can explain the fire in his house? By the way, Peter, the fire brigade got there very quickly. Downstairs is a bit of a mess, but they stopped it spreading too badly beyond the lounge.'

She turned back to face Collins. 'A fire? I don't know anything about that,' said Collins. 'And Bill here was with me when we visited Peter. Do you know anything about a fire, Bill?'

Bill shook his head and managed a smile.

'Oh yeah, Bill. You wouldn't know anything about a big fuckin' bump on my head would you?' said Angela, glaring at Collin's friend.

'Have you any other questions, officer, or can we get back to work?' Collins sounded impatient.

Angela took the pen out of her pocket.

'Do you recognise this? This was the pen Peter wrote his supposed suicide note with and then left both outside. Quick thinking, by the way, Peter. This is no ordinary pen, Mr Collins, it is actually a video pen and I had the chance to view some of its recording on the way over here. Considering how small the pen is, the picture quality is very good, and the audio is almost perfect. Now what did you say again? Oh yes, something along the lines of *and why should I want to risk more than I have already by having one more person killed?* Yes, that's fairly accurate I'd say. Unfortunately, we didn't have time to watch it all, but I'm sure it will make fascinating viewing for a jury.'

Collins continued to smile, but he was looking much less confident.

'I doubt if that will be admissible as evidence,' he said.

'Well, we'll see,' said Angela. 'But to be honest it's not really necessary. You said your colleagues will back you up, and perhaps they will, but you've forgotten about me. I'll admit I don't remember much after the second thump on the head, but my memories before that are fairly clear. So, I reckon that evens things up a bit. What do you think now, smart arse?'

Collins didn't say anything, he just continued to smile.

'Read them their rights then cuff 'em,' said Angela to the officers. 'Take my mobile, Peter, and give your son a ring; you're going to need somewhere to stay tonight.'

Peter Turner slowly got to his feet and Angela took his arm to help him. One officer started speaking to Bill while a second walked over to Collin's desk.

Collins got to his feet just as the policeman reached him, but he suddenly pushed the officer, catching him off guard and causing him to fall over the desk. Collins ran to a door at the far side of the room, a door Angela hadn't even noticed. He pulled it open and rushed out. There were a few clangs as his feet rang out on the metal grill. He clattered into Greg and both fell to the ground. Collins quickly got to his feet and attempted to make for the stairs. Greg recovered and grabbed Collins round the knees. Both fell and cartwheeled down the rickety steps to land at the feet of the be-mused officers.

Angela helped Peter back into a seat.

'The switches over there put the warehouse lights on,' said John the driver nodding to a board on the wall.

Angela hurried over to the panel and threw the switches.

'Have you got him?' shouted Angela as she hurried to the open door. No answer.

As the warehouse lights began to flicker to life Angela could see the two figures lying at the bottom of the stairs. Both seemed to be moving. 'Someone phone for an ambulance,' shouted Angela as she made to go down the stairs.

'Are you OK?' asked Angela as she reached Greg.

'I think so,' said Greg. 'Everything happened so quickly. He appeared suddenly and before I had a chance to react, we were both on the floor. I made a grab for him and we both ended up down here.'

'Well don't try and move too much until the ambulance gets here.'

The ambulance arrived within ten minutes and after the medics checked out both men they were helped into the vehicle. 'A couple of you guys go in the ambulance with them,' said Angela to two of the policemen. 'Get the officer checked out first and read the other guy his rights. Whatever you do don't let him out of your sights.'

Angela watched as the ambulance sped out of the warehouse, then made her way back up the stairs to where Peter was still sitting in a chair. The uniformed officers had handcuffed Bill and John and were leading them out of the office.

'Did you manage to reach your son?' asked Angela.

The ex-policeman looked up at her and nodded, and then he slumped forward and fell off his chair onto the floor.

Angela rushed out of the office and looked over the railing. 'Get another ambulance quick! When it arrives get the medics up here right away!'

After what seemed like an age, the medics arrived and clanked their way up the stairs and started to treat Peter Turner.

Another couple of cars arrived, one patrol car and one un-marked vehicle. Angela quickly outlined to DS Wallace, the officer put in charge of the scene, what had happened. She didn't cover all the details, just the salient points the Detective would need to direct the personnel processing the scene.

'I'm afraid quite a few people have been milling about, espe-cially the guys tending to Peter.'

'No problem,' said DS Wallace, 'preserving human life always takes priority over preserving the scene. I just hope he's going to be OK. Do you know if the suspect has any relative who should be informed?'

'No idea,' said Angela, 'you could turn over a few rocks and see who crawls out.'

DS Wallace gave her a strange look.

'It's been a long day. You could try asking his two pals before we take them away. The uniformed boys'll have them in one of their patrol cars. Collins fell after a brief scuffle with DC Anderson. I'll make sure he gives the full details in his statement, but you should talk to the officers who were on the ground level; they can confirm what happened.'

Wallace nodded and went to speak to Collin's companions.

The detective who had examined Collins watched as Turner was strapped to a gurney to be taken to the ambulance.

'I sure hope Peter's OK. He's a really nice guy,' said the detective.

'Do you know him quite well?' asked Angela.

'Fairly well,' said the detective. 'He's always interested in what I'm working on. Lately, he's been following the serial killer hunt. I think he'd have liked to have been a detective.'

'So, you were able to give him a little inside information,' said Angela.

The detective looked a little uncomfortable. 'Not really, well, nothing very important. There really wasn't much to tell as you know. I hope he's going to be OK.'

The ambulance staff quickly and efficiently moved Peter down the stairs and into the ambulance with Angela and the detective following close behind them.

'He's stable for the moment,' explained one of the medics, 'but we really need to get him to the hospital asap.'

Angela turned to the detective who knew Peter. 'I'll go in the ambulance with him.'

Angela phoned Brian from the ambulance. She quickly explained that Peter was being rushed to the hospital but didn't go into any more detail. Brian said he would contact Roy.

They had only been at the hospital for ten or fifteen minutes when Brian, Elizabeth and Roy arrived. A doctor told them that Peter was stable but didn't want them to visit him until the next day. Roy decided to stay in case there were any further developments, and Brian and Elizabeth decided to stay with him for a while. Angela gave them a very condensed version of events and promised to provide more details later.

Just as she was trying to decide whether to buy a cup of something from the vending machine Greg hobbled along the corridor.

'How're you feeling?' she asked.

'Bumps and bruises, that's all they say. Probably one for every step I hit.'

'You should have let him go. The guys at the bottom would have got him.'

Greg shrugged. 'I didn't really think of that. Probably my rugby instincts took over. How's Collins?'

'No idea,' said Angela. 'I've asked the officers watching him to give me an update as soon as they know anything.'

'Did I hear you say that you were conscious in Peter's house?'

'Yeah.'

'And you heard everything back at Turner's house?'

'Everything? I didn't hear anything. I didn't know if it was New Year or New York. The only thing I heard was some bastard thumping in my head as if he wanted out. I remember going in the back door and hearing voices, I vaguely remember someone pulling my hair, and then I was outside the house and you were there along with lots of other people.'

Chapter 33

Angela and Greg went back to the station to write up their reports after collecting Greg's car. They found a message waiting on them from the Boss.

'He wants to see us in the morning,' said Greg. 'Before the briefing.'

They finished their reports, and Greg gave Angela a lift back to Glenmavis to collect her car.

'At the risk of you moaning at me again, how're you feeling?' asked Greg.

'I'm actually feeling quite tired. I could do with getting to bed.'

'If you're not feeling too well later, give me a ring and I'll come round. You might have a reaction to all the smoke and the bangs on the head.'

'I appreciate that, Greg, but I'll be fine. Let me ask you something. Weren't you tempted to rush after Peter when he left with Collins? You could be getting yourself a new partner.'

'Yes, it did cross my mind, but I'd miss all the lunchtime treats and the hours of fun we have making up the law as we go along.'

'Yeah, that would be pretty boring.'

Angela had a lot to think about when she lay in bed that night. Her plan had put both her and Turner in danger. She had come out OK, but there was no telling if Peter would be so lucky. She thought of phoning the hospital, and then changed her mind. There were so many questions running through her head, and these caused her to toss and turn more than her frequent bouts of coughing. Had Peter gone along with her plan because she knew of his involvement in the decade old accident? If she had stayed away from Peter's house, would Collins have simply walked away with the book? If so, Peter wouldn't be in hospital. She cursed her impulsiveness. Everything had happened so quickly, but when people had time to reflect, how would Roy Turner and the Reids view her strategy? She turned to lie the other way in bed. Was she hoping Peter would survive to get her off the hook? She hated herself for even allowing that thought to come into her head.

Her bedside clock seemed to be ticking more loudly than usual. Normally, she found the constant rhythm soothing, but tonight it seemed to be harsher and to have an almost accusing sound to it. Frustrated at being unable to sleep, she got out of bed and walked into her kitchen to get a drink. Outside it had started to rain. She shivered against the cold as she poured herself a glass of water. Her reflection stared back at her from the window where droplets of water on the outside wound their way down to the sill. Her bravado of earlier seemed to be trickling away with the drops of water. The report she had filed gave the official story, but this could fall apart very quickly under questioning of all the people involved. Everything would depend on the Boss.

She finished her glass of water and took another stare at her reflection. The video pen Peter had used to record his conversation with Collins was safely back in its drawer. The video it contained could be crucial in the case against Collins and his henchmen, but this would depend on her coming up with a reason for Peter having it. She walked to the drawer and took out the pen. Switching on her computer, she connected the pen and watched the video again.

There was nothing in it that contradicted her story or explained her real relationship with Peter. But there was quite a lot that showed what Collins and his thugs had been up to. She decided to hand it in, but this brought her back to explaining how Peter Turner got it in the first place. There was also clear footage of Collins looking through the recipe book. Questions would be asked about this. That was also tucked away in her drawer until she decided what to do with it. Again, it was evidence. If she destroyed it or didn't turn it over, she was committing an offence. Another one to add to the growing list.

Lifting a hand, she gingerly touched the lumps on the back of her skull. They were still sore to touch, but at least her head felt much clearer, and the man inside was hammering a bit quieter than previously. She went back to bed to try and get some sleep.

As Angela prepared for Greg coming to collect her the next morning, she couldn't make up her mind whether she was going to the station as a hero or taking a walk to the gallows. A lot would depend on the attitude of her superior officer when she got there. She made sure she had the pen and the recipe book and stood by the window looking for Greg.

'Did you sleep OK,' asked Greg.

'No,' she said truthfully, 'how about you?'

'Not much,' he said, 'Too sore.'

'Yes, me too. I've decided to hand in the pen and tell everything apart from the plan I had hatched with Peter.'

'Well, I'll tell my story exactly as it happened. I didn't know anything about your arrangement with Peter.'

'But you do now?'

'Well, you babbled something last night, but you had been through a traumatic experience and I wasn't paying a lot of attention. I think I'll be very concise and just mention things that are directly relevant to the case. I went to Peter's house to follow up on a few points, saw your car, and also noticed Collin's car. As I approached the house, I saw Collins leave with Turner, but no sign of you. I found you unconscious and the house on fire. I called the fire service then we followed Collins, and so on.'

Angela nodded. 'I still haven't decided how to explain about Turner having my pen. I don't want to invent something especially since Peter may well tell a different story. By the way, I phoned the hospital this morning and they say he's stable.'

'Yes, that's what they told me as well. I also spoke to Roy. He said that he and the Reids would like to talk to us when we have the time. I said we might be able to catch up with them tonight. It crossed my mind that I should perhaps go to the hospital and ask after Peter.'

'Yeah, a good idea. I'll come as well, assuming I'm not in jail.'

'Quite a day yesterday,' said Russell, 'have either of you any update on Peter Turner's condition?'

'We both phoned the hospital this morning,' replied Angela, 'they said he's in a stable condition.'

The DCI nodded.

'His son would like to speak to us when convenient,' added Greg. 'We spoke to him briefly last night, but things were a bit hectic then.'

'Yes,' said the DCI, 'they would have been. I think you should both go and speak to him as soon as you can. I imagine he'll have a lot of questions. And how are you feeling, Angela?'

'Not too bad. My cough's improving and my head's fine unless I touch it.'

He nodded again and leaned back in his chair, shuffling some papers he had on the desk in front of him.

'I've read your reports,' he said eventually. 'It appears you've both been in the right place at the right time. Very fortunate.'

'I would like to add to my report,' said Angela. 'A couple of things that might clarify matters.'

She produced the recipe book and pen.

'This book is the reason Collins went to see Peter Turner.' She handed the book over to the DCI.

'It's a book we found in Chief Inspector Stewart's house, and I believe it contains information pertinent to the failed raids carried out on premises Steve Collin's was involved in providing security for. I recognised the handwriting as being that of Robbie Stewart, and the dates tied in with the dates of the raids.'

The DCI looked at her seriously. 'Are you suggesting that Chief Inspector Stewart was passing information to Collins?'

'I'm afraid it looks that way, sir. I believe he was being black-mailed by Collins over something that happened a number of years ago.'

'That's a very serious accusation, Angela. Have you anything other than this book to back up your suspicions?'

'Yes sir. There was an accident ten years ago involving a police car and two members of the public, which resulted in one person being killed, and another seriously injured. In the police car at the time of the accident was Chief Inspector Stewart, Peter Turner and Steve Collins. The subsequent inquiry apportioned no blame to either of the officers, but I believe something may have been said or happened that gave Collins leverage over the Chief Inspector. The family which suffered the deaths ...'

Russell's phone rang and he picked up the receiver. 'No calls,' he said briskly, and then nodded for Angela to continue.

'James Reid, the father of Brian and Elizabeth Reid, died in the accident. The youngest daughter, Caroline, was in a coma as a result of the accident. The mother went to pieces and eventually committed suicide. Elizabeth and Brian then allowed the life support system keeping Caroline alive to be switched off. A few months ago, Brian and Elizabeth began to investigate the events surrounding the accident. One person they spoke to died soon after they had spoken to her, and another couple were lucky to survive a house fire. Elizabeth herself ended up in hospital after a suspicious brake failure on her car. Brian Reid also spoke with Robbie Stewart and, as we know, he died in an incident that was made to look like the work of the serial killer we've been chasing.'

'So, you're suggesting Chief Inspector Stewart was murdered by Steve Collins, and that he carried out the other attacks and started the fire?'

'I think that's a distinct possibility.'

'But have you anything other than this book to back up what you're suggesting?'

Angela produced the pen and handed it to Russell.

'This is a video pen Peter Turner used to record some of his meeting with Collins. You will find that Collins mentions the accidents, although doesn't specifically talk about Stewart's murder.'

Russell looked at the pen. 'I haven't seen this thing before,' he said. 'Is this part of our surveillance equipment?'

'No sir, it belongs to me,' said Angela. 'Peter Turner had spoken to the Reids, and believed Collins was behind the supposed accidents that the Reids told him about. He felt anxious that Collins might try to threaten him in some way. I felt he was being a bit paranoid, but to set his mind at rest I loaned him the pen and he took it with him to the Stewart funeral. I didn't have the opportunity to get it back from him, but this turns out to have been very fortunate as he managed to operate it when Collins arrived at his house. It could have been destroyed in the fire, but Turner had the presence of mind to use this pen to write his supposed suicide note and then to leave it outside where Greg found it.'

Russell slowly rocked back and forward in his chair.

'I can't make up my mind if that's the biggest load of bullshit I've ever heard, or if it's all strange enough to be the truth.'

Angela opened her mouth to speak, but the DCI held up a hand to stop her.

'I'm going to view the video contents of this pen, and then I'll want to speak to you both again. In the meantime, I don't want either of you to submit any clarifications of your reports. If what you suspect regarding Robbie Stewart is true, then we have a problem. If other parts of your story are true, then we have at least one murder and another two or three attempted murders on our hands, and that's not including the attempted murder of a police officer.'

He looked thoughtful for a few moments while Greg and Angela sat in silence.

'We still have the two men who were with Collins last night held in custody?'

'Yes,' said Angela.

'And we're planning to charge them with kidnapping and attempted murder?'

'Yes,' said Angela again. 'Certainly, we can charge Gibson. I'm not so sure about Briggs. Sir, I should clarify something that was in my report. I told Collins that I had been conscious while he was talking with Turner. That may have been what caused him to make a run for it. His companions also heard me make that statement, but as I pointed out in my report, I didn't actually hear anything.'

'So, it was a bluff?'

'Yes sir.'

'Well, it certainly had an effect on Collins. I want you two to question these men. But you've not to repeat your statement about hearing what happened, is that clear? We don't want that on tape.'

He swung forward in his chair and stood up.

'OK.' He looked at his watch. 'We still have a few hours before we have to either charge or release the men. I'm sure they'll be screaming for their lawyers, so we'll have to move quickly.'

'Where do you think the Boss will go from here?' said Greg when they had returned to their desks.

'I'm sure he'll be pretty worked up about the fact that Stewart was helping Collins,' said Angela. 'That could really put the cat amongst the pigeons, and I'm pretty sure he'll take that much higher up the tree. Anyway, let's see what history these guys have. You have a dig around in the files while I see if I can find out what their official roles are in Collin's company.'

Angela felt she owed it to Peter Turner, Betty White, the Scotts and the Reids to pin everything they possibly could on the men in custody. Collins was likely to have been the one giving the orders, but Angela didn't believe his employees would have had much regret in carrying them out.

After a couple of hours of digging, Angela had little to show for her efforts. John Briggs, the driver, seemed to do little other than what his title suggested. He was 48 years old and had worked with Collins for as far back as she could trace. Bill Gibson was 38 years old and was listed as a private assistant.

'How'd you get on?' asked Angela, throwing her pen onto her desk in disgust.

'Not much better than you by the look of things,' said Greg.

'I reckon Gibson is a tougher nut than Briggs,' said Angela.

'I've managed to dig out a few details,' said Greg. 'Gibson is single. Briggs is married and has two daughters, one aged twelve and the other nine.'

'That's interesting,' said Angela. 'I suppose it's just possible he was simply a driver for Collin's company. I'm not saying he didn't know what was going on, but he might not have been directly involved in the violence,' said Angela. 'I think he's the one to tackle first.'

'OK,' said Greg, 'I'll go along with that. Are the guys being held here?'

'Yeah. Hopefully in separate cells. Do you know the saying that there's honour amongst thieves?'

Greg nodded.

'Well, don't believe a word of it. Most of the thieves I've met couldn't even spell honour.'

'Especially the American ones,' said Greg. He noticed Angela looking at him in a strange way. 'Americans spell honour without the 'u',' said Greg by way of explanation.

'I got the joke, Greg. It wasn't funny when you told it, and it's even less funny when you explain it.'

'Mr. Briggs, we're here to ask you some questions regarding your relationship with Steve Collins.'

'I'm not saying anything until I've spoken to my lawyer,' said Briggs, leaning back in his chair and folding his arms.

'That's a pity, Mr Briggs, we hoped we might be able to clear up a few things then let you return to your family.' Angela started to gather up her papers and got to her feet. 'But have it your way. I'll see about getting in touch with your lawyer if you give me the details. But I don't think I'll be able to contact the firm until early next week.'

'Now wait a minute,' said Briggs desperately. Angela paused and stared at him impassively.

'There's probably no harm in helping you clear up some things,' said Briggs slowly. 'I mean, it's not as if I've done anything wrong. I was just doing my job.'

'Does your job normally involve kidnapping?' said Greg. 'And what about attempted murder and arson? Exactly what qualifications do you need for your job?'

'Now hold on!' said Briggs. 'You're not going to drag me into any of that stuff! I thought you said you hoped we might clear up a few things and then I'd be able to go home?'

'You must excuse my colleague,' said Angela, sitting back down. 'It's been quite a stressful few days. We're getting a bit ahead of ourselves here.' She gave Greg a less than friendly look.

'Let's start again. Can you tell us how long you've worked for Steve Collins?'

Briggs shuffled a bit uneasily in his chair trying to decide if he should answer. He looked at Angela and she smiled at him.

'About six or seven years,' said Briggs eventually, 'as a driver. That's all I did.'

'What type of driving jobs?'

'Pick-ups and drop offs. Sometimes I had to go to the airport or bus station to pick up business associates, then take them back again.'

'And that's all you did? You just drove for him?'

'Yes. That's all I did.'

'Did you drive for anyone other than Mr Collins?'

'I told you, I sometimes picked people up and dropped them off again.'

'What about Mr Gibson? Did you drive for him?'

Briggs snorted. 'No. He's nothing special. I just drove for *important* people.'

'So, you didn't drive Mr Gibson around? Even locally, around Airdrie?'

'I told you. I rarely drove Gibson anywhere.'

'And what is Mr Gibson's role in the company?'

'He looks after Mr Collins.'

'What do you mean by looks after? Is he a butler or a secretary?'

Briggs snorted yet again. This seemed to be his way of saying *no*, and it was really beginning to annoy Greg.

'I'd say he is more of a bodyguard type of guy.'

Angela raised her eyebrows. 'Really? And why would a businessman need a bodyguard?'

Briggs shrugged. 'Lots of people in business have enemies.'

Angela opened the files in front of her. 'Can you tell me where you were on the afternoon of 6th January?'

'I can't remember,' said Briggs.

'How about the evening of 26th January?'

Briggs shrugged again. Angela waited. 'No idea,' said the man eventually. 'On evenings I would be at home. I don't work nights.'

'What about the afternoon of January 28th?'

'No idea.'

'And the evening of 31st January? Oh, I forgot. You didn't work at night.'

'That's right,' said Briggs.

'And if we asked your wife about those evenings, she would be able to back up your story?'

'Yes, I'm sure she would.'

'But you have no idea where you were on the dates I've mentioned?'

'I told you I don't know. What happened on those days anyway?'

Angela looked at Greg then back at Briggs. He sat with an inquisitive look on his face.

Angela slowly opened a folder that contained photographs.

'On the 6th of January Betty White apparently fell down the stairs in her house and died from a broken neck.'

Angela pushed a picture over to Briggs. She watched his face closely as he looked at the photograph.

'On the 28th of January there was a car accident in which a young woman was taken to hospital in a coma.' She slid another picture over to him and again watched his face intently.

'On January 31st an ex-policeman, Robert Stewart, was murdered in Motherwell.' A third photograph was handed to him.

'I know him,' said Briggs, pointing at the last photograph. 'I've seen him with Steve Collins a few times.'

'Was the last time recently?' said Angela.

'The last time was probably a few months ago.'

'Did you ever give Mr Stewart a lift?'

Briggs shook his head. 'Not that I can remember.'

Angela looked at her file. 'I've missed a couple out,' she said. 'On the night of January 26th there was a fire at a house not far from here. Terry and Pamela Scott's house. Perhaps you read about it in the papers?'

'I didn't read anything about it,' said Briggs. 'I only buy a paper for the horses. I throw the rest away.'

Angela slid another picture over to him.

'You can't see their faces very well as they're wearing oxygen masks.' She looked in her folder again.

'You've got children, haven't you Mr Briggs?'

'Yes, I've got two girls.'

Angela took a last picture out of her file and looked at it.

'These are the daughters of Terry and Pamela Scott. Unlike their parents who had only suffered from smoke inhalation, the girls suffered burns in the fire.'

She slid the picture over to Briggs.

He took a look at the picture, then suddenly turned his head to the side, made a grab for a litterbin, and threw up, partly in it, and partly on the floor.

'Get someone to clean that up, Greg,' said Angela quietly. 'And get Mr Briggs a glass of water.'

They quickly ushered Briggs into another room and continued the interview. Angela had brought the pictures with her and idly flicked at the edge of the folder as she spoke.

'The two girls will be scarred for life, Mr Briggs. They face long and painful hours of plastic surgery. As to how this will affect them mentally...' Angela didn't finish the sentence and just shook her head while continuing to flick at the corner of her folder.

Briggs didn't look at her. His eyes were fixed on the folder.

She opened the folder and looked inside. Briggs recoiled back into his chair.

'The doctors think that their hair caught fire and they tried to put it out with their hands. Of course, their hair will grow back, or at least it'll grow back in the parts where their scalps aren't too badly burnt. They both had very long hair. They probably turned their heads from side to side in an effort to put the fire out, but this caused the burning hair to come into contact with their faces, perhaps even to stick there causing more burning. The fire brigade say it was a miracle that their clothes didn't catch fire. If that had happened...well, it didn't.'

Briggs looked at her. He shook his head. 'You've got to believe me. I had nothing to do with the fire. I wasn't there. I didn't know it was going to happen.'

'Yes? What would you have done if you'd known?'

'I don't know,' said Briggs sadly. He sat idly picking at the corner of the table.

'I don't think you'd have done anything,' continued Angela. 'You may not have been there, but I reckon you know a lot more about this these events than you're telling us.'

'I don't. I really don't.'

'So, you don't know anything about how Betty White died? You don't know how Robert Stewart died? And you've never been to the Scott's house before in your life? You've never even driven past it on your way from your home to Collin's place?'

'I never drive through Calderbank. I come into Chapelhall from the other side,' said Briggs.

'What's in Calderbank?' said Angela.

'The Scott's house. Where the fire was,' said Briggs.

'I thought you hadn't read about it in the papers?' said Angela.

'I didn't.'

'So how did you know the house was in Calderbank?'

'You told me.'

'No, I didn't. I just said that it was close to here.'

Briggs shrugged, but didn't say anything more.

Suddenly Angela slammed her hand down on the table, causing Briggs and Greg to jump.

'You knew the house is in Calderbank because you've been there, haven't you Briggs? Perhaps not on the night of the fire, but you've been there all right.' Angela had got to her feet and was shouting now. 'Maybe earlier when you were getting the lie of the land, or perhaps you followed Elizabeth Reid when she went to visit the Scotts.'

Suddenly she stopped talking. 'Yes, that's it isn't it?' she said in a quieter voice, but with more menace. 'That's the connection between all these events. You were asked to find out what inquiries the Reids were making, weren't you? You followed Brian Reid to Betty White's house, and you followed Elizabeth Reid to the Scott's house.'

'No!' said Briggs.

'Yes!' shouted Angela. 'Steve Collins had you follow them to find out what they were up to. He knew they had been digging about because Robbie Stewart told him, and you were given the job of keeping an eye on them, weren't you?'

'How could I?' said Briggs desperately, 'they had two cars. I couldn't be in two places at the same time.'

'Greg,' said Angela, turning to her young partner, 'gather all the CCTV footage we have of the Reid's movements and check out the other cars within a hundred yards of them against all the vehicles belonging to Collins and his associates.'

'I'll get right on to it,' he said and turned to leave.

'Wait,' said Briggs. Greg stopped and waited. Angela sat back down in her chair.

'I did follow the Reid woman to Calderbank, but that's all I did. I told Collins where she'd gone and that was that. I'd nothing to do with the fire.'

'And Betty White?' said Angela.

Briggs shook his head. 'I don't know anything about that. And I don't know anything about the car accident or that guy, Stewart's murder.' Briggs folded his arms and appeared to be in a huff.

Angela recognised the protective pose.

'So, you followed Elizabeth Reid to Calderbank and then reported back to Collins?'

Briggs nodded.

'And you had no idea what he planned to do with that information?'

Briggs shuffled in his seat, but kept his arms folded.

'Mr Briggs?' urged Angela.

'No. I had no idea. He told me to watch her and tell him where she went. That was it. You've got to believe me! There's no way I'd get involved in starting fires or murder! I swear it on the lives of my kids! Listen, I've nothing more to say. If you want to keep me here, then charge me with something. If not, then let me go. Or at least get me my lawyer.'

'We'll think about it for a wee while, Mr Briggs. There'll be a lot of press hanging about looking for an update. We don't want them pestering you, but it might be best if we tell them you're still helping us with our inquiries and that you've provided a lot of useful information. But we'll tell them you're not a suspect, just a witness in our ongoing investigation.'

The colour had drained from Brigg's face.

'No, no,' he stammered, 'you can't do that! Just leave me out of it! You don't have to tell them anything. You don't know who you're dealing with here!'

'Oh, we need to tell them something, Mr Briggs,' said Angela.

'Just tell them I'm not a suspect and I've been released. You don't have to say anything about helping with your inquiries.'

'Why not? What's the harm in that?'

'Because I've got a wife and two kids.'

'Well, what do you think?' said Greg when the interview had been concluded.

'I'm pretty sure he's telling us the truth,' said Angela. 'I doubt if he was directly involved in any of the attacks.'

'So where does that leave us? And what was all that stuff about the press?'

'A very good question, Greg.'

'So, what do we tell the press?'

'Absolutely nothing. I never had any intentions of telling them anything, I just wanted to see how Briggs would react to being in the limelight, and he certainly didn't disappoint me. We'll keep him here for a while yet. I'd like to talk to him again, but after we've interviewed Gibson.'

'Well, that was a waste of time,' said Greg. 'You'd think he'd get fed up continually saying *no comment.*'

'Never mind Greg. I didn't expect anything else, but we had to check.'

Chapter 34

'How did they get the story?' said Greg.

'It's no great surprise,' said the Boss. 'There are so many people who know what's happening it was only a matter of time before it reached the papers.' He glanced down at the newspaper again and read the headline *police charity shop sting operation*.

'Will we try and find the source?' said Greg.

'There's not really any point,' said the Boss. 'I'm just disappointed that the paper printed the story without checking with us first.'

'So, it's all been a waste of time,' said Greg quite despondently. He looked at Angela. 'You're taking this very calmly,' he said.

'It's maybe not as bad as it appears,' she said slowly. Greg stared at her in disbelief. 'Go on,' said the Boss.

'I think he'll view our charity shop ploy as a challenge.'

'You think he'll still try and buy the boots?' said Greg.

'Yes, I think he will.'

'I agree,' said the Boss. 'He may even think that we'll abandon the operation now the paper has the story. In fact, it might be an idea to see if the paper will run a story to that effect. I reckon the powers that be will be coming down on them like a ton of bricks, so the paper might be put in the position of owing us one. No. I don't think we abandon the operation.' He picked up the paper and read some of it again. 'I'll do a bit of phoning around and find out if any of the other papers are planning to run a follow up. You might be correct, Angela, this sort of thing could well be an ego boost to our guy.'

Chapter 35

The killer paced up and down his lounge, an open paper lying on his settee. Now and again, he stopped pacing, took another look at the report, then started pacing again.

He had run through a whole range of emotions since first reading the newspaper. His annoyance developed into anger, then he felt pride at the respect he had been shown, then a reluctant admiration for the plan, then defiance. But there had been no fear, definitely no fear. However, every different emotion suggested a different plan of action, and that was no good. He would have to pace some more until he could decide how he *really* felt. Then he would work out what to do. A different periodical lay on his coffee table. In the lead article, a study had revealed that domestic abuse suffered by women was increasing. A major contributory cause of this was alcohol.

He had decided not to write his diary while unsure of his mood, but he realised that this was exactly the time to write.

Sometimes I feel like King Canute trying to turn back the tide, but I have to try. If men are so weak that they need alcohol to deal with their problems, then that is up to them. But when wives and children suffer as a result of their drinking, that is a different matter. I know. I have seen it first-hand. And where were all the agencies, the police, the social workers, and the alcohol councillors when my father came home and closed the door to keep the world out? None of them did me or my mother any good. No one could enter my world behind the door into my hell that lasted until the brutal bully collapsed to sleep it off. Then my mother would comfort me and tell me it was all right as she tried to wipe the blood off her mouth and stop the bruises from swelling up. Through tears I had pleaded with mum to get help. But she shook her head violently and her eyes filled with fear. She had such lovely blue eyes. I try to visualise her face but can't. I almost have it, but just as the picture begins to develop it becomes distorted. It becomes a mass of bruises, black and blue, and blood, deep red blood. Her eyes I try so desperately to imagine are almost closed due to the bruising, and her lips that whispered such comforting things to me are swollen and streaked with blood. I open my eyes and banish the picture from my mind. Fortunately, she is free from the pain now, but so many others aren't. How many children and mothers are sitting at home dreading the return of the monster? The feeling of frustration grows inside me as I write. I can only do so much. Yes! That's the feeling to concentrate on! Determination. A crusade driven by determination. I will challenge the authorities, the authorities that did nothing to help me or save my mother. My crusade will be stepped up.

Chapter 36

'If Turner's telling us the truth, it's a mixture of good and bad news,' said Russell.

The Boss pursed his lips as he turned over what Angela and Greg had told him.

'The good news is that Stewart looks to have been the only copper involved in this scheme.' Russell shrugged as he voiced his thoughts. 'As if we didn't have enough on our plates with this serial killer, we now appear to have a major crime gang involved in serious drugs business right on our doorstep.'

'Couldn't we just pass on what we know to the drugs boys and let them get on with it?' suggested Angela.

'That would be the sensible thing to do, I agree,' said Russell.

'But you're not going to do that,' said Angela, stating a fact rather than asking a question.

'I'm not prepared to hand over the whole thing just yet,' agreed the Boss. He glanced at Angela rather warily. 'I know you're not one for police politics, Angela, but I've got to keep it at the back of my mind. If we go to the Drugs Squad, we'd have to come clean with everything we know.'

'You mean we'd have to tell them that one of our own was dirty?' said Angela.

'As I said Angela, you're not one for police politics. You call a spade a spade. In politics you have to find half a dozen ways to describe a spade.' He sighed and seemed to find something interesting to stare at on the floor. 'I don't really expect you to agree,' he said, having gathered his thoughts, 'but I'd like to hand this over when we have enough information to allow the Drugs Squad to follow it up without them having to be aware of Robbie Stewart's involvement.'

'But I do agree,' said Angela.

Russell raised his eyebrows, then leaned back in his chair and stared at her.

'Let me hazard a guess,' he said eventually. 'Would your agreement have anything to do with Maureen Stewart?'

'Did what I think just happen, actually happen?' said Greg as they sat down at their desks.

'That depends on what you think happened,' said Angela.

'We agreed to suppress evidence so that the reputation of an ex-cop can be protected.'

Angela feigned surprise. 'Did we do that, Greg? Really? Now think carefully, because what you're suggesting is very serious."

'Oh no,' said Greg, 'you're not going to play your mind games with me. You know damn well that's what we agreed!'

'No, we didn't. We agreed to inform the Drugs Squad when we had more evidence. We need to follow this a bit further down the road.'

'Yes, further down the road away from Stewart.'

Angela shrugged. 'Stewart's not the story here. We need to get more on this whole drugs business. If everything we know at present got out to the press, the only real story is that an ex-cop was feeding information to crooks. The Drugs Squad would go in heavy-handed and round up a few of Collins' guys and pick up a few pills here and there, but that's about it. We really need to be able to hand them something they can get excited about.'

Greg grunted. 'That all sounds great, but I still think you're taking that view to protect Maureen Stewart.'

'It's doubtful if we'll be able to protect her no matter how much we might want to,' admitted Angela. 'But is it such a bad thing to try and keep her out of it? Thankfully that decision isn't up to us.'

'So where do we go from here?' asked Greg.

'Home, I think. We'll get a relatively early night and that'll give the Boss some time to work out how we proceed.'

Angela switched her television off for the third time since she had left Greg and looked at the clock. The time was just after seven, approximately twenty minutes later than the last time she had checked. She thought about picking up her book again, then decided against it. Getting up, she walked into the kitchen and decided to wash her dishes. This would take all of five minutes, then she would be back to alternating between her book and the television to try and find some distraction. It was unusual for her to be home so early in the day, and she put her inability to settle down to that fact. But she knew that the real problem was the case she was working on. It left a bad taste in her mouth and reminded her of the one and only time she had tried hill climbing. Just as she reached what she thought would be the summit, another stretch of the same, boring mixture of rock and plant life lay ahead. 'It'll be worth it for the view,' she had been told. Eventually she reached the top and took in the view. It was OK if you like that sort of thing, but all she could think of was the long trip back down again. This case was panning out that way. She tried to look at the positives of what had been achieved. Steve Collins had been stopped; Robbie Stewart's involvement had been ascertained within reason; and they had the man in custody who was likely to have been behind the incidents with Elizabeth Reid, the Scotts and Betty

White. But even as she turned this over in her mind, the doubts returned. Would someone just pop up in Collins place? Would they be able to prove Gibson's involvement in the crimes? And what would be the outcome for Maureen Stewart? Greg had been correct; they *were* looking at a strategy to protect the memory of ex-Chief Inspector Stewart.

Angela watched thoughtfully as the water swirled clockwise and carried the remainder of the soapsuds down the plughole. She dried her hands, walked into her lounge and slumped back down into her chair after picking up her book. *This case is a lot more complicated than we first thought.* Angela read the line from her novel and smiled wryly. Then her doorbell rang.

She hurried to the door.

'Who's there?' she called out.

'Jim Russell,' came the reply.

'Who?'

'Jim Russell, Detective Chief Inspector Russell.'

Angela opened the door feeling a bit stupid and found her boss waiting patiently. She could have passed him in the street without recognising him, as he was wearing an open neck shirt, jeans and a casual jacket.

'Can I come in?' he said, after Angela had studied him for a few moments. 'I'm not a Jehovah's Witness or collecting for a charity, I just need to have a word with you.'

'Ah, of course, yes,' said Angela, standing aside to let her boss pass.

'I'm sorry to call on you like this,' he said as he walked into the lounge and waited for Angela to invite him to sit down. 'But I thought it might be a good idea to have a chat with you out of the office. I hope you're not busy. I probably should have phoned ahead in case you had company.'

'Oh, that's OK,' said Angela, 'Do you want some tea or coffee?'

'If you were planning to make some for yourself, that would be great,' said Russell.

A few minutes later she set a cup of black coffee down in front of him. 'I'm afraid I'm out of biscuits,' she said.

Russell patted his stomach. 'Probably just as well,' he said with a laugh. He took a drink of his coffee, gave an approving smile, and then placed it on the low table in front of him.

'There's something I want to discuss with you,' he said. 'Briggs has been released. But he wants to talk to you. Informally.'

'What about?' asked Angela.

'He wouldn't say. But I have a suspicion you showing him the photographs of the Scott children struck a nerve with him, what with him having two young daughters. I suspect he's terrified of being charged in relation to the fire. And I think he's more frightened of his wife's reaction to the charge.'

'I can understand that,' said Angela thoughtfully. 'But could this not have waited until we're on duty?'

'It's unlikely we will be able to find excuses to keep Collins and Gibson out of circulation much longer. When they get out I suspect they'll be looking to close ranks on this business. I think we need to try and get more out of Briggs before that happens.'

Russell reached into his pocket and produced a slip of paper. 'This is Brigg's phone number. I'd appreciate it if you could give him a call. Tonight would be good.'

'I can do that if you think it's urgent.'

'I do. And I suggest you arrange to meet him somewhere outside the station.'

'So we won't be recording the meeting?'

'No. As I said, he wants it to be informal. But I'm hoping he will give us something we can follow up on. And meet him alone. Leave Constable Anderson out of it.'

Chapter 37

'So, what do you want to tell me, Mr Briggs?' asked Angela. Although it was just after 8am, the Cosy Café was fairly busy. They had managed to find a table tucked away at the back, but even so Briggs looked extremely nervous.

'Are you recording this?' asked Briggs.

'This isn't a US cop show, Mr Briggs. We don't do things like that.' When Angela finished talking, she remembered the video pen and hoped Briggs wouldn't pick her up on that.

He didn't seem to notice, but still didn't relax.

'If anyone claims I said what I'm going to say I'll deny it. I'm caught in the middle of something I don't like and if word got out, I'd spilled the beans, well…'

'There's a problem,' said Angela slowly. 'If you were involved in these attacks there's little we could…'

'I haven't done anything! You've got to believe that! I had no idea what was going to happen to all these people!' He pushed his egg roll around on his plate as if fearing it would jump up and bite him.

'Ok. Let's say I believe you,' replied Angela in her most conciliatory tone of voice. 'So who was responsible? I'm pretty sure you know more than you've told us otherwise we wouldn't be here.' She took a bite of her bacon roll and waited.

Briggs took a few deep breaths.

'OK. I told you I was only a driver and that's the truth. I was asked to take people to places and wasn't encouraged to ask any questions.'

He paused, seemed to consider starting on his roll but left it and took a drink of his coffee instead.

'I can't remember all of the dates but I do remember the places. I drove for Gibson once or twice after being told to do so by Mr Collins. I dropped Gibson off once in McKenna Drive, but couldn't find a place to park so had to turn into Kipps Avenue. I waited until he phoned me to go back for him. I followed the blue Mondeo to the house in Calderbank and reported this back to Mr Collins. He seemed surprised to hear that it was a woman driving. I didn't know why I had to follow the car.'

He glanced at Angela and couldn't miss seeing the incredulous look on her face.

'I didn't ask questions! I just did as I was told!'

'Go on,' said Angela.

'I waited in the car until she came out of the house then followed her again. She drove onto the motorway heading south. When she stopped at a service station for fuel, I phoned Mr Collins and he told me to come back to the office.' He took another drink of his coffee.

'I know Gibson was in Calderbank on January 29th. I was asked to take him, but it was my eldest daughter's birthday, so I was excused. I assume he drove himself that night.'

'And that's all?' said Angela. Briggs nodded.

'What about the kidnapping of Peter Turner?'

'I didn't know it was a kidnapping! I drove Collins and Gibson to the house of what they said was an old friend. Gibson came out with the guy and got into his car. Collins came back to the car I was driving, and we set off for the warehouse. It wasn't until we got there that I realised things weren't what I had thought. Then you guys arrived.'

Angela watched the man as he started to eat his roll. She was pretty sure he was telling her the truth and she felt herself beginning to feel sorry for him. His reaction when he was shown the photos of the Scott children displayed empathy. She was beginning to believe he was caught in the middle of the whole affair. However, she was also sure that he would refuse to give evidence at any trial of Collins or Briggs. She would have to use the information she had been given in some other way.

'There's no way we can use the video pen as evidence. Our legal advisors reckon we would be accused of entrapment.'

Russell slumped back in his chair clearly frustrated.

'So where does that leave us?' asked Angela.

'We have Peter Turner's evidence to the effect that Collins admitted to the attacks. And I'm afraid that's pretty much all we have. And I've no doubt that Gibson will back up Collin's denial that he said anything of the kind. Even if Briggs did testify to what he told you, he can't say who did what to whom. I doubt if we'll be able to keep them in custody; we just don't have enough solid evidence.'

'No luck from the search warrants?'

'Absolutely nothing I'm afraid.'

As difficult as she found Russell's statements, Angela couldn't think of any way to refute what he said.

Russell's prediction turned out to be accurate, and Collins and Gibson were both released on bail.

'Do you think Briggs will be in any danger from that pair?' asked Greg.

'I doubt it,' said Angela. 'I'm sure they'll talk to him, but I don't think there's much he can tell them. Unless he knows more than he told me. But I don't think that's the case.'

The following morning Greg was on his way to collect Angela when a newspaper billboard caught his eye. He pulled over and bought a copy of the paper.

While he waited on Angela, he managed to read the bulk of the front page article.

'What do you think about this?' said Greg as Angela got into the car.

'Considering you've just stuck it under my nose I don't think anything about it. Why don't you drive while I read it?'

Greg tried to engage Angela in conversation a few times on the way to the station, but she ignored him while she read the paper.

Greg parked as precisely as usual, but neither made any move to get out of the car.

'Was it you?' asked Greg.

'Was what me?'

'The leak to the paper.'

'Do you really want me to answer that?'

'No. Perhaps you'd better not. I don't want to get dragged into this.'

'Very wise, Greg. But nothing in the article isn't true.' She ran her eyes over the article again. '*Prominent businessman and associate being investigated regarding two murders, arson, malicious damage, kidnapping and possible other charges.* Nothing libellous.'

'I don't think whether the article is true or not is really the question. It's one matter to tell a reporter to *fuck off*, but this is entirely different.'

As they entered the station room it appeared that every officer had their own copy of the same paper. It also appeared to Angela that almost every one of them gave her a knowing look and quite a few grins.

Russell had called a meeting and when he appeared to address the group, he had a copy of the paper in his hand.

'I see that we're all catching up on the news.' Russell waved the paper as if there was any doubt what news item he was referring to.

'I am only going to make one statement regarding this matter, and I want you all to take it to heart.'

He paused. When he started talking again, he spoke slowly and deliberately. 'I know for a fact that the leak did not come from any of the officers here.'

He paused to allow his statement to sink in. 'So, let's carry on with the investigation. We will no doubt have plenty of interest from the press trying to follow up this story. The only comment I want to read about from any officer involved in this investigation is *no comment*. Am I making this perfectly clear?'

There was general nodding of heads.

'So, who could it have been?' asked Greg as they made their way back to their desks.

'Does it really matter?' said Angela. 'The public will now be expecting charges to be brought so that puts us under more pressure.'

They spent the rest of the day going over what evidence they had, hoping they would find something they had overlooked.

'Greg. We're going round in circles. Let's call it a night.'

Greg collected Angela at the usual time the following morning and they drove to the station in silence.

Just as they reached their desks Angela's mobile rang.

'Good news?' said Greg when she finished the call.

'Yes. Peter Turner is going into hospital today and they hope to do the operation sometime in the next few days.'

'Well, that's good news.'

Angela's phone rang again before she could answer.

'That's interesting,' she said when she finished the call. 'That was Briggs. Collins called him and told him to stay at home for a few days as he and Gibson were going to a meeting in Manchester.'

'I'd like to be a fly on the wall at that meeting,' said Greg.

'At least that takes some of the pressure off Briggs. He sounded quite relieved on the phone.'

'I still can't believe the Fiscal won't bring more serious charges against Collins and Gibson. It's so frustrating.'

'Without the video pen we've got next to nothing. I know how you feel. We just need to hope we come across some other evidence or Briggs can be encouraged to testify.'

'None of Collins' other employees gave us anything?'

'Not a bean. They're pretty much all ex-cons and know the way things work. They know we have nothing.'

They spent the rest of the day catching up on the latest on the serial killer hunt. The whole unit was in danger of being swamped with information from the public. No matter how ridiculous some of this information appeared to be, it all had to be painstakingly checked out. Normally the more ridiculous statements would give the two detectives a bit of a laugh, but neither were in the mood. For once Angela couldn't come up with anything to lighten the atmosphere. They were both relieved when the day finished.

After another two days of making no progress they arrived at work and were immediately called into Russell's office.

'I've had a call from a senior officer from Greater Manchester police. Our friends Steve Collins and Bill Gibson were found dead yesterday.'

Greg and Angela looked at each other.

'Details are sketchy, but it appears that our two suspects had been seen in a Manchester nightclub in the company of individuals who are well known to the local police. A large quantity of drink, and possibly drugs, were taken. CCTV has shown the two being helped to their hotel rooms by some as yet unknown individuals. They were clearly the worse for wear. When they failed to vacate their rooms, entry was forced, and both were found dead.'

'Is foul play suspected?' asked Angela.

'Nothing obvious,' replied Russell. 'Clearly there will be autopsies carried out, but the feeling at the moment is that the deaths were due to a mixture of drink and drugs.'

'I'm trying very hard not to jump to any conclusions here,' said Angela.

'Let me guess what you're thinking,' said Russell. 'The Manchester guys were behind the drug shipments that came up to Collins. They read the newspaper report about our two guys. Not having any idea of what evidence we had against them, they were concerned that Collins and Gibson might try to do a deal with us to save their necks, a deal that might bring unwanted attention onto the Manchester boys.'

'That pretty much sums up what I was thinking,' said Angela.

'I don't think that's far off the mark.'

'So, what happens now?' Greg asked.

Russell sat back in his chair and shook his head. 'It's really none of our concern. I've been asked for what background information I can provide, but it's not our investigation.'

'I can't say I'm unhappy about that,' said Angela.

'I agree,' said Russell. 'We've enough on our plate just now. No matter what the autopsies reveal, we can draw a line under our investigation into the Collins affair. I propose to declare that we hold Collins responsible for the murder of Robbie Stewart. Although I wouldn't say that until we catch this serial killer.'

Chapter 38

It's a bit of a nuisance to go buying boots in disguise but needs must as they say. Anyway, I now have everything I need to continue my work. I must admit to a grudging admiration for the authorities. They are really trying to up the ante with their quite ingenious charity shop plan. I must commend the newspaper that ran with the story. It really was a big help to me. My latest plan is complete. I do not have a particular target in mind, but my chosen location will give me a good choice of suitable victims.

The killer got back into his car cursing his luck. Everything had been going according to plan. Deed done. Walking back to his car. Then the bloody dog saw him. And just as he was taking off his mask and shower cap. He didn't know it was there until it started barking. But the question is, did the woman walking the dog see him? If she did, would she recognise him? He started the engine and took a few deep breaths. It was dark. He turned away as soon as he saw her. She could only have had a brief moment at best to see him. What the hell was a woman doing walking her dog in a dark park so late at night? Don't people realise that there are dangers out there?

He sat for another few moments composing himself. Even if she did see him and would recognise him, there's no way she will have the opportunity to identify him until he was caught. So, stick to the plan. Don't make a silly mistake at this stage.

He put the car into gear and pulled away. A few minutes later he parked at the side of the road. He got out of the car, collected the bag of discarded clothes, crossed the road to the bins and dumped the bag. As he made his way back to the car, he was still debating with himself the possible outcomes of the evening.

He had no idea where the other car had come from. He wasn't aware of it being there until it hit him.

'Greg? Are you busy?'

'I'm actually in the middle of a cocktail evening with some friends.'

'Well get their carers to take them home and come and get me. There's been another murder.'

'Where?'

'Right on our doorstep. Dunbeth Park.'

'Coatbridge? OK, I'm on my way.'

Greg turned right at the cenotaph and then left to drive down Centenary Avenue, past the site of a previous killing. He had only negotiated the fairly sharp right-hand bend when they saw flashing blue lights at the bottom of the street.

They stopped, identified themselves and asked what had happened.

'A hit and run. It looks as if the victim was struck as he was crossing the road.' The young female traffic cop was clearly making an effort to appear calm.

'How is he?' asked Angela.

'He was alive when the ambulance picked him up, but it's not looking good. There was blood everywhere…'

'Try to stay calm and concentrate on doing your job officer. You'll be fine. Can I assume that is his car?' Angela nodded at the Ford Fiesta parked half on the pavement and half on the road.

'Yes. He had the keys in his hand. We've ran the plates, and it's a company car.'

'Any ID on the victim?'

'None. No wallet, driving licence. Not even any money in his pockets. He did have a set of keys we assume are for his house. There's one strange thing. But maybe it's nothing.'

Angela encouraged her to continue.

'Well. As I've said it might be nothing. But there's a wristwatch on the passenger seat.'

'And?'

'Well. The victim was wearing a wristwatch.'

'Do you think it could be the killer?' asked Greg as they reversed and left the scene of the accident.

'It's possible,' said Angela. 'But what was he doing crossing the road? There are no shops anywhere near and he didn't have any money on him anyway.'

'Maybe he needed the toilet and was going into the park. Or maybe he was just going to go behind the bins.'

'Greg! Turn round and get back to the accident!'

Greg did as he was asked and a few minutes later they were back where the traffic police were still investigating.

'Gimme your torch and gloves. Get one of the traffic guys over here with a camera.'

Before he could answer she jumped out of the car. She pulled the gloves on, switched on the torch and made for the bins.

Just as Greg and another officer reached her, she had hauled a black bin bag out of one of the bins.

The officer with the camera looked at Greg with a puzzled look on his face.

'What do you want me to take a picture of?' he asked.

'You're either going to get a photo of crucial evidence or a picture of a detective making an arse of herself.'

She ripped open the bag and tipped the contents onto the ground.

'Jackpot!' she said. 'Take a shot of the pile, then take a few as I separate the clothes.'

'I suppose this is evidence in a crime?'

'Exactly, Officer. Very important evidence.'

'Shoplifting from Oxfam?'

'You probably wouldn't believe me if I told you,' said Angela. 'Greg. Get some evidence bags from the car.'

Angela arranged the items carefully and the officer took all the pictures she asked for. She returned to speak to the young female officer.

'Did the victim say anything?'

'He was barely conscious. He just kept muttering *my diary, my diary*. I assumed he was suffering from shock.'

Angela asked to speak to the officer in charge. 'There's been a murder along at the park. That's where we're going. I want this car taken to the station and examined forensically. I want an officer stationed at the hospital.'

'I don't think the victim is likely to be in a state to go anywhere,' replied the officer.

'It's not for the victim. It's to keep other people away from him.'

As they reached the park entrance where various police vehicles were parked the heaven's opened and the rain started to pour down.

'Why isn't this scene being protected?' she asked when they arrived at a cluster of officers.

'No one could climb trees,' muttered one of the officers.

'Oh, a smart arse! Any more comments like that and you'll be issuing parking tickets for the next month! Did you find any footprints?'

The officers looked at one another. 'You'll have to ask the forensic boys,' said one eventually. He pointed to where a couple of white suited individuals were sitting in a van.

Angela strode over to the van and battered on one of the passenger windows. A young man opened it.

'Why aren't you guys examining the scene? This rain will be washing away evidence!'

The two guys in the front seats looked at each other.

'We've finished,' replied one.

'Did you find any footprints?'

'Quite a few. But mostly all overlapping.'

'Shit!' exclaimed Angela.

'I said mostly,' said the same man. 'We did get a couple of partials in pretty good condition.'

'And you took casts?'

The two guys looked at each other as if Angela had just arrived from Mars.

'Of course we did. We have done this before, you know.'

Angela took a deep breath and relaxed. 'Sorry guys. I didn't mean to come across so strongly, but these casts could be the most important ones you've ever taken. Please make sure they get back to the station intact.'

'What size would you say the boots we found were Greg?'

'I know you're wanting them to be size 11,' he replied.

'You're bloody right I am! Did you take the number of the car we assume was being driven by the accident victim?'

Greg nodded.

'OK. Let's try and find out who was driving it tonight.'

They managed to discover that the car was owned by a local confectionary company, but they couldn't get any answer to their phone calls.

'We'll try again first thing in the morning, Greg.'

Greg looked at his watch. 'You mean in five hours?'

'Shit! Is it that late? OK, let's get some sleep. We need to be very careful everything is done by the book.'

Greg smiled. 'What's funny? Angela asked.

'I just never thought I would hear you say that,' said Greg.

Less than a mile away a man sat in his chair deep in thought. He was telling himself that the person he hit had been in the middle of the road and he couldn't avoid him. He shouldn't have left the scene. But he had been drinking. Normally he wouldn't dream of taking the car to the pub. But his wife insisted that it would be safer with the serial killer on the loose. He didn't plan to drink so much, but one thing led to another.

When Greg arrived to collect Angela the next morning he found her standing on her doorstep waiting on him.

'Am I late?' he asked.

'No. I'm just keen to get started. Did you sleep much?'

'Hardly a wink,' replied Greg.

'Me neither. I'm hoping the boss hasn't heard any details of last night's events. I'm looking forward to filling him in on our suspicions.'

They arrived at the station and were pleased to find Russell available to see them.

Trying to remain as calm as possible they detailed the previous evening's events.

'But of course, we still have to check that the evidence backs up our suspicions,' concluded Angela.

Russell had listened carefully to what they told him, but he couldn't stop a wide grin gradually spreading across his face.

'This could be the break we've been hoping for,' he said softly. 'It's important we follow procedure very carefully.'

'That's what Angela said,' answered Greg.

'Really?' said Russell. 'My goodness!'

They all laughed.

'Well done both of you. Having the foresight to check out the bin was... Well, that was real detective work. I'm proud of you.'

Greg managed to get in touch with someone in the office of Kidds Confectionary. He explained that there had been an accident and that the car was being examined. The receptionist had checked their records and confirmed that an employee named Arthur Blackwood had been using the car. Greg told the lady on the phone that Blackwood was in Monklands Hospital in a critical condition.

Greg and Angela drove to Blackwood's house with a search warrant. They used his keys and entered the house.

'No mention of Blackwood having a partner?' asked Greg.

'No. He seems to be a bit of a loner.'

'Wouldn't it have been better to have a squad here doing the search?' asked Greg. 'This could take us ages.'

'A fair point Greg, but we are more likely to recognise anything significant.'

'How about this?' said Greg. He read the title of the book. '*The Diary of Jack the Ripper*. Could this be the diary the officers heard him mumble about?'

Angela took the book and examined it. 'Unless he was asking for something to read being brought to the hospital, I don't see what the connection could be. Let's keep looking.'

After five hours the only thing they had turned up was a hand-written diary. However, this only contained dates and times of meetings. These all looked innocent enough but would be checked out anyway.

'If this is the home of our serial killer then he's been extremely careful.'

'You can say that again Greg. I really don't know what I was expecting to find. We'll get his computer checked out, but I don't hold out a lot of hope. Have some of our boys checked out his workplace?'

'They're doing that just now.'

Angela's phone rang. She listened for a few moments.

'Let's pack up here Greg. Blackwood has died.'

They carefully locked Blackwood's house and returned to their car.

'So, it's over?'

'Yes Greg. The casts of the partial footprints matches perfectly the boots we found in the bin. I will be very surprised if we have any more murders by the *Careful Killer*.'

'I'm pleased you found time to see me,' said Peter.

'Even if you hadn't asked me to call, I planned to visit to give you my best wishes before the op.'

'I appreciate that. And how is Detective Anderson?'

'We're both feeling much better,' said Angela.

Peter opened the small drawer in his bedside cabinet and took out an envelope.

He was silent for a few moments and then looked at Angela. 'This will shed more light on events. I decided to write it rather than explain to you verbally. Just in case things don't turn out well for me.'

Angela accepted the envelope but made no attempt to open it.

'Let me ask you something,' she said. 'Some time ago Greg had checked up that you were here undergoing tests on the two days you mentioned. He assumed the two days included an overnight stay. Would I be correct in saying that you were allowed to go home on the Monday night?'

Peter smiled. 'You are wise beyond your years Angela. That letter,' he nodded at the envelope Angela was holding. 'That explains everything as far as I know it. From the time of the accident involving the Reid family up to the death of Robbie Stewart. I always thought that the people who say that confession is good for the soul didn't know what they were talking about. But they're correct. I'm prepared to face the music. If I come through this OK, I won't deny what I've written.'

Angela thought for a few moments. 'You won't have heard yet, but Steve Collins and Bill Gibson are dead. The Boss intends to draw a line under the Stewart killing by declaring that Collins was behind it. But keep that to yourself for the present. And we strongly suspect that the serial killer is also dead after a car accident.' She got up to leave.

'I hope everything goes well for you Peter. As regards this letter, I'll file it carefully.'

With that she ripped the letter in two and dropped it in the bin.

Printed in Great Britain
by Amazon